HARD WARE

MISHA BELL

♠ Mozaika Publications ♠

Copyright © 2021 Misha Bell
www.mishabell.com

Published by Mozaika Publications, an imprint of Mozaika LLC.
www.mozaikallc.com

Cover by Najla Qamber Designs
www.najlaqamberdesigns.com

Photography by Wander Aguiar
www.wanderbookclub.com

e-ISBN: 978-1-63142-627-8
Print ISBN: 978-1-63142-628-5

Chapter One

*I*s that a *bear?*

The Kegel balls feel like they're on the verge of escaping my vagina. I squeeze my well-trained muscles to keep the toy inside. The pair of balls are of my own design, so I know if I squeeze them one more time, the vibration feature will activate, and this isn't a good time for that.

The leash jerks in my hand.

"Bonaparte, behave." The sternness in my voice is futile. My Chihuahua keeps tugging, his gaze glued to the bear and his tail wagging so rapidly I half expect him to helicopter into the air like a drone.

To my relief, the bear merely sniffs the fire hydrant, oblivious to the delicious four-pound appetizer a mere leap away.

Digging in my heels, I pull back on the leash. "Seriously, Boner. Do you *want* to get eaten?"

The pulling stops, and my dog looks up at me, a

mixture of sadness and indignation in his green eyes. As usual, I can imagine what he'd say if I were a dog whisperer:

"*Ma chérie*, that dog is ignoring me. *Moi*! Unthinkable."

I toss him a biscuit. "That bear clearly has no manners. In its defense, though, would *you* be able to resist sniffing that hydrant? We're next to Central Park. Millions of dogs have peed there. The smell must be heavenly."

With a leap, Boner catches the treat, swallows it without chewing, and returns his attention to his gargantuan quarry.

My own gaze shifts to the man holding the beast's leash, and my jaw drops as my inner muscles involuntarily squeeze the Kegel balls.

The vibration activates, but I ignore it, my eyes hungrily roaming over the tall, athletically built male specimen in front of me.

The bear's owner is hot.

Scorching, panty-melting, uterus-exploding hot.

The kind of hot that I'm going to end up masturbating to.

Wait. Strictly speaking, I *am* masturbating to him —the vibration inside my vagina is building my climax with every passing second. Thankfully, he's not looking at me, so I can gobble him up without shame.

The man checks all my boxes, even ones I didn't know I had.

Thick, silky-looking hair the color of mink's fur.

Short, neatly trimmed dark beard that emphasizes his regal nose and carved features. Broad shoulders padded with just the right amount of muscle and a chest to die for, all tapering down to a lean waist and narrow hips. He's even wearing a turtleneck, for fuck's sake—and everyone knows that's the guy equivalent of a sexy black dress.

Oh, and his lips. I want to make a mold of those lips and turn that mold into a sex toy.

Speaking of sex toys, the balls are getting me ever closer to the edge. Though I've been accused of being blasé about such things, even I recognize that coming here and now, in front of a stranger, isn't the most socially acceptable move on my part.

I've got to disable the balls, which can be done if I squeeze them three more times. The problem is, each squeeze also changes the vibration speed, so my situation will get worse before it gets better.

No helping that, I suppose.

I squeeze.

The vibration intensifies.

Twice more to go and—

Boner barks.

The bear's massive snout unpeels from the hydrant, and giant brown eyes zero in on the dog-shaped hors d'oeuvre at my feet.

Finally getting the attention he craves, Boner rapidly wags his tail and tries to sprint to his doom.

I squeeze the balls again, involuntarily. One more time, and they're off. Except the vibration is now on full speed, and it feels amazing. So, so amazing...

Crap. What am I doing?

Have to squeeze one last time.

Except the prerequisite muscles have turned to jelly, and I'm having trouble squeezing.

Is this it?

Am I going to have an orgasm just as my dog gets eaten—all in front of the insanely hot stranger?

Fleetingly, I wonder if I should let the bear eat my best friend to distract from my imminent combustion —and maybe so that the bear's owner will sleep with me later as recompense for my loss.

No, that's madness.

I tug on the leash, stopping Boner's noble sacrifice in its tracks.

Except now he's on the bear's radar.

The beast lunges—and the swift jerk of its leash catches the hot stranger off guard. By the time he realizes what's what and digs in his heels, the bear's maw is mere inches away from Boner's tennis-ball-sized head.

Clutching my handbag, I back away, pulling my overexcited friend with me. Not that I'm not overexcited myself. My heart is pounding, and I'm sweating from the effort of holding back the orgasm as the balls continue to vibrate on max.

Squeezing isn't working. Maybe I just ride it out, keeping a poker face?

The stranger says something to the bear in a

language I don't recognize, though the guttural quality makes it sound like a distant relative of Russian. Then his eyes narrow on Boner, and still without looking at me, he growls in perfectly unaccented English, "Keep that rat away from my dog."

His voice is deep and as ridiculously sexy as the rest of him, but thankfully, his words make me angry enough that the impending orgasm recedes.

Such a shame. All these gifts wasted on a man who's clearly an asshat.

I tighten my grip on Boner's leash and narrow my own eyes at the stranger. "I'll keep my *dog* away from your *bear.*"

There. Not a bad comeback considering my situation.

He finally deigns to look at me—and I'm once again struck dumb.

Those eyes, set beneath a pair of thick, dark eyebrows, are the most beautiful color I've ever seen, a mercurial sort of hazel that seems to shift between dark green and amber-tinted brown.

Said eyes widen as they travel over my body, lingering for a moment on my short skirt and bare legs, but then his gorgeous face takes on an imperious expression. "Oh, please. She's more of a dog than yours will ever be."

His rich, deep voice conspires with the balls inside me to get me even closer to a place I don't want to be.

Maybe I could do what guys do in this situation— think unsexy thoughts.

Goop from the eyes. Ear wax. Squeezing a whitehead. Smelly armpits. Flaky scalps. Gray stuff dug out of belly buttons. Nail fungus.

Nope. None of those are working.

Mother?

That seems to do the trick.

Speaking of her, I channel what she derisively calls my "Snow Queen demeanor" and finally find the words to reply to the stranger. "Dogness isn't about quantity; it's about quality."

His thick eyebrows lift just a smidge. He's clearly never had anyone talk back to him before. "Why is that yappy little thing out of your purse in the first place?"

Ugh. Definitely an asshat. At least the annoyance is keeping the orgasm at bay. I hate that Chihuahua stereotype. Despite having been named after Napoleon, Boner doesn't actually have the complex that so many of his brethren do and isn't yappy in the least. He's been to doggy school, so he's well behaved. Mostly. He *is* a dog.

Fine. Ms. Nice Bella gloves are officially off.

I level a cold glare at the crotch of the stranger's jeans, then look back at his face, one eyebrow arched villainously. "Let me guess. The big dog is there to compensate for something?"

Whew. Where's my Oscar? I doubt even Angelina Jolie can tell someone off while holding back an orgasm.

The bastard just smirks. Those mercurial eyes gleaming, he drawls, "Want to bet?"

Oh, no.

With the picture of a gargantuan cock in my mind, I finally lose the fight against my balls and come.

Chapter Two

*I*t's a miracle that I'm able to suppress my moan—a miracle that deserves yet another Oscar. All the women who fake orgasms should try the reverse. It's harder than I would've imagined.

The big question is: did he see it on my face?

The last spasm deactivates the balls, so at least I'm spared a repeat performance.

A loud bark rings out somewhere in the park.

Both of us glance down at our charges—I guess on the off chance they've learned to project their voices long distance, a feat that even I, a skilled ventriloquist, am not capable of.

Boner's nose is pointed in the direction of the distant bark, tail wagging with excited curiosity. "*Ma chérie*, I think that dog barked because there's a squirrel there, in Béchamel sauce. Can we please, please go there? Please!"

In contrast to Boner, the bear is cowering pitifully,

giant fluffy ears drooping and three-hundred-pound body shaking like a furry brown leaf.

Crap. Now I feel sorry for the bear, but also vindicated.

Who's the bigger dog now?

The stranger croons something soothing in his language, patting the bear's head, and the beast snaps out of her panic.

With a small wag of her tail, she turns her snout toward Boner and takes a big sniff.

Forgetting the other dog, Boner looks up at the bear and also sniffs the air.

With a huff, the stranger says something in that Russianesque language again and drags the bear away without giving me the chance to mock his "real dog's" cowardliness.

Boner longingly eyes the bear's rear end. "*Ma chérie*, that is a lot of butt to sniff. What a *tragédie*."

"I feel your pain," I whisper, my eyes roaming the tight, muscular tush outlined by the jeans of the irksome stranger—a tush that looks extra tempting in the orgasm afterglow. "I'm not sure if I want to sniff it, per se, but I think having that butt attached to that brain is a loss for womankind."

We resume our walk, and every time Boner stops to sniff something, I sneak a glance at the annoying stranger and make sure not to accidentally squeeze the Kegel balls again.

He's taking the bear to Boner's favorite spot, a

doggy playground—though on occasion, I've seen human toddlers on those ramps as well.

Great. Now we can't go there.

Unless we should?

No. Forget that guy.

Unfortunately, as we continue on our walk, I find that forgetting him is hard work, especially in light of the warmth still pulsing in my core.

Why does the universe have to be so unfair? I so rarely come across guys I'm attracted to, and when I finally find one, he turns out to be an ass. Then again, given my past relationships, the mere fact that I'm attracted to someone might be a red flag. According to my friend Xenia, I'm an asshole magnet. Case in point: my most recent ex.

There's a reason I prefer my sex toys to real men.

A sixth sense pulls me out of my daydreaming just in time to spot Boner sniffing a snail on the ground.

"No!" I shout just as he—unsurprisingly—shoves the snail right into his maw.

"Spit that out."

He looks up at me with a guileless expression. "Why? It's *escargot*."

I channel the alpha in our little relationship. "Spit it. You could get the French heartworm."

Looking contrite, Boner spits the creature out and watches it crawl away, unbothered by dog drool. "French heartworm sounds like my kind of heartworm."

I toss him another treat. "Good boy. I bet that

bear isn't nearly as well trained. She would get a parasite in a heartbeat, but not you."

"*Touché.*" He resumes his walk, ears drooping.

Poor guy. First he couldn't sniff a bear; now he's not allowed to eat a snail. I can relate. I was denied premium man candy myself.

Guiding Boner toward a fire hydrant, I watch him forget all his worries as he hikes up his leg impossibly high and pees at a level only a big dog should be able to reach.

If only my key to happiness were so simple—I'd hike up my leg in a heartbeat. Well, not right this moment—my balls would fall out.

Happy with his urinary work, Boner resumes his trot.

Not for the first time, I wonder why he has such ambitions when it comes to his pee. Is it part of a delusion where he thinks he's a much, much bigger dog? Or could it be that all dogs want to shoot for the stars, and being small and limber helps Boner not tip over as he hikes his leg higher than his head?

Boner stops and looks wistfully in the direction of the playground.

Since the bear is still there, I say, "How about we feed John first?"

At John's name, Boner approvingly wags his tail. John either doesn't have a home or has some other reason why he never bathes—which makes him a fun human to smell, for a dog.

Halfway to John's bench, a black cat crosses our

path. Since the cat is bigger than Boner, he pretends not to see it. I, on the other hand, halt in my tracks and nearly squeeze the balls too hard once again.

Thank goodness my brothers aren't here to mock me. A black cat crossing the road is a major Russian superstition that I find difficult to ignore. The MIT-trained engineer in me can't fathom how the bad luck from the cat would even work, yet I keep standing there, hoping someone crosses the cat's path and therefore takes the bad juju onto them.

With the business venture I'm launching, I can't chance any bad luck.

A squirrel suddenly dashes right over the tainted path. Since it's not bigger than him, Boner tries to give it a chase, but I hold him back just in time.

Whew. The squirrel will now get the bad luck instead of me or some nice old lady.

As we resume the walk, a king poodle walks toward us.

I grin. With that lion haircut, this dog looks a lot more French than mine—not that Boner has anything French in him besides his name and his soul. He actually looks like he could be in those "¡Yo quiero Taco Bell!" commercials, and with his Mexican ancestry, it's anyone's guess why he doesn't have a Hispanic accent when I picture him speaking to me.

Boner tries to be friendly with the poodle.

The bigger dog shows its teeth and growls.

Boner halts in his tracks and looks at me. "How *impoli*!"

I give the lady owner a dirty look.

She shrugs at me guiltily and hurries past us.

The rest of the way to John is uneventful, and when we get to the bench, he's there as usual, just staring blankly into the distance.

Tucking Boner's leash under my armpit, I take out the sandwich I made for John from my handbag. "Hi."

"Great. The commie is back," John grumbles before bending down to fluff Boner's fur.

I thrust the sandwich at him. "I was born after the Soviet Union had already collapsed, and I came to this country when I was five years old, so I'm much more of an American capitalist pig than a commie."

John frowns at the sandwich. "Once a commie, always a commie."

I guess that's fair. From what little I know of John's story, he's a Vietnam vet and is thus justified in his opinions on commies.

He's also too proud to accept charity, so I tread carefully, as usual. "This is from my parents' restaurant," I say, nodding at the sandwich. "They brought me too much food again, and in Russian culture, it's considered bad luck to throw out bread."

That last bit is actually true, which is why I only buy the frozen variety.

Mumbling something about dumb commie superstitions, John snatches the sandwich and begins wolfing it down.

There. Over time, I've learned how to make this

transaction go pretty smoothly. When I first met him, John was unhealthily thin, but now he's—

The leash escapes from under my armpit as Boner suddenly torpedoes forward.

Crap.

"Later, John," I shout over my shoulder as I launch into a run. "I've got to catch him!"

I don't hear what John says, but I do see where Boner is headed.

The playground.

"Boner, stop!" I yell.

He doesn't. So much for that doggie school.

As I pick up speed, I curse myself for my constant desire to multitask. Though I've taught myself to leave my phone at home to avoid getting distracted by work emails, I just had to test out the Kegel balls on this walk.

Squeezing my pelvic muscles for all I'm worth, I speed up some more. Juggling balls has nothing on trying to keep them inside one's privates while sprinting.

Boner vaults up the ramp right next to the bear.

No. He can't mean to—

But he does.

Using the height advantage of the ramp as an assist, my Chihuahua mounts the bear and begins to hump.

Chapter Three

"*B*oner, stop, I say!"

That doggy school owes me a serious refund—this scenario should've been a part of their curriculum.

Oblivious to the world, my Chihuahua thrusts his tiny butt at the bear's gargantuan behind. From a distance, Boner looks like a bird hitching a ride on a hippopotamus.

Damn it. Silly dog. Why would you even attempt to have sex with something a hundred times bigger than you?

The thrusting accelerates.

My lungs burn as I pick up speed despite the obstacle of my tight skirt. At least I'm wearing my cute new sneaks instead of my usual high-heeled boots—those would make this impromptu track session impossible.

"Boner, stop it!" I pant.

He does the opposite. His humping grows frantic, making it look like he's having a sex seizure.

I further pick up the pace and my thong shifts, creating an unpleasant draft on my lady parts.

Why is the bear not eating him for this? Not that I'm complaining. Maybe Boner's tiny wiener isn't even in that cavernous vagina. I have no doubt that if a beast that big felt assaulted, Boner would be a dead dog.

Crap. Is this an assault? Is my little buddy a rapist?

But no. The bear's fluffy tail is up, providing Boner with easier entry. That has to be her way of consenting to this—along with the fact that she's not crushing him with her massive jaws. For all I know, they came to an agreement when they sniffed each other.

He must've seduced her with his mighty Chihuahua pheromones.

Of course, none of this will save Boner from the bear's annoyingly hot asshat of an owner. When he sees what's happening, he'll undoubtedly turn murderous. Luckily, his attention is on the guy he's currently talking to—or, more accurately, gesticulating and shouting at. The guy is holding a camera, which I hope he won't use to take a picture of Boner's misdemeanor.

My leg muscles burn as I sprint faster. I'm now only twenty feet away.

The camera guy loses whatever the argument was, and slinks away.

This is it.

The stranger turns and his gorgeous eyes widen as he registers the bear's situation.

Leaping for the ramp, I finally grab Boner's leash. Before I can drag him away, he disconnects of his own free will and looks up at me, tail wagging with masculine satisfaction.

As expected, the stranger's jaw turns to stone, his regal nostrils flaring.

With effort, I restrain myself from yelling "bad dog" at Boner. I don't want to give my little friend a sex complex, the kind my mother gave me when she caught me masturbating in my early teens.

Dogs deserve to be sexual beings just like humans do.

The bear owner's flinty gaze shifts from Boner to me. "Did your rat just—"

"My *dog* is sorry about what he did." It requires tremendous restraint to sound placating. "As am I. I got distracted, and he escaped."

Boner looks at me uncomprehendingly. "Why apologize, *ma chérie*? This is *le grand amour*."

The stranger regards me with a withering stare. "Let me guess. You got lost in your phone?" Under his breath, he mutters something about Americans with their incessant posts and tweets.

My hackles officially rise, and it's an effort to keep myself from squeezing balls—his and the ones inside me. "Let *me* guess. You like to judge people without a shred of evidence? As it so happens, I don't bring my phone on my dog walks. Nor am I an American in the strictest sense of the word. Nor do I use social media, for that matter."

Curiosity replaces some of the anger on his face. "Then how did you let him escape?"

I give him my signature icy glare. "I don't have to explain myself to you."

I might've been too intense there. The bear's ears droop, and she hides behind the stranger.

His eyes narrow again. "Your dog violated mine. The least you can do is be civil."

Like me, Boner doesn't like his tone. Putting himself between us, he growls at the stranger.

"Easy, boy," I mutter, then take a deep breath to calm myself. Sometimes you win by taking the high road. "I do want to apologize."

"I don't need your apology. I need to know if your dog has any STDs."

Somehow, I still keep my cool. "This is the first time he's had real sex, so I highly doubt it."

Immediately, I want to smack myself for emphasizing the "real" bit; the last thing I want to get into is how I've built my dog a sex toy.

The stranger looks a bit calmer now, as does the bear behind him. "That's good. Still, semen can harbor a wide range of viruses. How do we know your dog isn't infected with something?"

I shrug. "He hasn't been sick? Besides, we don't know if he actually penetrated her—or if there was any semen."

Dog semen. Now that's a subject I didn't think would come up when I started my day.

"That's not good enough," the guy says. "I'd like you to take him to a vet and do a thorough checkup." He pats his pockets and comes out with a wallet. "I'll pay."

How does he get under my skin so easily? "I can pay for my own vet. Thanks."

"If you insist." The wallet disappears.

I straighten my spine. "I insist."

He gives me a more thorough once-over, his gaze once again lingering on my legs. "And you'll let me know the vet results?" His voice is a shade huskier as his hazel eyes return to my face.

My treacherous heart skips a beat. "I'll need to put my number into your phone. As I said, I don't have mine."

Is that a hint of a smile quirking his sexy lips?

"That would be great, except I also don't bring my phone on my dog walks," he says. Wryly, he adds, "Nor do I use social media. Nor am I an American."

That last bit I could've guessed, but no social media? I thought my paranoid brothers and I were the only ones abstaining in this day and age. And no phone on a walk? Even said brothers make fun of me for doing *that*.

"Do you have a business card?" I ask, ignoring the temptation to tally up our similarities. Just because we're having a civil conversation doesn't mean he's not still an asshat.

I'd offer him my own business card, but for some reason, I don't want him to know I own a sex toy company. There's something about him—maybe the understated yet obviously expensive cut of his clothes, or the imperious angle of his jaw—that makes me think of Fortune 500 boardrooms and ten-course dinners under crystal chandeliers. Men like this tend to look down on nontraditional entrepreneurs like me —though why I care what he thinks is a mystery.

Typically, I'm out and proud about what I do.

He reaches into his pocket and pulls out a pen. "I don't have a card." He looks around and spots a couple of coffee cups some litterer left on a nearby bench. Grabbing the cleaner-looking one, he writes something on it and hands it to me.

Dragomir, it says in a bold, masculine scrawl, alongside a phone number with a Manhattan area code.

Dragomir? Is that Drago for short? Sounds like a Harry Potter villain.

"I'm Bella." Setting down the cup, I politely extend my hand.

His eyes gleam as he accepts the greeting, his much larger palm engulfing mine—and my breath catches at the electrifying warmth of his skin.

It's a wonder it doesn't activate the balls inside me.

"Dragomir." He pronounces the name with a Russian-sounding accent.

I reluctantly reclaim my hand. "Where are you from, originally?"

"Ruskovia," he says, again with that same pronunciation.

Hmm. I've heard of that place. If I remember right, it's smaller than any of the New York boroughs, and kind of backward, at least insofar as they still have a ruling monarchy. I have no clue where it is on the map, what their customs are, or whether it was the inspiration for Sokovia in *The Avengers*.

What I do know is that if this guy is anything to go by, Ruskovia might be the best-looking nation in the world.

I must be looking kind of blank because he says with a slight eye roll, "Ruskovia is a country in Eastern Europe—in case your knowledge of geography is that of a typical American."

My brothers always say my geography could be better, but who is this Dragomir to criticize me or the American educational system?

"I know where Ruskovia is," I say, only slightly fibbing. "I was born in Russia myself. That's also in Eastern Europe—in case *your* knowledge of geography is subpar."

His eyes tighten at the word *Russia*, and I belatedly recall that a lot of Eastern European countries don't like my motherland thanks to the efforts of the Soviets back in the day to bring communism to them, usually at gunpoint.

"I was little when I moved here," I add, before I can ask myself why I'm trying to get on his good side.

He cocks his head. "That *would* explain your perfect English."

Was that a compliment? It sure feels like it.

"How about you?" I ask, deciding to take it at face value. "How come you don't have an accent?"

"I had great teachers," he says and glances down with a frown.

I follow his gaze and suppress a snort. While we were talking, Boner and his bear got together, and she's just given him a lick—a big, slobbering lick.

Boner seems like the happiest dog in the world.

Dragomir says something to the bear in what must be Ruskovian. The only words I can make out are *Winnie* and something like *Pooh*.

Or was it lower-case "poo?"

Sheepishly, the bear scoots away from Boner.

My good humor evaporates. "Did you just insult my dog again?"

"No. I told Winnifred not to lick him. Don't Russians use the command 'fu' as well?"

Fu. Not *poo*. And yes, my parents always yell "fu" at Boner when they see him doing things they don't like. To me, it always seems like they're trying to teach him martial arts, à la *Kung Fu Panda*.

Then something clicks. "Your dog's name is Winnifred? As in, Winnie, for short?"

He nods.

"You realize that's a bear's name, right? As in, Winnie the P—"

"I wasn't the one to name her. What's the name of yours?"

Who doesn't name their own dog? "Bonaparte."

He arches his eyebrows. "You don't think that's a little too ambitious for a dog with a brain the size of a pea?"

I cross my arms over my chest. "Chihuahuas have the biggest brain-to-body ratio of any breed."

"Still." He looks Boner over with skepticism. "Winnie's brain might just be the size of his whole body."

"Or it might be puny if she has a very thick skull," I say, adding under my breath, "like you."

He gives me his imperious stare. "Winnie is of the misha breed. They've rid Ruskovia of wolves and bears and are the smartest dogs in the world."

"This breed is actually called *misha*?" I suppress the urge to ask how exactly Winnie would be able to hunt wolves when she was scared of some random dog's bark.

He sighs. "They are called that. So what?"

"Misha is associated with bears in Russia. You know, like Olympic Misha… the bear?"

"Well, in Ruskovia, misha is only associated with majestic, highly intelligent dogs."

"I bet you Boner is more intelligent than Winnie." As soon as I say it, I picture a lecture from my mother. When I was little, she tried to convince me that men don't like to be challenged and wouldn't want to go near a competitive girl like me.

Not that Dragomir wants to go near me in any case. Given the way this encounter has gone so far, my competitiveness is unlikely to make the top of his cons list—assuming he has a list with any pros on it.

He looks at Boner, then at me. "Are you serious?"

I decide to double down. "As taxes. I know a decent intelligence test for a dog, and I'm confident Boner will ace it before Winnie."

The gleam of battle enters his eyes. "I, too, know a test. And Winnie will wipe the floor with your Napoleon wannabe."

"So, it's official." I rub my hands together. "We have ourselves a competition."

Is that a cocky smile on his lips? "What does the winner get?"

The Grinch would be envious of my answering grin as I think of the perfect thing. "If I win, I want you to get down on your knees and—"

I stop as his eyes widen. He glances at the hem of my skirt, a hungry expression appearing on his face.

Wow.

I know what he's thinking, but it's not what I had in mind—until this moment, that is.

Chapter Four

*H*e steps close enough for me to detect the cinnamon notes in his sensual cologne. "Get on my knees and do what?"

My own knees feel oddly weak. I clear my throat, but my voice still comes out huskier than is wise. "Get down on your knees, face Boner, and tell him he's the smartest being you've ever met."

Is that disappointment on his face?

Is there some on mine?

He shrugs. "As unpleasant as that outcome would be, I don't need to worry about it because Winnie will win."

"Well then, on the off chance she does, what would you want *me* to do?"

He rubs the short, dark hair of his beard. It's more of an overgrown stubble, really—something he might've grown in a week or two, I realize as I peer at it closer. His hair is just so thick and luscious that it looks like there's more of it than there really is.

Wait, why am I obsessing over his hair? I just asked him an important question, and he's taking his sweet time answering. Does that mean he's going to demand something indecent? I can almost hear his deep voice growling in reply, "Get down on your knees and unzip me, then take out my—"

"*When* I win," he says, interrupting my lewd imaginings, "we'll walk together until Winnie defecates, and then you'll clean it up."

He looks smug.

Damn. Those are big stakes. Literally.

Does he use ten-gallon garbage bags to contain all that poop? Will I need a shovel?

The one part of that scenario I like is that we'd walk together. And depending on Winnie's fiber consumption, we might get a chance to get to know each other. Maybe stop butting heads for a change. Maybe even—

"Are you chickening out?" The words carry a clear-cut challenge.

I glare at him. "No way. It's on. What's the test?"

He pets Winnie's head. "You put a towel on a dog's head and time how long it takes them to get out from under it."

I don't show my glee. I've done that with Boner once. He got free in less than thirty seconds, which was very good according to the article I was reading. "Where do we get towels?"

Please say "your place."

The stubble gets another rub. "Our clothes?"

Before I can reply, he grabs the hem of his turtleneck, exposing a flash of toned abs, and pulls it over his head.

Fuck. Me.

As in, *fuck me, please.*

I almost activate my balls once again.

Under the turtleneck, he's wearing my second favorite article of male clothing, albeit one with an unfortunate name: wifebeater. More importantly, he's ripped. His shoulders are perfectly round with muscle, his arms crazy buff, and his pecs are the kind that can dance.

I want to change my ask if I win to something inappropriate. Also, would it be so bad if I activated the balls on purpose and had another orgasm right here and now?

"You don't have to take off your top," he says, misinterpreting my stunned expression. "Given your Chihuahua's size, my handkerchief will do."

A handkerchief? What is this, the eighteen-hundreds?

Thanking the fashion gods for my decision to wear a bralette under my shirt, I begin to unbutton.

As his eyes widen again, the light brown in them seems to turn into molten gold.

I'm not shy, but by the time I shrug my shirt off, I'm on the verge of blushing at what I'm seeing on his face.

"I don't want Boner to lose because he doesn't recognize the scent on your hankie." There. Voice unruffled. And my getting undressed has nothing to do with trying to, say, seduce anyone. Nope. Only a truly devious woman would do *that*.

He pulls out the aforementioned hankie and dabs his forehead. "Do you have a watch with a stop clock?"

"Why? We don't need it to see who gets free first."

"I want to record the time for posterity. Under thirty seconds is considered a very good result."

Does this mean he's also done this test on his dog?

I guess I should get ready to shovel giant doodoo.

I wave my empty wrist. "Sorry, no watch here."

"How about we use mine?" He tilts his muscular forearm so I can see the piece.

Under the pretext of seeing the watch better, I sidle up to him until I'm within kissing range. This close up, his scent is intoxicating, all warm male skin and rich, cinnamon-y spice. My mouth literally waters as X-rated images fill my brain again.

"Are those hand-drawn penises on your handbag?" he asks, forcing me to snap out of yet another lust-induced fantasy.

Why is everyone an art critic when it comes to this? Yes, I like decorating my possessions this way. Sue me.

"Do you have a problem with my drawings?" I angle my body so he can't see my bag. In the process, I accidentally step on his foot.

Damn it. Stepping on a foot is a bad omen. It means the person doing the stepping is going to have a conflict with the person whose foot was stepped on.

Or in this case, more conflict.

"No problem," he says—and it's unclear if he means the foot or the penis drawings.

I hesitate, then decide to just go for it. "Can you step on my foot?" According to Russian tradition, this annuls the bad juju.

He raises an eyebrow. "Russian superstition?"

I nod, flushing slightly.

"In Ruskovia, if a woman accidentally steps on a man's foot, it is said they will end up together. Of course, I don't believe in such nonsense myself."

Yet he gently steps on my foot, then shows me the watch again and smiles.

That smile. Would it be too obvious if I fanned myself? More importantly, would I be a perv if I activated the vibration now? I really want to. Not only does he smell all masculine and yummy, but at this distance, I can feel the heat radiating from him, as though he were a fire-breathing dragon.

Maybe that last bit is why he's named Dragomir?

Realizing I've completely forgotten about the watch, I give it an exaggerated once-over.

Wow. It's by Patek Philippe, the makers of the world's most expensive wristwatches. This particular masterpiece appears custom made, with Cyrillic-looking writing that must be Ruskovian and a strange design made out of diamonds.

No wonder I got the old money vibe from Dragomir. This thing must cost millions.

"So," he murmurs, causing my gaze to jerk up to his face. "Will you trust my watch?"

Some instinct is telling me not to trust anything about him, period. Still, without a rational comeback, I simply nod and rip myself away from the gravitational pull of those mercurial eyes.

"On my mark," he says, turning his attention to the watch.

I hold my top over Boner.

He tosses his turtleneck on Winnie's head. "Go."

Chapter Five

*a*s I drop my shirt on Boner, I realize this test isn't going to be fair. My Chihuahua is so tiny that my shirt is a much bigger obstacle for him than Dragomir's turtleneck is for Winnie.

I should've agreed to the handkerchief, after all.

Oh, well. If I bring this up now, Dragomir will accuse me of being a sore loser.

Let's just hope Boner is that much more intelligent —or good at this particular test.

Both dogs begin their struggle to get out.

The seconds tick by.

Realizing I'm holding my breath, I loosen my tightly bunched shoulders and gulp in some air.

Suddenly, a paw appears from under my shirt, then another, then Boner's head.

I point excitedly. "He's done!"

Boner wags his tail. "*Ma chérie*, did you have any doubts I would emerge *victorieux*? Not cool."

"Twenty-five seconds," Dragomir growls, his gaze on his turtleneck.

A few more seconds pass, yet Winnie is still not out.

Then a few more.

Suddenly, the turtleneck begins to shrink, though it's unclear how... at least at first.

"Is she eating it?" I ask.

He starts, then grabs the turtleneck and tugs on it.

Yep.

The bear has decided the best way to get out is by eating the obstacle.

A few tugs and a few soothing words in Ruskovian later, the turtleneck is in tatters, but at least none is in the dog's stomach.

For no reason at all, Dragomir gives *me* a glare.

Talk about a sore loser. The guy must be even more competitive than I am.

"At least she found a creative way to get out," I say, figuring an olive branch never hurt anyone.

His chilly gaze warms a few degrees. "You still won this round. What's *your* test?"

I walk over to the bench and pick up the two left-over cups, combining them with the one with his digits on it.

"This is meant to test their memory," I say.

A cocky smirk flashes across his face. "I think I know this test too."

Damn it. I was hoping to have an advantage here. But hey, at least I'm in the lead so far.

"First, we teach them that a treat will be under a cup." I demonstrate this by taking out a gourmet doggie cookie and sticking it under the cup to the left. "Boner, get it."

With a wag of his tail, he pushes the leftmost cup over with his nose and gobbles up the treat.

"Winnie can do that too," Dragomir says, then takes out a treat and sticks it under a cup.

Winnie cocks her head.

He says something in Ruskovian.

She points her giant snout at the cup.

Smiling warmly, he lifts the cup and lets the big girl eat the treat.

Something inside me squeezes. That smile looks good on him, but then again, pretty much everything does.

"So," I say, fighting the urge to activate the balls, "now that they know the protocol, we hide a treat so they can see the right cup, turn them around for thirty seconds, then test their memory by turning them back to see if they go for the right cup on the first try. Or the second. The more guesses, the worse the test performance."

He nods. "Ladies first."

"Dog or human?"

He grins. "Your team goes first."

I get another treat, put it under the middle cup, turn Boner around, and count thirty Mississippis.

"Thirty seconds," Dragomir says, reminding me about his watch.

Oops. I'm glad it's Boner's memory we're testing and not mine.

"Sweetie, get the treat," I say.

Without hesitation, Boner knocks over the middle cup and swallows the treat. *"Savoureux."*

Yes! Who's a smart boy?

"Your turn," I tell Dragomir, unable to keep the smugness from my voice.

He puts his treat under the middle cup and turns Winnie away.

Another thirty Mississippis later, he turns her back.

She cocks her head again.

He gives the Ruskovian command.

She looks up at him, as if confused.

His next command sounds a little sharper.

She turns back toward the cups, seems to concentrate, then puts the rightmost cup in her mouth and begins to chew.

Wow. She really buckled under the pressure.

"Winnifred, fu!" Dragomir orders, his tone that of someone whose every command is obeyed without question.

Ears drooping, Winnie spits out the chewed-up cup, then points her nose at the middle one.

He lifts the correct cup so she can eat her treat.

I wait a few beats to make sure I don't sound like I'm gloating. "I guess we win."

"It was the smell of coffee on the cup." He sounds defensive. "She loves coffee."

I meet his gaze. "Are you welshing on our bet?"

He blows out a breath. "Let's get this over with."

Since he's about to kneel, I step away, else he might see up my skirt—a problem, especially since I haven't had the moment of privacy required to fix my thong.

Placing what's left of his turtleneck on the ground next to Boner, Dragomir gets on his knees, towering over my dog's tiny body.

"Pick him up so the two of you are eye to eye," I say, trying not to laugh. "Assuming he's okay with that."

This is also a test. Two actually.

First: Will Dragomir be an ass about it and refuse?

Second: Boner is a decent judge of character when it comes to letting people touch him. For instance, he growls at both of my parents when they try. So if Dragomir is evil on *that* level, this won't go smoothly.

To my shock, Dragomir croons something in Ruskovian and gently scratches Boner behind the ear.

Am I jealous of my own dog?

Boner wags his tail.

Operation Pick-Up is clearly a go as far as he's concerned.

Dragomir lifts him gently, looks him in the eyes, and with impressive sincerity says, "Napoleon Bonaparte, I'm sorry. You're the smartest dog—nay, being —I've ever met."

In reply, Boner licks Dragomir's face.

I start laughing, all the tension between us popping like an overfilled balloon.

Dragomir gently puts Boner back on the ground and grins at me.

I wasn't the only one who felt jealous, apparently. Winnie rushes to Dragomir and also licks his face—leaving a giant jellyfish worth of slobber on his chiseled features.

My laughter is now out of control. My eyes tear up, my nose runs, and then, to my horror, the muscles in my vagina suddenly fail at their job—and I feel the Kegel balls slipping out.

Crap. I was able to run and have an orgasm without losing the slippery things, just to be done in by laughter?

Boosted by adrenaline, I catch one of the balls by my knee. The second one, however, drops to the ground and rolls in Winnie's direction.

No.

Please don't—

Without a second of hesitation, Winnie snatches the ball with her mouth.

"Fu!" I yell.

The command doesn't work.

Winnie swallows the ball.

Chapter Six

*D*ragomir looks at me questioningly.

Of course. He's just heard me say "Fu."

How do I explain what happened? *Gee, your dog must like the taste of my girl juices because she just swallowed a sex toy I've been hiding in my vag.*

Do I even need to tell him?

Won't Winnie just poop the ball out?

Ugh, but what if there are some complications?

I can't not tell him.

"You're going to be mad," I say, frantically trying to come up with the least embarrassing way to deliver the news.

His thick eyebrows snap together. "What happened?"

I show him the ball I caught. "I was trying to relax using these… err… Chinese meditation balls, and one fell and Winnifred swallowed it."

There. Sounds believable.

Unfortunately, it doesn't take a linguist to know that the next thing Dragomir growls in Ruskovian is a curse. Squatting next to Winnie, he urges her to upchuck the ball—to no avail.

He mutters another curse under his breath and jumps to his feet. Darting a glance at his watch, he starts dragging her away without so much as a good-bye, his long legs eating the ground in furious strides.

Crap. "Is she going to be okay?" I call after them.

"How the fuck should I know?" The question is thrown over his shoulder with such intensity that both dogs flatten their ears. "That's why we're going to the vet."

I grab Boner and run after them. "Let me come with you. I feel terrible about this."

"You've done enough." He lengthens his strides.

I give up chasing him. "I'll call to check on her!" I yell to his back. "And I'll let you know if Boner has any STDs."

I might've yelled the word *STDs* a bit too loudly, because I get a bunch of strange looks from the passersby.

If Dragomir hears me, he doesn't show it.

"Well, that sucked." Going back, I grab the cup with the writing on it and lead Boner away.

When I get home, the first thing I do is locate my phone so I can enter Dragomir's number into my contacts.

Turning the cup over, I stare at it, dumbfounded.

There's no number or name on it.

Well, there is a name, but it's Barbara.

Grr. When I grabbed the stupid thing, I didn't double-check to make sure the writing on it was actually *his* writing.

"I'll be back," I tell Boner and run back to the park.

As I approach the spot where I first met Dragomir, I notice a garbage truck driving down the street, which gives me an unpleasant feeling in the pit of my stomach.

The feeling deepens as I get to the doggy playground.

The two cups I left behind are now missing.

As I feared, someone has cleaned them up.

Heading back home, I picture Dragomir waiting for my call, then assuming I'm a terrible person who doesn't give a crap about the fate of his dog—which couldn't be further from the truth.

By the time I enter my apartment, I'm so upset I need a mood boost, so I ask Alexa to play Boner's favorite song: "Who Let the Dogs Out."

As always when it comes on, Boner begins to howl-sing to the music and bark at the *woof* parts. Though I've seen lots of other Chihuahuas sing to music on YouTube, none seem as talented as mine.

He's so good, in fact, I half expect him to compose a doggy opera one day—and call it *La Bonerhème*.

"You're a genius," I tell Boner when the song is over.

He wags his tail. "Tell me something I don't know, *ma chérie*."

With a grin, I go get his snack, and when I come back with it, I catch him licking his butthole.

"So much for genius," I mutter.

Seeing the treat in my hand, he darts over and eagerly gobbles it down. Afterward, as he often does, he rushes over to Remy, the sex toy I designed for him, and begins humping it.

Remy is a plush rat that looks a lot like a female Chihuahua, only with a tiny sleeve-style faux vagina built in. Bringing this product to market is on my to-do list, though for now, human sex needs are a bigger priority for my business.

"Dude, you just had sex in the park," I say gently, to avoid giving him that sex complex. "Minutes ago."

"This is what a healthy libido is like, *ma chérie*. Envy doesn't look good on *vous*."

Grinning, I go to my office to give him privacy.

That turns out to be a mistake. Now that I'm alone, thoughts of Dragomir resurface.

Jumping on my laptop, I look up Ruskovia and Dragomir.

Nope. Too many results, and none of the top ones point in his direction.

It's official: I don't have a way to get in touch. The

best I can do is hope that we'll meet again in that section of the park, but Boner and I have always gone there and this was our first time running into Dragomir. He must not come there often—and after what happened, I wouldn't be surprised if he'd outright avoid that spot from now on.

With a sigh, I check my calendar.

Great. I almost forgot an important meeting with my brother later today.

I need to clear my head, pronto. But how?

One option is to masturbate while thinking about Dragomir. I have a whole suitcase of toys—all designed by me and produced by my company, Belka.

No, bad idea. That would only make me think of him more.

It's time for the big guns.

I turn on my TV and put on a movie that never fails to cheer me up: *Frozen*.

Ever since I was a little girl, I've been compared unfavorably to the Snow Queen, a villainous character from a Danish fairy tale that is popular in Russia. And then Disney came along and made that same character into a kickass princess, turning the whole thing on its head. I love it, and not just because I'd lived by the key lesson of *Frozen* even before I saw it—being yourself without apologizing for it.

Or in the words of my favorite song from the soundtrack: I don't care what they're going to say… about my sex toys.

As always, the movie lifts my spirits. Afterward, I

get some food and coffee, then work on designing a new toy. I make great progress, getting as far as sending a prototype to my 3D printer.

When it's time, I grab a gift for my bro, put on my sharpest business suit and most kickass boots, and head to his office.

Chapter Seven

Stepping out of the elevator, I grin at the plaque that proudly proclaims, "1000 Devils."

This is my brother's way of owning our last name, Chortsky, which means "of the devil." He's made it so that "a thousand chorts" is no longer just a Russian curse, but also a cool video game development company.

I've done something similar myself. "Belka" is what our mother calls me when she's unhappy with me—which is all the time. So—in part because that word also means *squirrel*—I've decided to claim that name for my sex toy company.

Before I advance any deeper into the lobby, I take a sharp turn into the armory and choose a couple of my favorite guns. This office has a tradition of its employees shooting Nerf guns at visitors, and I like to dish out as good as I get.

Holding my weapons Lara Croft style, I dash onto the floor, eyes scanning for foes.

For some reason, the male employees here rarely, if ever, shoot at me. The female employees, on the other hand, are always out for my blood.

I have a big advantage, though. I was a tomboy growing up, and I have two brothers, one of whom created this shooting tradition in the first place. If there were a SEAL Team Six of Nerf assaults, I'd be on it.

The first woman to leap out at me is not even trying. She's got her gun in one hand and a coffee in the other.

Without aiming, she shoots.

I duck, then launch a dart at her collarbone. As I'd hoped, the projectile drops from her shirt and into her cup.

That should teach her.

The next lady is older, so I'm more respectful as I unload my gun into her, aiming for the legs.

The next two I get before they even get the chance to pull the trigger.

Suddenly, a dart smacks me between my shoulder blades.

So it's like that now? Hit me in the back?

Pivoting on the attacker, I shoot without aiming.

Oops.

I happen to know this lady's name is Karen, and she must've been about to yell a war cry or something because the dart is in her mouth now… or maybe her throat.

She's making gagging noises and flapping her arms like a headless chicken.

Dropping the guns, I rush over and prepare to do the Heimlich maneuver. Since my parents own a restaurant, everyone in my family has learned how to do this, just in case.

Karen doesn't seem to need the help, though. After a few more gagging sounds, she spits out the dart, clears her throat, and gives me a sheepish smile.

The incident puts a damper on the shootout, so no one bugs me as I collect my guns and make my way to the meeting room.

Alex, my oldest brother and the owner of 1000 Devils, gives me a warm hug as I walk in.

Pulling back, I grin at him. With his blue eyes, black hair, pale skin, and symmetrical facial features, he's like my gender-bending mirror—especially if you ignore the perpetual scruff on his face.

Sitting down, he shakes his head. "If Karen sues, you'll owe me."

I take a seat in front of him. "She shot me in the back. Mess with the bull, get the horns."

He grins. "Wouldn't you be a cow in that scenario?"

I pull his gift out of my bag. "Why is everything cattle-related so sexist? Why does *cowed* mean *submissive*? Why is it a bullish market instead of a cowish market?

Bullshit instead of cowshit. Bull Terrier instead of Cow Terrier. Bull in a china shop instead of cow. Did you know that cows kill more people per year than sharks?"

He shrugs. "Hey, given how many get slaughtered for our pleasure, it's only fair they even out the odds sometimes."

"I've got a gift for you." I slide the box across the table.

Cringing, he peeks inside.

I put on my ventriloquist hat. "Like, hello." I make my voice low and creaky, throwing it so it seems to be coming from the box. "I'm, like, totally your new girlfriend. You seriously better use me or else."

He rakes his hand through his messy dark locks. "Another sex toy?"

My grin is evil—I get to make fun of both of my brothers in one go. "That's a sleeve made out of Belka's patented material. More importantly, it's Vlad's favorite."

Vlad, our middle sibling, recently got embroiled in testing my products—with his employee, no less. Now said employee, Fanny, is his girlfriend. So naturally, Alex and I will never stop teasing him about it.

Alex's chuckle is uncomfortable, to say the least. "Thanks. I think. Just know that the world at large can twist your good intentions to make us look like the Lannisters—or the Borgias."

"Couldn't care less about rumors," I say breezily.

"What if I told you I can get my own toys?" he says. "I can even buy them from your website."

Another evil grin. "I'll make you a deal. Get your-self a girlfriend, and the gifts might stop."

He rolls his eyes. "Double standard much? When will you start dating?"

I feel a pang of regret. If I hadn't lost that cup, maybe—

"Hey, sis, I'm sorry," Alex says, misinterpreting my expression. "I forgot that it's a sensitive topic."

He's talking about my last disastrous relationship. The ass turned out to be married—a lie by omission that left me devastated.

"I'm fine," I say, shrugging off the unpleasant memories. "How about we get down to business?"

"Right." He stashes my gift under the table. "This has something to do with the business venture you've been trying to launch? The sex suit that works with VR?"

"I prefer thinking of it as an immersive sexual experience, but yes. The idea is to democratize plea-sure. To bring sex to people who have trouble getting it for whatever reason, or who don't want it with real people. Burn victims, people with disabilities, those with an extremely contagious sexually transmitted disease or crippling social anxiety—the list goes on and on. The same product can also help people in long-distance relationships, as well as astronauts and—"

"Dude, you don't need to sell me on it," he says. "I think the venture sounds really cool, and might make you the richest one in the family."

"You know I don't care about money—though having said that, money is kind of why I'm here."

In an eyeblink, he's got a checkbook in his hands. "How much do you need?"

I smile. "You don't have the kind of money I need. VR hardware is big leagues."

He whistles. "You plan to design a VR headset? I thought it was just the suit."

I shake my head. "Off-the-shelf VR companies are prudish when it comes to their app stores, and their headsets are not that friendly to people with smaller heads—like women. Besides, the best kind of suit would have the VR gear built in anyway. I found a promising company that makes adjustable headsets that's not doing so well. I want to buy it and integrate them into my venture."

He puts the checkbook away. "Wow. Buying a VR company? Didn't Facebook pay two billion for Oculus?"

"This won't be at the same level, but yeah. This is why I've been looking for investors."

"And?"

I sigh. "I've been at it for months, but no luck. I don't know if it's Belka's core business, or my gender, or my pitching abilities, but no one is biting."

He steeples his fingers. "How can I help?"

I dig a flash drive out of my bag and slide it over to him. "It's all there. To sum up, I want to start a joint venture with you that might sound more appealing to potential investors than one that's solely mine. The sex stuff doesn't need to be overly prominent in our presentation."

He pockets the flash drive. "A bait-and-switch strategy?"

"Kind of. What we'll tell them is the truth: I'll build the hardware, and you'll head the team that writes the software. The project will still be labeled as adult entertainment."

He scratches his scruffy chin. "So what will the software do, officially?"

"Your call. I'm thinking casino, or life simulation à la Second Life or the Sims."

He grins. "And we just don't mention that the casino will have a strip club section, or that the most popular activity in this VR second life will be hooking up?"

"Yep. At least not if they don't explicitly ask about that."

In other words, it will be a lie. I have no illusions on this front. Not telling someone something important—like their marital status—*is* a lie.

Alex drums his fingers on the table. "That's a lot to think about."

I stand up. "Please review everything on that drive and let me know your decision. If you're not interested, I'll go to Vlad. It just sounds more like your cup of tea."

He also rises to his feet. "It does. I have experience making VR games already. They're PG, but still. Also,

I have to say, this sounds very promising, both as a coding project and financially."

I give him a line from my current spiel for investors. "Porn is a hundred-billion-dollar industry. It's been shrinking because of piracy and free content, but that wouldn't be an issue for this venture because we're going to be selling special suits. Plus, VR apps and games are more challenging to pirate."

He walks to the meeting room door and opens it for me. "If the investors worry about piracy, I can tell them the steps we take for 1000 Devils games."

I give him a peck on the cheek as I leave. "I knew you'd be useful. Let me know as soon as you decide either way."

Chapter Eight

"*A* standard shipment of anal beads?" I double-check with the rep on the phone.

"Yep. Also, we want to double our order of butt plugs," she says.

"I'll get my people on it."

"Thanks," she says and hangs up.

I sigh. I made a point to hire a person to deal with adult toy superstores, yet I still occasionally have to field the calls myself, especially from the bigger clients.

Before I forget, I write an email to the person who should've gotten that call and copy the whole Belka logistics team for good measure. I use our item number codes in place of words like "anal beads" and "butt plugs," as this greatly cuts down on unnecessary giggles, especially among newer employees.

Since I'm already in business mode, I check on our Amazon sales, as well as our other major retailers.

Business is great, though the line of smart toys

isn't yet selling as well as I want. Our bestsellers are still the Cucumbernator, the cucumber-shaped dildo I designed on a lark, and the Squidinator, a mollusk-shaped clit massager made from our patented material that actually makes it feel like a squid.

For the rest of the day and the two days that follow, I wait for Alex to make his decision and keep myself from thinking about Dragomir by designing new toys and working on the VR suit.

I also walk Boner in the same part of the park, but no luck. I have yet to come across the bear and her gorgeous owner again. I'll just have to hope Winnie pooped the ball out without any problems.

As I arrive home from the park the next morning, I receive a text from my best friend, Xenia. It's in Russian but written with English letters:

Come have brunch with me. I found a place where they allow dogs.

I haven't seen Xenia in a while, so I eagerly reply in the affirmative, pick out a gift for her, and rush out with Boner in tow.

———

The dog-friendly restaurant turns out to also be kid-friendly—which isn't very friendly to Chihuahuas.

"*Ma chérie*, keep those giant *monstres* away," Boner's frightened eyes seem to say as I shoo a five-year-old boy and girl away from our table while cursing Xenia under my breath for being late.

Once the kid threat is averted, I resume doodling on the paper tablecloth. By the time Xenia finally arrives, our table is completely covered in small penises. Besides looking cute, they provide the added bonus of motivating most moms to keep their offspring away from my dog.

"Hi, honey," Xenia says in Russian and pecks me on both cheeks.

"Hey, babe," I reply in English.

A mix of English and Russian is how we always talk; this way, she can improve her English and I my Russian.

"Happy belated birthday." I thrust a box into her hands. "And don't worry, I won't ask how old you've turned. Only your current weight."

Somewhere in her mid-sixties, Xenia is my oldest friend—both in terms of her age and in how long we've known each other. In fact, we go all the way back to when she was a chef in my parents' restaurant. We stayed in touch after they fired her for "being vulgar" and "corrupting" me. Of course, the truth is just the opposite. Even as a teen, I was a much worse influence on her than she was on me.

"Thank you." She shakes the box skeptically and lowers her voice to a whisper. "Is it yet another dildo?"

"Open it to find out."

She does, after first looking around furtively. "It *is* a dildo."

"A custom-made one I printed just for you. I

designed it a week before your birthday but waited until after to give it to you."

She nods approvingly. Even more superstitious than I am, Xenia knows that giving someone a birthday gift or congrats before the actual date is a huge no-no. In the Russian tradition, you can only do it on the day of or after.

"See that evil eye thingy at the tip?" I ask.

She pulls the dildo halfway out so she can examine its mushroom-like head.

Since Xenia is always worried about jinxes and evil eye curses, she wears a nazar amulet in the shape of an eye to ward off bad spirits and malevolent intentions. Now she also has a toy decorated with the same design.

As she examines it, her face flushes and her eyebrows pull together. "Do you think someone could cast an evil eye down there?" She glances down her body. "Only Boy Toy ever sees it. Well, and the doctor."

I shrug. "Better safe than sorry."

Xenia is a widow who was single for many years. But recently, she met a forty-five-year-old guy whom she's dubbed her "boy toy." According to her, he looks like Liam Neeson, Xenia's celebrity crush. Having met Boy Toy, I personally think that with his beer belly and bushy gray beard, he looks a lot more like Santa Claus, but I'll never mention this to Xenia since I highly approve of her dating.

"Mommy, what is that?" A little girl points at Xenia's gift, her eyes widening.

I deepen my voice and throw it so it appears to come out of the box my friend is holding. "I'm the nice lady's very special new best friend."

The kid goggles at the dildo until her mom drags her away, muttering something about crazy people.

Xenia laughs and stashes her gift away. "When are you going to find yourself a man instead of playing with these toys?"

Before I can reply, a waiter arrives and we both order mimosas and the Eggs Benedict.

When he leaves, I tell Xenia about Dragomir.

"Wow," she says. "You should, as they say in English, 'hatefuck the guy.'"

She looks up to find the waiter with a tray and blushes. He's clearly caught the last bit of her wisdom.

Once our food and drink are on the table and we have privacy again, I say, "I can't do anything with him. I lost his number."

She waves dismissively. "If it's meant to be, it's meant to be. Remember how you put that top on backward last month? I told you that meant you'd meet someone new."

Xenia knows some extra-obscure superstitions, many of which are clothing-related for some reason. Recently, I accidentally wore a T-shirt inside out, and she claimed I'd get beaten unless a friend punched me first. So she whacked me. Talk about a self-fulfilling prophecy.

"I'll keep walking Boner in that section of the park. Maybe he'll show up." I toss my little friend a treat, and he gratefully wags his tail.

Smacking herself on the forehead, Xenia rummages in her bag and takes out a plastic bag. "It's for the little devil," she says with a grin.

Xenia's new business is gourmet dog food, so I know Boner will appreciate the contents of the bag.

Since we have company, I throw Boner's voice under the table for Xenia's pleasure. "*Ma chérie*, let me sample the goods before you hide them."

I toss him one of Xenia's creations.

"Ah, Xenia. You're a *génie culinaire*."

"Merci," Xenia says to Boner, then looks up at me. "Do you think this Dragomir could be the one?"

She doesn't mean one true love. At least I don't think so. She's one of the few people who knows about a problem I've developed since my last bad relationship: I can't seem to achieve an orgasm with a guy. So, when Xenia says "the one," she usually means "the one who can make you come without the aid of sex toys."

I shrug. "He could've been. I *did* already have an orgasm next to him."

Her eyes widen, and I tell her about the Kegel balls.

"You're not wearing those things here and now, right?" she asks with a slight wrinkling of her nose.

"No, but you probably should be. Boy Toy would appreciate the results."

"I've found them to be too tickly," she says. "Now, how about you tell me some more about this guy."

"Like what?"

"Well, with a name like Dragomir, is he Russian?"

"Nope. Ruskovian."

Xenia's eyes widen. "Ruskovian, huh? They have a reputation."

"For being rude?"

She looks around. "For being well-endowed."

I nearly choke on my mimosa.

"Don't move." She narrows her eyes on my face, then reaches in and grabs something from my cheek.

"An eyelash." She shows it to me. "Make a wish."

I blow the eyelash away as the superstition dictates. As I do, I wish to run into Dragomir again, so I can check if Xenia's statement holds true for him —purely for science, of course.

Hold up. I should've used up the wish on the new venture instead. Oh, well. Hopefully, I'll shed another eyelash someday soon.

For the rest of the brunch, we give each other updates on our work lives. As I'm about to leave, Xenia stops me from using lip balm by saying, "If your lips are dry enough, they'll itch, which means you'll be kissing someone soon."

Hmm. I wonder if purposely drying your lips annuls that. Just in case, though, I don't apply the lip balm.

"Keep me posted on Dragomir," Xenia says as we hug goodbye.

I sigh, stepping back. "I doubt there will be updates, but sure."

————

Before getting home, I take Boner into the park on the off chance the eyelash magic actually happens.

Nope.

When we get home, I check for messages from Alex.

Aha. He wants to talk, so I call him up.

"Hi, sis."

"Hey. Did you decide?"

"It's a go. We should talk details."

A cab ride and a shootout later, I'm back in his office, where we discuss the logistics of the venture and the fundraising for the rest of the day. Since his company is the respectable one, and he's the one with the penis, we decide that he'll be the first to meet with the investors, then pull me in as needed.

We also divvy up some tasks. I'm to continue working on the suit, and he's going to put together two demos of the software: sexy and vanilla.

————

Alex's first meeting with the investors takes place the next week, and our strategy works. We get our first backers. Unfortunately, they only commit a modest sum.

Still, when I get home that evening, I feel like I should celebrate, so I pour myself a glass of wine and put on a movie that never fails to turn me on: Michael Fassbender playing Steve Jobs.

It's not that I like either of these men. I just love a guy in a turtleneck.

Pulling out my favorite vibrator from my suitcase of toys, I get myself off, though instead of the movie, it's a mental image of Dragomir in a turtleneck that I actually orgasm to.

Thank fuck for toys. As a teen, I nearly got carpal tunnel from masturbating to the album cover of *With the Beatles*—the one where the whole band wears turtlenecks. I also used to do it to the very old *Cosmos* show, in which the host, Carl Sagan, always wore a turtleneck.

The latter might also be how I developed a passion for science, which later led to an obsession with engineering, and then, naturally, the designing of high-tech sex toys.

To quote *The Lion King*, it's the circle of life.

Chapter Nine

"Which sounds better: a dildo attachment for a drill, a clit stimulator attachment for an electric toothbrush, or a saddle that goes on top of a washing machine?" I ask my focus group over Zoom. "Or none of the above?"

The toothbrush attachment turns out to be the winner, so I design a few that can work with the most popular electric toothbrush brands.

As I'm eating lunch after my design-fest, I get a videocall from my brother Vlad.

"Your new venture," he says as soon as I see his face, one nearly identical to Alex's, only way less scruffy and with glasses. "I want in on it."

I grin into the camera. "And hello to you too."

"Sorry. Hi, sis. I was just a little annoyed to be kept out of the loop."

"Oh, sorry. I just didn't want to put you in an uncomfortable position. We both know that if I'd asked for money, you would've wanted to say yes regardless of what it was for."

His stern expression softens. "I didn't think of that."

My grin widens. "After all the testing you've done for Belka, I figured it was time I imposed on Alex instead."

He rolls his eyes. "Well, Alex told me about your project, and I want to invest. Let's talk details."

So we do, and in the process, he agrees to help me and Alex with cybersecurity—his specialty. He also comes up with a cool name for the venture—Project Morpheus—and last but not least, he commits a cool mil, bringing me a little closer to my goal.

———

For the next week, we attempt to hunt down more investors without much to show for it. Nor do I bump into Dragomir in the park—a double bummer.

I do get hiccups on Thursday, though, which means someone is remembering me. I hope it's him.

The week after that is the same: no new funding and no Dragomir. Though on Wednesday, my ears do feel hot, which means someone is thinking of me—again, hopefully him.

Thursday night, Xenia comes over to my house for a Liam Neeson marathon. Turns out, he and many other hot male actors wear turtlenecks in *Love*

Actually—info that goes into my ever-growing turtle-neck-related spank bank.

The last movie we watch is *Star Wars*, and something about her favorite actor with long hair and Jedi powers must really do it for Xenia, because she fans herself every single time his character is on the screen.

When the credits roll, I attempt to get her to try VR games—one of my favorite leisure activities.

"You'd like *Beat Saber*," I say, holding out the VR headset. "It's a game where you hold two lightsabers, just like Liam did in *Star Wars*, and swing them at notes to the beat of a song you like."

She reluctantly agrees, so I put the headset on her head and thrust the game controllers into her hands.

Boner steps aside—he clearly remembers how I'd nearly trampled him during my last VR session.

As soon as the game starts, Xenia screams bloody murder in Russian and flaps her arms so wildly that one of the remotes flies out of her hand and smashes into my boob.

Massaging the injury, I help my friend escape the evil headset.

"I guess VR isn't for you," I say as she glares at me.

Too bad. Until now, Xenia was on my short list of beta testers for the Project Morpheus VR sex suit.

Is that amusement in Boner's eyes?

"*Ma chérie*, I'm suddenly craving some chicken, ideally with the head cut off."

———

On Friday of the following week, Alex tells me he's found a "whale"—a venture capital firm with deep pockets that might commit all the money we need in one fell swoop. They liked what he had to say, and now they want to meet with me to get all the technical details about the hardware.

I'm so excited I give myself three orgasms using my best toys, then stay up all night ironing out my presentation. By morning, I'm a little bleary-eyed but bushy-tailed and prepped to the max.

I put on my most conservative business suit, slip my feet into my favorite stilettos, slather on some war-paint-quality makeup, and take a cab downtown.

All the dough to fund my dream, here I come.

Chapter Ten

*E*verything about this company screams swanky, from the gleaming glass-and-steel building to the immaculate marble floors and the giant, testosterone-filled meeting room I step into.

Alex winks at me, then addresses the room of eight other men with a serious expression. "Gentlemen, this is Bella Chortsky, my partner and the hardware expert we've been waiting for."

The guy who seems to be the leader had been eyeing me like a piece of candy. Now his look shifts to undisguised disappointment. "She's going to explain the hardware?" he asks, with way too much emphasis on *she*. His accent sounds Eastern European, and his face looks vaguely familiar for some reason, though I'm sure I've never met him before.

I reward the asshole with my Snow Queen glare.

Alex's hands bunch at his sides. "Indeed. She *is* the expert. An MIT graduate, mind you, with——"

"I didn't mean anything." The guy takes a step back from my brother, who despite his general laid-back-ness, can be pretty frightening when angry. "Why don't we go over the technical specs of the suit as we wait for Mr. Lamian?"

Alex's expression goes back to congenial. "Sure. I cede the floor to Bella, my sister and the co-owner of Project Morpheus."

The guy extends his clammy hand to me, and I shake it with a fake smile.

"I'm Marco Fluroff," he says. "Please, call me Marco."

"And you can call me Bella," I say, extracting my hand and resisting the urge to wipe his sweat off my palm.

Wait. Marco? *That's* who he reminds me of. The villain from *Taken*, the movie I re-watched with Xenia during our Liam Neeson marathon. Even the name of the human trafficker from that film was the same: Marco.

Taking over the big screen, I open my presentation and launch into my carefully rehearsed spiel about the hardware. As I go through all the technical details, I can't help picturing myself delivering a paraphrased version of the ultimatum from *Taken* to this Marco:

"I have a very particular set of skills—skills making sex toys. I have acquired them over a very long career helping horny people. These skills make me a nightmare for people like you. If you commit the money now, that will be the end of it—I will not look for you, I will not pursue you... but if you don't, I will look for you, I will find you... and shove a giant dildo up your ass."

"Any questions?" I say with a bright smile when I've gone through all the salient points.

Shrugging, Marco glances at a dude in glasses. "Eugenius?"

The guy stands up. "Just to clarify, the haptic feedback you've designed into the suit will allow users to experience a touch as light as that of a feather?"

Feather, if you're into tickle play, or a lover's kiss, or a lick as well—but I don't say any of that. "That's right. As you can imagine, this will allow for extremely life-like sensations when wearing the suit."

"Interesting stuff," Eugenius says approvingly. "Is it customizable for sensitive users?"

"Definitely," I say, and he sits back down. I level a challenging stare at Marco. "How about you? Does everything I've explained make sense?"

Based on how his eyes had glazed over when I got technical, I highly doubt it.

He clears his throat. "I'm more of a financial guy, but it all seems clear to me. And I just got a text from Mr. Lamian. He's about to step into the—"

The doors open, and a tall, powerfully built man dressed in a dark suit strides in.

His piercing hazel eyes land on me—and immediately narrow into catlike slits.

Fucking fuck.

My heartbeat leaps into overdrive, and my entire body flushes.

This is Mr. Lamian?

I know him by a different name.

His first name.

Dragomir.

Chapter Eleven

"*Y*ou?" Dragomir growls, crossing the room toward me in long strides.

"You?" I exclaim almost at the same time.

Everyone looks at us with confused expressions.

I can't blame them. Dragomir looks like he's on the verge of spitting fire.

"I lost the cup with your number," I blurt before he has the chance to accuse me of something awful.

"A convenient excuse." He sweeps his gaze around the room and commands, "Leave us."

His company isn't run as a democracy, that's for sure. Marco and the rest leap to their feet and scatter like hunted quail.

Only Alex stays. He puts himself between me and Dragomir, his face twisting into something scary. "Who are you, and what the fuck do you want with my sister?"

"It's okay," I say in Russian. "I've met him before. He's got a reason to be upset. A misunderstanding. I'll clear it up."

If my ovaries don't explode, that is. Dragomir looks so damn good in that suit—maybe even better than in a turtleneck. No, that's blasphemy. But maybe a suit over a turtleneck? Yeah, that would be—

Wait, what am I thinking here? I have to focus. My dream project is at stake.

"I don't give a fuck what his reason is," Alex growls back at me in Russian. "If he so much as—"

"I just want to talk," Dragomir says in accented Russian. "I'd never harm her. What kind of a savage do you take me for?"

He's trilingual? I guess I shouldn't be surprised. A lot of folks in Eastern Europe learn Russian as a second language. English too, for that matter.

"Just talk?" Alex's fierce expression eases slightly. I think he's recalled that I'm not a preteen, and that this is a corporate environment, not a playground riddled with bullies. Not that I needed my brothers to handle bullies for me, much to my mother's chagrin.

"Probably a short chat at that," Dragomir says, switching to English. "Can we please have some privacy?"

Alex reluctantly heads toward the door. Before exiting, he turns and gives Dragomir another glare, just in case. "If you hurt my sister in any way, it won't end well for you."

He sounds so convincing that I have to remind

myself he's a software engineer and not a mafia enforcer from *Eastern Promises*.

"Is Winnie okay?" I ask as soon as Alex closes the door. "Did the ball come out?"

Dragomir nods. "Everything got resolved that same day." He studies me intently, his mercurial eyes seeming to fluctuate between green and gold-flecked brown. "Have you tested Bonaparte for STDs?"

Crap. I'm tempted to lie, but that wouldn't be cool. I opt for the truth. "I'm sorry. I didn't have your contact info, so I didn't think it was necessary."

Now that I think about it, I should've done it anyway—and I would have, if things hadn't gotten so busy with all the fundraising.

Dragomir's lips twist. "Like I said, a convenient excuse."

I step toward him, trying not to think about how sexy those lips seem even now. "Listen to me, please. I know how this looks. If I were you, I'd probably be skeptical too, but I swear this was a mix-up. I took a cup that had writing on it, but it turned out to say 'Barbara.' I ran back immediately, but they'd just cleaned the park and picked up the trash. I went back every day after that, trying to find you and Winnie so I could make it right."

And so I could see him again, but I don't tell him that. It's way too soon. Also, getting closer to him was a strategic miscalculation—at least as far as keeping my thinking clear. With that subtle hint of cinnamon tickling my nostrils, all I want is to jump into his arms and—

Wait, did his hard expression just soften?

Score!

Maybe he's remembered seeing the name *Barbara* on one of the cups.

I press my advantage. "Now that we've reconnected, I will of course test Boner for anything you want and as soon as possible."

He tilts his head. "Is that so?"

"Of course."

"How about now?"

I blink at him. "As in, right now?"

"You said as soon as possible."

"Fine, let's do it now," I say, belatedly realizing how big of a bust this investment meeting is—which really sucks, as I was hoping to be done with the fundraising part of the venture so I can get to the fun bits, like actually building the suit.

He steps over to the door and opens it for me.

As we walk out, everyone looks at us questioningly, especially Alex.

"The meeting is adjourned," Dragomir says in that uncompromising, boss-of-the-world manner of his.

"We have a private matter we need to attend to," I whisper to Alex in Russian. "Don't worry. He's not a threat to me."

At least not to my physical wellbeing. To my

hormones, Dragomir is kryptonite, but that isn't something my brother needs to be worried about.

"Text me whenever your matter is concluded," Alex says, and it's clear I'll have to tell him the whole story, sans the balls in my vagina.

"Deal," I say, and we all ride the elevator down in the most uncomfortable silence I've ever participated in.

Marco is the first to escape the elevator at the lobby, with Alex and the rest of the investment crew filing out after him. Dragomir and I stay to ride down to the parking lot.

"This is us." Dragomir gestures at a strange vehicle already waiting by the curb.

I gape at the thing.

If a bus, an RV, and a limo blew up, and the parts randomly got reassembled into a single hybrid car, it might look like this.

"Is this even allowed on the streets of New York?" I ask. "It looks like a mobile home... for an eco-tech billionaire."

His mouth quirks. "It's legal. Parking can be a challenge, but thanks to Fyodor, I don't have to worry about that."

A door opens and a ladder descends. A man wearing a tuxedo jacket with tailcoats greets us in a deep, British-accented voice. "Please, come inside."

The RV has a butler?

"Thanks, Fyodor," Dragomir says and gestures for me to go first.

Impossibly, the vehicle looks bigger inside than outside—like the TARDIS from *Doctor Who*. I spot a treadmill large enough for a bear to run on—which is exactly what Dragomir's bear is currently doing—a sleek computer desk that's designed to alternate between sitting and standing positions, a plush leather couch bigger than the one in my living room, and a full-sized bar that appears to be stocked with every drink imaginable.

"There are studio apartments in Manhattan smaller than this," I say in awe as Dragomir joins me.

"Winnie gets lonely when I leave her at home," he explains with a shrug. "This way, I can take her with me on most trips."

And I thought my Boner was spoiled rotten. Turns out he doesn't know the meaning of the word.

"May I get you something to drink?" Fyodor asks.

"I'm good," I say.

"We're in a hurry," Dragomir says. "We're headed to Ms. Chortsky's home." He looks at me. "What's the address?"

I grimace. "Please don't call me Ms. Chortsky. That sounds too much like my mother."

"Shall I call you 'mistress' then?" Fyodor asks without a hint of humor.

"Unless you want me to spank you, please call me Bella," I say, and to halt any further discussion on this topic, I rattle out my address.

With a bow, Fyodor scurries away to take a seat at the wheel, and as soon as the vehicle gets moving, a partition between us and Fyodor goes up, blocking him from view.

The treadmill stops, and Winnie notices Dragomir.

A whoosh of fur, and she's on her hind legs, licking his face.

Lucky bitch. I'd like to do that myself.

As Dragomir deals with his bear's affections, I scan the room.

Besides all the comforts I've already noted, on the shelf near the treadmill is the latest and greatest VR headset—better even than the one I own, and I splurged.

This really sucks. Besides rolling in dough, Dragomir is into VR. He would've been the perfect investor for our venture if I hadn't screwed everything up. Now who knows how long it'll take to find another investor like him.

It'll probably be as difficult as finding another man I'd be this attracted to. Even with that slobber on his face, if he wanted to kiss me right now, I'd let him.

Finally freeing himself, he pulls out a pack of wet wipes, cleans his face, and mops up the residual moisture with his handkerchief.

Odd. The initials on the hanky are D.C. Shouldn't that be D.L. for Dragomir Lamian?

"Take a seat." He gestures at the couch.

I obey and he joins me—though, sadly, he ends up on the cushion farthest from me.

"Are you into VR?" I ask, waving in the direction of his headset.

He nods. "That's what had caught my attention about your venture. Headgear is almost mainstream now, and there are some special-purpose treadmills on the market too." He glances at the one Winnie was running on. "A whole-body VR suit is the logical next step."

"It is," I say enthusiastically. "And I plan to be the one to bring it to people."

His sexy lips curve in a smile. "You don't lack confidence, that's for sure."

Is that a compliment? I'll take it.

"What's your favorite VR game?" he asks before I can steer the conversation toward the possibility of him investing in Project Morpheus after all.

"*Beat Saber*," I reply with a grin. "You?"

His eyes seem to shift from light brown to green. "Same. What's your favorite song?"

"'Radioactive' by Imagine Dragons. You?"

"Again, same. Have you beaten it on Expert?"

"Of course." I examine my bright red nails. "I've also done it on Expert Plus."

He lifts his eyebrows. "You have?"

Trust issues much? Why would I lie about something like this? Since I want to stay on his good side, I say, "Definitely. My name is on the worldwide scoreboard in the top ten: BabushkaPwned. Check me out. Or better yet, I can demonstrate my skills."

He shakes his head. "In a moving car, that'd be dangerous."

Yeah, sure. The ride is buttery smooth. I bet he just wants to master Expert Plus when I'm not around. That's what I'd do if I learned that someone I know in real life is better than I am at my favorite song. Or any song. Or any game.

I guess I am a bit competitive.

Since I doubt that challenging him would incentivize him to invest, I change the topic. "How old were you when you moved to the US?"

"Twenty-four," he says. "How about you?"

Wow. Those teachers who taught him English must've been really good—or he has a knack for languages.

"I was five," I say. "I barely remember Russia."

He grimaces. "I remember Ruskovia just fine."

So, he doesn't like something back home. I guess that's normal for folks who left one place for somewhere else.

"How about your family?" I ask. "Did they all move with you?"

At the word *family*, his face turns cold and expressionless.

Interesting.

Before I can ask anything else, the car stops.

"Go get Boner," he says, his tone once again coolly imperious.

As I make the trip, I ponder his reaction, and an unsettling idea jumps into my head.

Could he be married and hiding it, like my asshole ex?

It's feasible. A guy that hot and rich would usually be with someone. The lack of a wedding band on his finger doesn't mean squat based on my painful experience, nor does the lack of family pictures around his RV.

Once in my apartment, I immediately go to my computer and type "Dragomir Lamian" into Google.

Nothing.

There's zero information on him.

That's bizarre. My brother Vlad is almost pathologically paranoid about his digital profile, and even *he* has more data out there, like a mention of him on his company's website.

Dragomir's venture capital fund doesn't say who's at the helm.

"Isn't that sketch?" I ask Boner as I ready him for the trip.

"*Oui.* He might have *une femme.*"

Crap. The possibility of a wife means I need to stop being attracted to him. Actually, even if it turns out he's not married, there are just too many other issues. It's obvious he's filthy rich and moves in high-society circles—he's got a butler, for fuck's sake—so he's probably going to look down his regal nose at my sex toy company. Also, if his firm does end up investing in our venture, as unlikely as that seems right now, business and romance don't mix.

I square my shoulders.

Decision made.

No matter how much I want to lick his face, bear style, I will not give in to that urge.

Chapter Twelve

*B*oner in my arms, I step back into the RV-limo.

Damn it.

Seeing Dragomir's chiseled features once more, I realize that merely telling myself not to be attracted to him is going to be tricky. If I'm really serious about this, I'll have to avoid him after the STD test.

Yeah. That'd be the smart thing to do.

When Boner and Winnie spot each other, their tails begin to wag, with his repeatedly smacking my chin and hers nearly tripping up Dragomir.

Unable to help myself, I throw my interpretation of Boner's voice a few inches down to where his head is.

"Ah, Winnie, *ma petite*. I haven't been able to get our last *rendezvous* out of my mind."

That's definitely a smile that dances in the corners of Dragomir's eyes.

In the worst example of ventriloquism in history, Dragomir makes Winnie's voice sound much too deep, as if it's coming from his crotch—and gives it a Russian accent for some reason.

"How dare you, Napoleon Carlovich? Take a woman's virtue and then no call, Facebook message, or even a tweet?"

I grin. "Carlovich?" Is he trying to give the dog a Russian-style patronymic? Unless… do they have those in Ruskovia too? Mine is Borisovna, as in *daughter of Boris*. Does that mean—

"Carlo Bonaparte was the famous general's father," Dragomir says, answering my unspoken question. "Speaking of history, if anyone should be called anything petite, it's your dog. One of the real Napoleon's many nicknames was *Le Petit Caporal*."

"I hate to tell you this," I say in a conspiratorial whisper, "but my dog isn't actually a reincarnation of the real Napoleon. I know it seems uncanny, given how intelligent he is and all."

The smile spreads to Dragomir's lips. "You have to admit, put a bicorne on his head and they'd be like twins."

I laugh. "Do you mind if I let him hang out with her?"

Dragomir's smile disappears. "Let's make sure he's clean first, then we'll see."

Both Boner and Winnie look miserable at not being allowed to interact, so we distract them with treats and belly rubs as much as we can.

Thankfully, the ride to Dragomir's vet is brief.

"Stay with Fyodor," Dragomir says to Winnie as soon as we park. "We'll be back soon."

Winnie makes a strange whining sound and looks at the door.

"Fyodor!" Dragomir shouts, then rattles out something in Ruskovian.

The butler appears and puts a leash on Winnie. After we all step out of the vehicle, Dragomir turns to me and says, "Hold your breath."

Huh?

Before I can clarify what he means, he looks at Winnie and issues a command in Ruskovian. It sounds like "Kraken"—though that word could be on my mind because of Liam Neeson/Zeus in *Clash of the Titans.*

THPPTPHTPHPHHPH.

The fart coming out of Winnie's rear end goes on for what feels like an hour.

Boner tenses in my arms, his eyes widening.

I'm so shocked I forget Dragomir's order to hold my breath and accidentally inhale.

Fuuuuuck. My eyes water, and I begin to gag.

To say that the bear's flatulence smells like rotten eggs would be a disservice to rotten eggs. If I'd eaten fermented cabbage infused with pure hydrogen sulfide all my life and held in a fart for a decade, the final product still wouldn't have approached this level of foulness.

Is this how this dog breed rid Ruskovia of wolves and bears?

Shaking his head, Dragomir holds a handkerchief to his nose, surgical mask style. "Sorry about this. As you can imagine, if she'd done this in the car, I would've had to get a new one."

A new car or a new dog?

He strides to the building, and Boner and I hurry after him.

When we're inside, I finally take a breath.

Impossibly, the stench has managed to follow us in, but at least it's now diluted and merely reminds me of the worst fart I'd previously had the displeasure of smelling.

Boner looks longingly at Winnie through the glass door. Knowing dogs, the Kraken incident might well have made his infatuation with Winnie that much stronger.

"*Ma petite*, cruel *destin* has ripped us *à part*."

Hurrying to get farther away from the fart epicenter, we leap into the elevator.

By the time we enter the doctor's empty waiting room, the smell is finally gone.

"Why haven't you simply tested Winnie for STDs?" I ask Dragomir after I suck in a grateful breath of stale medical office air.

"I have. But what if Boner has something with a long incubation period?"

I barely resist rolling my eyes. "Like what?"

He shrugs his broad shoulders. "I don't want to

take any chances. In fact, after Boner is done, I'll get Winnie tested one more time."

Before I can ask what the point of that is, the doctor—a bewhiskered man who looks vaguely like Einstein—comes out. Looking at Dragomir though a pair of glasses with the thickest lenses I've ever seen, he says something in Ruskovian.

"In English, please," Dragomir says.

"Large apologies," the doctor says with a thick accent. "Allow me decoding of my tongue. I asked, 'What's with bitch?'"

I narrow my eyes. "What did you just call me?"

"*Winnie* is with Fyodor," Dragomir says. "We're here for the other matter."

Ah. The good doctor was enquiring about his female dog patient. I guess he gets to live another day.

The doc reaches for Boner with a mad scientist's leer. "So, this was stud?"

"*Ma chérie*, I hereby decree everyone refer to me as 'stud' going forward."

I arch an eyebrow at Dragomir.

"I told Dr. Delomalov what happened in the park."

With a nod, I hand Boner to the doctor.

Boner looks at me pleadingly.

"*Ma chérie*, don't let them take my manhood, *s'il vous plaît.*"

"It's just a test," I tell him.

"Dr. Delomalov has assured me the test will be completely painless," Dragomir chimes in.

The vet croons something in Ruskovian that seems to somewhat reassure Boner, but as soon as they disappear, I find myself anxiously pacing.

When I bump my shin on the table with the magazines, I stop and whip out my phone so I can check if the vet was lying about the pain level of the test.

Weird.

My phone has no bars.

"It's like a Faraday Cage in this place," Dragomir says. "I usually bring a paper book if I know something will take a while."

Huffing with disappointment, I resume pacing.

"Don't worry," Dragomir says when I make the tenth back-and-forth. "Dr. Delomalov is the world's most renowned dog expert."

I force myself to sit.

He pulls out his phone. "How about we exchange our contact information? Properly this time."

My heart performs an excited backflip. I'm sure this is for our dogs and potential future business collaboration, but my hand still shakes slightly as I create a new contact and have him fill in his digits. He then does the same.

I pocket my phone, and my mind turns to said business collaboration. I consider the best way to approach it, then decide to just go for it. "If Boner is clean, would you consider investing in Morpheus?"

His thick eyebrows pull together. "I would consider it either way. Business is business."

I blow out a relieved breath. "I was worried that with everything that's happened—never mind."

He rubs the stubble on his chin. "There *is* a caveat."

Crap. Does he know about my sex toy company already?

"I'll need to recuse myself from the decision process," he says.

Whew.

"You'll be working with Marco instead of me."

Spoke too soon.

Dealing with Marco will be a terrible experience, I know. Based on our interactions thus far, I might have an easier time convincing Marco to kidnap the daughter of a man with a certain set of skills.

Naturally, telling any of this to Dragomir would be opening a can of worms, so I just ask, "Why are you recusing yourself?"

He studies me with those changeable hazel eyes. "I like to avoid making business decisions based on emotion."

I draw back, irrationally wounded. "You hate me for Winnie's mishap that much?"

He quirks a dark eyebrow. "Who said anything about hate?"

Chapter Thirteen

I blink at him.

If not hate, what emotion would mess up his business decisions?

Before I can ask, the doctor comes out holding a rather wild-eyed Boner.

"*Ma chérie*, it was *terrible, horrible*. Let's never come here again."

"Stud was champ." Dr. Delomalov hands me my dog.

"Will you let us both know the results?" Dragomir asks. "Assuming Bella doesn't mind?"

"I don't mind," I say, stroking Boner on the head to calm him down.

"Great," Dragomir says. "Now I'd like to take care of the payment."

Right. Payment. I totally forgot about that.

"I can pay my dog's bills myself," I say. My company might not be a fancy venture capital fund with offices in a swanky building—or any formal offices, really, as my employees and I work from home—but it's nicely profitable and growing fast, with this year's revenues already in the low seven figures.

Dragomir touches my wrist, sending shivery energy down my spine. "Bella, please, allow me. I dragged you here, after all."

I just stand there, rendered mute. It's possible I'd say yes to anything after that touch. Even some unspeakable things. *Especially* unspeakable things.

"I vote Dragomir pay," the doctor says.

I frown. Is he being sexist, or is my money no good here for some reason?

With a knowing smile, Dragomir takes out an honest-to-goodness golden coin from his pocket. I catch a glimpse of an older man's face on one side before Dr. Delomalov stashes the coin in his wallet.

What the hell was that about? Have I fallen asleep and ended up in a *John Wick* movie? The criminal underworld uses gold coins in that franchise.

Come to think of it, Dragomir has other things in common with John Wick. For example—spoiler alert—it's easy to picture him going on a revenge spree if someone were to kill *his* dog. In fact, he might be capable of murdering someone for simply looking at Winnie the wrong way.

"*Ma chérie*, by that *critères*, you're also John Wick."

"Almost forgot." The doctor hands me a form. "Need stud and your information."

"Right." I set Boner down and begin to fill out the form.

"I'm going to go downstairs to make sure Winnie is ready for her test," Dragomir says. "See you soon."

I rush to complete the form so we can ride down together, but he's gone by the time I finish.

"Thank you, doctor," I say, handing him the form. "Now if you'll excuse me…"

The doctor takes the form from me and then, to my shock, presses a light kiss to the back of my hand. "I had pleasure with Napoleon and you meeting. Such beauty and grace not often found in this country."

Yeah okay, whatever, dude. I barely prevent myself from rolling my eyes as I reclaim my hand. Older Ruskovians must be even worse than their generation's Russian counterparts, though my parents' friends are also prone to cringy OTT compliments.

Boner and I take the elevator down and run into Dragomir and Winnie in the lobby. Spotting her, Boner begins a drone impersonation with his tail.

"*Ma petite. Ma petite.* Has it been a year since I've last seen your *beau visage?*"

Winnie's tail smashes into Dragomir's thigh with such force I half expect the man to stumble. "*Da,* Napoleon Carlovich. I lost count of time, yearning for our encounter."

"Fyodor will take you home," Dragomir tells me. "No need for the two of you to wait as Winnie is tested."

So much for the doggies hanging out. Or the two of us.

Hiding my disappointment, I nod and exit the building.

Impossibly, it still smells like the bear's fart outside.

"Le bouquet, ma chérie. Le bouquet exquis."

Holding Boner tight, I dash to the RV limo. Fyodor opens the door just as I reach it, then waits politely while I catch my breath inside.

"Ready to go, madam?" he asks.

I inhale blissfully fart-free air. "Take us home."

Chapter Fourteen

*a*s soon as we're back at my place, I make a sandwich and take Boner for a walk.

After the trauma of the vet and separation from Winnie, he clearly needs his spirits lifted.

The walk is a success. Not only does Boner speedily do his business, but John accuses me of being a commie only once as I give him the sandwich—a new record.

When I get home, I find a message from Alex:

Good news. They've rescheduled today's meeting. What was that between you and the owner?

I videocall Alex and explain how I met Dragomir —skipping the Kegel balls part so as not to traumatize him.

"Sounds like you want to date this guy," Alex says when I'm done.

I grimace. "That would be a bad idea."

"You said he's recused himself. What's the problem?"

"So many things, but the main one is that I think he's hiding something."

Alex drums his fingers on his desk. "You should talk to our snoopy sibling."

Now *that's* not a bad idea. Besides hiding his own private info from the world, Vlad is scary good at uncovering things other people want hidden. Stalin would've found him very useful.

"Wouldn't it be an invasion of Dragomir's privacy?" I ask, arguing with myself as much as with Alex. "I wouldn't like it if a guy *I* was dating did a deep dive on me."

He waves his hand dismissively. "As you said, you're not dating. More importantly, we're about to go into business together, which makes this fairly reasonable. I bet he's looking into us as well."

Great. That means he'll learn about my company and pull out. And not in a birth control way.

I sigh. "I guess I'll talk to Vlad."

"Make sure it's face to face." Alex smirks. "You know how he is."

Vlad prefers face to face in general because, as he puts it, "Why invite the NSA to the conversation?"

"Thanks," I tell Alex. "I'll set something up with him. Now——"

"Wait. Are you going to Mom's birthday?"

"How could I not? What am I, Vlad?"

He grins. "He's been much better about attending family shindigs. Fanny is a good influence."

"Agreed. See you at the party."

Alex hangs up and I text Vlad.

His reply is instant:

Want to come visit me at Binary Birch tomorrow at 9?

I grin as I think of a gift for him.

Sure. See you then.

———

Exiting the elevator on the floor of Vlad's company, I glance at the serious-looking plaque.

Sometimes I wonder if my brothers set out to make their companies look like complete opposites. Binary Birch has a modern art feel, in that cold, utilitarian way. There are no nerf guns in sight, nor game rooms, nor sleeping nooks.

In fact, it looks a bit like the offices of Dragomir's venture capital firm.

I check my phone. No calls or texts from Dragomir.

Bummer. A part of me was hoping he'd get in touch first thing.

There are also no calls or voicemails from the vet about Boner's STD tests—something that would give me an excuse to call Dragomir myself. Not that I need an excuse. If this were another guy, I'd probably call or text, but given all that's happened between us, I want to see if he wants to get in touch.

So for now, I wait. Or rather, since it's almost nine, I rush over to Vlad's office.

When his employees spot me, they scurry out of the way—though I'm not sure whose reputation scares them so much: mine or his.

"Hi, sis," Vlad says when I step into his office.

We hug, and I kiss his cheek before thrusting a plastic box into his hands. "A gift."

Without looking inside, Vlad drops it into a drawer and pointedly slides it shut.

"Hey, don't you want to know what's in there?"

My brother's expression is unchanged. "I can guess."

"Fine, I'll just tell you," I say, pouting in disappointment. "That is a penis pump. Replacement for the one you and Fanny broke."

He shakes his head. "She had nothing to do with it. I told you, it was a sizing issue."

"Sure. Sure." I keep my face exaggeratedly serious. "That's why this unit I got for you is double the size of the one you shattered. Hopefully, it will be able to accommodate someone with your prodigious… gift."

He sighs in exasperation. "I suspect you came here because you want something from me. Do you really think teasing is the way to go?"

I give him my best puppy-eyed look. "Come on, don't be like that. You know you can't say no to your little Belochka."

His lips twitch. "There is that. Still, say one more

word about the size of my junk, and I'll find the willpower for that no."

"The favor has to do with the business you're now a part of," I say. "So you'll be helping yourself. And Alex."

"What's the favor?"

I explain the mystery of Dragomir's lack of online presence.

Vlad unlocks his computer. "Spell that name for me."

I do, then add, "Besides Dragomir, it might be worth checking what you can find on Marco Fluroff—he's the guy I'll be dealing with to get the funding."

Vlad nods. "I'll see what I can do."

"I assume I'm going to see you at Mom's birthday?"

He manages to make his nod reluctant, like I'm somehow forcing him to go.

I get up. "Later."

He leads me to the elevator, and this time, people dodge us even more thoroughly.

He must scare them more than I do.

———

After I get home and feed Boner, I check my phone again.

No calls.

Damn it.

I'm dying to learn what emotion Dragomir had

alluded to before recusing himself. Also, it would be nice just to hear from him.

Oh, well. Instead of waiting by the phone, I'll keep myself busy—Belka day-to-day operations won't take care of themselves.

I dive into emails first.

A client wants an order of our vibrating rubber duckies with attached dildos, so I email the right team. Another client wants our camera-enabled butt plugs and dildos, so I take care of that too.

Someone in marketing suggests we extend our reach into food-flavored lube and further expand our catalogue of BDSM paraphernalia.

Hmm. Would edible lube require FDA approval? Also, what flavors would people want? Bacon? No, that's more up Boner's alley. Strawberries?

In any case, flavored lube sounds like a headache for another day, so I look at what's popular in the BDSM sections of the online retailers to see what we don't already make and what the market might be missing.

Interesting.

We could start a line of spanking paddles that leave funny red marks on people's butts—something like faces of celebs. Oh, yeah. That should sell nicely. We already produce butt plugs that are shaped like politicians that people love and hate, and those do extremely well.

Since I'm on a kink kick, I spend the rest of the workday finalizing my design for another toy—a shoe with a dildo that's meant to allow someone to penetrate their partner with their foot.

If I play my cards right, I'll be the person who redefines the expression "playing footsies."

———

Nothing from Dragomir the following morning.

I prep what I'll say to Marco tomorrow, then spend the rest of the day working on the suit for Project Morpheus.

Turns out, nipple stimulation is a real head-scratcher. Vibration and air pressure that might work elsewhere on the body aren't enough in this case. I need to make sure the nipples can have the sensation of being caressed, touched roughly, pinched, licked, sucked—the list goes on and on.

Also, since we're branching into BDSM gear anyway, should the suit support something like nipple clamp play from the start?

As the day progresses, I have to whip out my nipples repeatedly and press them against different materials to see how well they approximate human touch.

No call from Dragomir when it's time to go to sleep.

Too bad.

Picturing him in a turtleneck, I use a range of toys to get myself nice and sleepy, then punch out for the day.

—————

"Let's talk financials," Marco says to Alex and rattles out a list of questions.

To say I'm annoyed with today's meeting would be an understatement. Not only was Dragomir completely missing from the room—a bummer in and of itself—but Marco hasn't asked me a single question today. I know he doesn't realize this venture is basically mine, but still, the whole thing chafes.

Since I want the funding, I stay cordial until the end.

"Thanks, Alex." Marco shakes my brother's hand. "We have a lot to think about. I'll reach out to you soon."

"We'll wait for your call," Alex says, emphasizing the *we*.

Marco looks at me as though he forgot I was there. "Of course. I meant the plural you."

Sure he did. Now that I think about it, only Alex got the new meeting request the other day.

Whatever.

Alex and I exit the conference room, leaving Marco and his team behind. When we come out of the elevator, I finally see him.

Dragomir.

He's waiting in the lobby—hopefully for me.

"I've got to run," Alex says with a wink, correctly assessing the situation.

I give him a hug and mumble something along the lines of, "See you later."

My heart is racing. Seeing Dragomir again is exciting. Maybe too exciting for my own good.

"Hi," I say when I reach him, unsure if I should give him a hug or a kiss as I would any other acquaintance.

He resolves my dilemma by extending his hand. I shake it—and receive a jolt of electricity that streaks right into my core.

He doesn't look unaffected either. His eyes are intent on my face, his lids lowering to a half-hooded position as he lets go of my hand with obvious reluctance.

"There's a very nice coffee shop next door," he says, his voice holding a hint of sexy roughness. "Or if you're hungry—"

"Coffee sounds great," I blurt.

Inside, I'm jumping up and down.

Is this a date?

I haven't been this psyched about a guy's attention since high school.

"Did you drive down here in your RV?" I ask as we exit the building.

"Sure did." He gestures at the street.

Yep. There it is, driving by slowly.

"Fyodor couldn't find parking, so he's making circles," Dragomir explains as we step into the coffee shop.

The place is empty, so it takes us mere moments to

order what we want. As we step to the waiting area, Dragomir's phone beeps with a text, and he excuses himself to check it.

Recalling that I put my own phone on silent for the meeting, I unmute it and check my messages.

I have a voicemail from the vet notifying me that Boner is clean, and a text from Xenia.

In the city. Want to grab sushi?

Before I can shoot her a reply, I see Dragomir looming over me, looking apologetic.

"What's up?" I ask, my pulse leaping at his nearness.

"Something's come up, and I only have a half hour before I have to run to a business meeting."

"That's fine," I lie. "I'll be having sushi with a friend around the same time as your meeting."

As in, I will be *now*.

Is that disappointment in his eyes?

Hey, he was the one who turned out to be busy first.

Excusing himself one more time, Dragomir gets back on his phone, so I text Xenia that I can meet her at our favorite place in forty minutes.

She instantly replies with an excited affirmative.

The barista tells us our drinks are ready. Before I can grab mine, Dragomir picks up both cups and carries them over to a comfy table.

A gentleman. I like it.

Taking a seat across from him, I blow on my

coffee in the most seductive way I can muster, but he seems oblivious to my subtle flirting.

Hmm. What's with such a serious expression? Not very date-like.

He puts down his cup. "We need to talk."

Damn. Now I know why guys dread those four words so much.

It's definitely a foreboding phrase.

"Sure." I set my own cup down. "What did you want to talk about?"

He captures my gaze, his hazel eyes mesmerizing in their intensity.

Whatever he's going to say is bad.

Really bad.

Has he already learned about my sex toy company? Or is it something even worse?

He takes in a breath. "We're pregnant."

Chapter Fifteen

I stare at him blankly. "Did you say 'pregnant?'"

He nods.

What. The. Fuck?

It seems to be the day of phrases guys dread. In fact, "we're pregnant" might often follow "we need to talk."

In any case, I thought I was supposed to be the one to say that to him—if we'd had sex and he'd knocked me up, that is.

"Remember how Winnie took the tests after Boner?" he says. "One of them was a pregnancy test."

Oh.

I want to smack myself on the forehead. Boner humped Winnie. That's why we've been testing them both for STDs. Humping can lead to babies—or puppies in this case.

I should've thought of this. The fact that I haven't might be an insult to Boner's virility, and I'm glad he isn't here to witness this exchange. He would be traumatized.

Oh, and when he learns about this, he'll want his name officially changed to Stud. After all, he's impregnated a freaking bear.

Dragomir puts his hand over mine. "I know it's a lot to take in, but say something."

The heat coming off his big, warm palm feels amazing, and more than a little distracting. With effort, I refocus on the topic at hand. "Are you sure it's his?"

He pulls his hand away. "How would you like it if you told a man he was the father of your baby and he questioned you?"

Good point. "I'm sorry. I'm just having trouble digesting this, that's all."

He nods, as gracious as a king granting pardon. "Winnie has only had sex once in her entire life, so Boner must be the father."

"Okay. Okay." So we're dealing with a near-virginal bear. I pinch the bridge of my nose. "Is she… err… keeping it?"

Crap. Why do I keep sounding like the guy who's just learned that his casual hookup is preggers?

Dragomir's eyes are now narrowed into slits. "If you're talking about an abortion, it's out of the question at this stage. And it's going to be a litter, so I'd say 'them,' not 'it.'"

I gulp down some scorching coffee. "I didn't mean it to sound like I *want* an abortion. I really don't. Boner having puppies sounds amazing. I just wasn't sure what Winnie's stance was on the whole pro-life versus pro-choice debate."

He regards me with a serious expression. "Winnie is a dog, remember? We can only guess at her stance, so the best I can do is assume she'd want to keep her pups."

"Sounds reasonable." I rub my temples. "This is pretty confusing."

He picks up his coffee. "I get it. When I first heard the news, I was a little taken aback. Bear in mind, even if Winnie magically learned to speak and said she wanted the abortion, it wouldn't be safe to do at this stage of her pregnancy. The doctor thinks the best option for her health is to proceed to the end. After the birth, once she's ready to part with them, we'll find a nice home for the pups. Or I'll keep them."

I picture what said pups might look like, and my mood rapidly improves. "I'll help you find the pups the best homes possible. Also, let me know if you need anything else at all. I can be there if there's an ultrasound. We can split the bills and——"

"Thank you." A genuine smile appears on his face, one so sexy that my panties all but dissolve under my skirt. "There was actually something along those lines I wanted to talk to you about."

"Oh?"

"A DNA test, for Bonaparte," he says. "I want to know if there's any genetic disease risk for the pups."

I cringe internally. "Another trip to the vet? He's still traumatized."

"It's just a saliva swab. I'll get Dr. Delomalov to teach me how to do it, and I'll come over to your place and perform it myself. Bonaparte won't even know he's being tested."

"Well, in that case, sure," I say.

Wait. He's just invited himself to my place. And I said yes!

He takes a sip of his coffee and regards me over the rim of the cup. "So, obviously, you haven't neutered your dog."

I grimace. "Yeah, sorry. I couldn't bring myself to do it. I have nothing against people who go through with it, but it's just a sensitive issue for me, personally. Boner is a sexual being, and he'd miss that if it were taken away."

Should I tell him I take this issue so seriously that I built Boner a hump toy?

Nah. Too close to the sex toy company topic that I want to avoid. Nor should I tell him why it's so personal. If it were socially acceptable, my parents would've spayed me when I was a teen. Not that I slept around or anything; any expression of sexuality on my part was taboo in their eyes.

"How about you?" I ask, pushing away the unpleasant memories. "Winnie was obviously not spayed."

It's his turn to grimace. "I couldn't bring myself to do it either. Also, there's the fact of Winnie's breed. She's of the purest misha bloodline—a part of Ruskovian history."

"Great. Boner has tainted a historical bloodline."

"That's not what I meant," he says. "Besides, he didn't really. Winnie can have purebred puppies later on. These ones can still find a loving home without being called 'mishas.'"

"Or we can start a mixed-breed trend. We'll call them Chishas. Or Mishuahuas."

He chuckles. "I kind of like the sound of Chishas."

I grin. "So, another pretty obvious question… You had no idea Winnie was in heat?"

He shrugs. "Maybe I'm not as comfortable as you when it comes to thinking of my dog as a sexual being. I've never looked into how any of that heat stuff works—figured I'd do so when there was a chance to continue the misha bloodline. Besides, now that I have read up on it, a lot of the signs are less noticeable due to how furry Winnie is." He looks slightly uncomfortable. "She was spotting around the time of the incident, but I mistakenly thought that meant she was less fertile as a result."

I keep a poker face. "Don't beat yourself up. That *is* how it works… for human females."

To his credit, he doesn't look grossed out at the mention of a human period. Instead, he leans back, draping his arm over a nearby chair in that king-of-the-world manner of his. "How about we talk about something other than our dogs?"

"Deal," I say. "But after this one last dog-related request."

He inclines his head. "Go ahead."

I watch his face as I say, "When you come over for the saliva swab, can you bring Winnie so she and Boner can spend a little time together?"

He frowns.

I knew it. He doesn't like the idea of them interacting. What a snob.

"Look," I say, getting angry on my canine friend's behalf. "Boner is clean of STDs. And it's not like he can make her any more preggers."

"Fine," he says, to my surprise. "It's a playdate."

A playdate?

Why does that sound so sexual?

I'm jealous of our dogs all of a sudden.

He smirks. "Now you owe me a topic of conversation that isn't dog related."

I match his smirk. "How about wolves? Is that too close to dogs?"

"No wolves, or bears, or rats," he says with a straight face.

"Are lions off the table too?"

"You can talk about lions if you wish," he says magnanimously.

"Finally. *Something* we can talk about."

His lips twitch. "That something being *lions*."

"Well, I've always found it weird how much fictional lions roar when they want to catch something. I think the real-world ones only roar to scare other lions away from their territory. During a hunt, I bet they're silent stalkers. I would be."

He nods seriously. "I think you're right. In Hollywood's defense, a roaring lion is more impressive."

"A lion with wings would be even more impressive, but they stick to reality on that front. Now that I think about it, this roaring thing happens with other fictional animals, too. Wasn't there a roaring barracuda in *Finding Nemo*?"

He shrugs.

"I think so. Forgetting the whole silent stalking bit, I doubt it's even possible to roar underwater."

"A submarine motor might roar," he says.

"Hmm." I consider it. "You might well be right."

He grins at me, and I'm about to say something else when I notice a man outside the shop, pointing a camera at us.

To my shock, I recognize him.

Dragomir was yelling at this very dude just as Boner was humping Winnie.

I didn't give it much thought before. I was too busy worrying about vaginas—as in, keeping Kegel balls in mine and my dog's penis out of Winnie's. Now I realize this guy's behavior was pretty odd.

Dragomir must notice something on my face

because he turns. Instantly, his powerful back tenses, his shoulders bunching tight.

Huh. I guess he and the guy are *really* not friendly.

Dragomir launches to his feet, but before he can step outside, the guy bolts, swiftly disappearing around the corner.

Dragomir looks as if he's debating giving chase.

Curiouser and curiouser. Who is that guy? What's with the camera?

A cold sensation settles at the bottom of my stomach. What if he's a private detective that Dragomir's wife hired because she suspects her husband of cheating?

That happened to my ex after I broke up with him —mostly thanks to Vlad's anonymous email to the wife suggesting that very thing.

Well, if there's a wife, I won't be the one the asshole will be cheating with.

Never again.

Apparently deciding against chasing down his enemy, Dragomir sits back down.

I'm all business now. I either get to the bottom of this marriage issue, or I can't see him ever again—no matter how hot he is. Or how cute the puppies might turn out.

"Who was that?" I ask, doing my best Snow Queen impersonation.

He shrugs. "I don't really know that creep. I've only seen him once before. I've told him to stay away, though."

Okay, that was too roundabout of a question. I need to just ask him point blank.

He looks at me intently.

I take in a big breath. "Dragomir, are you married?"

Chapter Sixteen

*H*e appears taken aback by the question. "No."

Just as he says the word, he sneezes.

I feel a huge sense of relief.

In Russia, we believe that when someone sneezes after making a statement, it means they're telling the truth. But we also believe in "trust but verify," so I'm not going to be completely happy until Vlad tells me what he's dug up. Also, I need a better answer about that creepy guy who ran away—something tells me Dragomir has no intention of really explaining that.

Since we're on this topic anyway, I might as well probe deeper. "Do you have a girlfriend? Boyfriend? Lover? Mistress?"

His eyes gleam with amusement. "No. I'm single. I have to say, this is a lot more personal than the chat about lions."

Crap. He's right.

I got very personal. Too personal, considering he's a potential investor.

"How about you?" he asks before I can apologize. "Married?"

I blow out a relieved breath. "Nope."

"How about a boyfriend?" he asks, matching my earlier tone. "Girlfriend? Lover? Master?"

I shake my head. "I've been man-free for almost three years."

His gaze sweeps over me in a way that makes me wish I had those Kegel balls to squeeze. "That's very hard to believe," he murmurs when his eyes return to my distinctly warm face.

Being a twenty-six-year-old woman, I resist the urge to flip my hair like a teenage girl in front of her first crush. "Okay then, we're both single," I say briskly instead. "I wonder what else we have in common."

He regards me speculatively. "Well, an Eastern European heritage is one thing, for sure. Some Ruskovian traditions are nearly identical to Russian. Architecture, too."

"There you go," I say, downing the rest of my coffee. "And let's not forget that we're both crazy about our dogs." *And want to fuck each other's brains out* —is what I want to add but opt to keep it inside my head, and not just in case that part is one-sided.

"We're both into VR." He reaches for a refill of his coffee at the same time I reach for mine—and our fingers brush, sending another mini-lightning sparking through my nerve endings.

My breath turns unsteady. "We're both competitive," I say, refocusing on the conversation with effort. "Though, of course, I'm much more so than you are."

His nostrils widen. "No way. I'm much more competitive than you. By a wide margin."

"Oh, please. I'm so competitive there's a picture of me in the dictionary under that word."

He leans in, eyes narrowed. "I invented that word."

"Yet you still don't know its meaning. Which is *me*."

He tsk-tsks. "Just admit defeat already. Competitive is my official middle name."

"Hmm… Dragomir Competitive Lamian—your parents must be worse than mine."

His smile falters.

Crap. Have I just stepped into something? Are his parents even alive?

His phone beeps.

"I'm sorry," he says. "This is that business thing I mentioned earlier. It's in a few minutes."

I check my phone.

Yep. I also have to run to meet Xenia.

I guess time flies when you discuss dog pregnancy with the guy you're lusting after.

He stands up. "I hope we can get to know each

other a little better when I come to take Bonaparte's DNA."

Speechless with glee, I nod a little too vigorously.

He picks up our empty cups. "Maybe the list of our similarities will grow?"

As he disposes of the cups, I wrestle with the urge to jump him right here and now, by the garbage can. It's not a good idea. He's still an investor. Still doesn't know about my sex toy company. More importantly, Vlad hasn't finished his snooping—meaning Dragomir could still be married, just outright lying about it. For all I know, he might be devious enough to have faked that sneeze at just the right moment.

Being Ruskovian, he could know all about truth and sneezing.

"Do you want a ride to the sushi restaurant?" he asks.

Given my thoughts a moment ago, a rational woman would say no, but I giddily bob my head. My agreeableness is rewarded when he puts his hand on the small of my back as he leads me out of the place.

I'd be game for him to lead me this way for a few hundred miles, but to my disappointment, the RV limo is already waiting.

Fyodor opens the door, and we climb inside.

Winnie stands on her hind legs and licks Dragomir's face again. Or rather, slobbers all over it.

As he's cleaning himself up, she transfers her attentions to me, perching her paws on my shoulders and going in for the kill with a huge, wet tongue.

I half laugh, half squeal—a mistake, as it gets slobber into my mouth.

The experience is equal parts gross and adorable. Plus, I think by some transitive property, I've just made out with Dragomir. Or at least exchanged some bodily fluids with him.

When I'm freed, he readies a hand wipe. "May I?"

He wants to touch my face?

"Yes, please." I hold my breath.

He rubs my face gently, and dog slobber or not, this is the most sensual experience of my life—and it goes on and on. He's really thorough, making sure he gets every last bit of drool off my skin. I give a brief thought to all the makeup coming off along with it, but it's worth it. Hopefully, he won't think I'm a troll without it. Or a goblin. Or an ogre. No, wait, Fiona from *Shrek* is an ogre, right? Yeah, ogres are cute.

Eventually, he stops the rubbing and ever so gently dries my face with his handkerchief. Judging by the heat glimmering in his hazel eyes, my troll-goblin concerns were overblown.

He steps back, and I exhale the breath I've been holding.

Does this RV have a shower? I could use a cold one right about now. Also, I know exactly what I'll be thinking about when I'm holding my vibrator tonight: his hands on my face.

"I'm sorry," he murmurs.

Sorry? For that? That's like Michelangelo apologizing for making his David statue. Unless he's sorry for ruining my makeup?

"She's never done that to anyone before," he continues.

Ah. He's apologizing on Winnie's behalf.

"It's fine," I say. "I hope it means she likes me."

He looks down at Winnie. She's now wagging her tail incessantly and gives us a doggy—or beary—grin. "To be honest, I always thought that greeting was a sign of love, not mere like."

"Well, what did you expect?" I say with a straight face. "Bitches love me."

Before he can reply, the car stops and the partition to Fyodor slides down.

"The sushi restaurant," the butler announces pompously.

"I'll walk Bella out," Dragomir tells Fyodor and opens the door for me.

As I step out of the vehicle, I feel light, like I'm floating. Dragomir walks me all the way to the sidewalk.

I stop, looking up at him. "That's the restaurant." I wave at the place. "My friend should be here any minute."

He steps close enough for me to detect the cinnamon notes of his cologne. His eyes gleam with warm amber undertones. "I had a great time hanging out with you."

"Me too," I say, my heart fluttering—just like it would after a date back in high school.

Maybe I've time-traveled without my knowledge.

"I'll get in touch about the playdate," he says softly.

I dampen my lips. "Looking forward to it."

His gaze falls to my mouth, and a peculiar tension seems to invade his body. Slowly, as if pulled by something, he bends his head.

My pulse skyrockets, and I rise on my tiptoes, swaying toward him. Our lips are just a breath apart now. If I just—

"Bella?" some evil person calls out in Xenia's voice. "Is that you?"

Dragomir pulls back.

I spin around and level an icy glare at the source of the noise.

Yep. The cockblocker is indeed someone I've always considered a friend.

"Dragomir," I say, my voice husky. "Meet Xenia."

Dragomir extends his hand. Xenia snatches it and shakes it like a wet towel, her eyes the size of tea saucers throughout.

"Nice to meet you," she finally manages in a thick accent.

"A pleasure," he says and looks down at the hand Xenia isn't letting go of.

"We should go," I tell her pointedly.

Xenia looks at me, then at her hand, then finally remembers that you eventually let people go when you do this sort of thing.

Dragomir's lips curve in a wry smile. "I'll be in touch," he tells me and disappears in his RV.

Xenia watches the RV's departure with a strange expression. Finally, she turns toward me. "It's against the rules of nature for a man to be that gorgeous."

For once, I agree with her—a woman who likes to say that a man needs to be only slightly better-looking than a gorilla.

Chapter Seventeen

"Tell me everything," Xenia demands as we take our seats and get two orders of Sushi Deluxe.

I fill her in on the whole dog pregnancy situation.

"His dog has the right idea," she says.

I pick up my glass of water and take a sip. "She does?"

"You should have that man's baby."

I nearly spew out the water in my mouth. "Baby?"

She nods sagely. "The two of you are the most beautiful people I've seen in real life. If you make a baby, it will be a movie star."

I use a napkin to wipe up the water droplets that went into my nose. "I'd expect this sort of thing from Mother, not you."

She gives me an insulted look. "You're comparing me to Natasha?"

"You're right. I'm sorry. That was too harsh."

The waiter brings out two boat-shaped plates, and we swap sushi pieces the way we always do: I give her all the boring things, like crab stick and cooked shrimp, and she gives me all the items she's too scared to eat, like uni, which is sea urchin gonads. Like the rest of my family, I'm an adventurous eater, while Xenia is noticeably less so—something that no doubt limits her as a chef.

For the rest of the meal, we chat about recent TV shows we've seen, and she gives me the latest scoop on her and Boy Toy, ending with her suspicion that he might pop the question soon.

"Will you say yes?" I ask, putting the last spoonful of my fried green tea ice cream into my mouth.

She shrugs. "I'm not a young chicken. This might be my last chance at this sort of thing."

I don't tell her that she once again sounds like my mother. Instead, I just say that she should only marry Boy Toy if she wants to, not to settle.

"I do want to. He's just so young…"

I roll my eyes. "He's forty-five and doesn't take good care of himself. Your life expectancy is probably the same—assuming that's what you're worried about when you talk about his age."

She sighs. "Who knows if he will even propose."

I strongly suspect that he will. Xenia is an amazing woman, and Santa—I mean, Boy Toy—doesn't strike me as a stupid man. Jolly, sure, but not stupid.

———

When I get home, Boner is extra excited to see me.

"Do you smell Winnie on me?" I ask him.

"*Oui.*"

"Can you tell from her scent that she's knocked up?"

"*Oui.* Call me Stud from now on."

I reapply the makeup I'd lost in my encounter with the bear, grab a sandwich for John, and take Boner out for a walk. When I return home, I get a message from Vlad requesting a meeting, so I make another trip to the Binary Birch offices.

———

"I couldn't find anything on Dragomir," Vlad says once we get the pleasantries out of the way.

"Nothing? That's suspicious in and of itself."

Vlad shrugs. "Who are we to say that? If he were to look into either of us, he wouldn't find much either."

I wince. "I actually *am* hiding something. My sex toy company."

My brother pushes his glasses higher up his nose. "Right, and they'd have to dig really, really deep to learn about that—we set you up with a New Mexico LLC and all that."

"Is there a way you could also 'dig deep?'"

He rubs his chin. "I'd need more info about him."

"Like what?"

"Names of people close to him, like siblings or parents. Maybe the name of his best friend. Anyone who might not be as paranoid as he is."

"I don't know any of that," I say. "But if I find out, I'll let you know."

"Just be subtle. If he's anything like me, he won't like it if he thinks you're snooping."

"Good point. Sucks that this has turned out to be so difficult."

Vlad nods sympathetically. "On the bright side, I found out something about that Marco guy."

I sit up straighter. "Is it juicy?"

"He's got two women," Vlad says. "Two families, in fact—one in Ruskovia and one here in the states."

Wow. Even my ex hadn't gone that far.

"Do you think they know about each other?" I ask. "Maybe it's a polyamorous relationship or something like that."

"Doubt it."

I shake my head in disgust. "What an asshole."

Vlad gives me a speculative look. "What do you plan to do with this?"

I blink at him uncomprehendingly. "What do you mean? I can't exactly confront him without letting Dragomir know that I'm snooping—and I don't think he'd like that."

"Well." Vlad glances at his office door and lowers his voice. "Someone unscrupulous might use this information to help themselves secure the funding they need."

"What? No! I'm not going to blackmail the guy. That's not my style."

Vlad gives me an approving half-smile. "I didn't think you would. Just throwing it out there. Alex tells me it's been hard securing more investors."

I clench my jaw. "Still not doing that."

Thankfully, Vlad drops the topic and asks me about the suit design—which I gladly tell him all about. I especially enjoy the way he squirms when I discuss nipple stimulation at length.

As I'm leaving, I can't help myself. "Once I have a working suit," I say ingeniously, "do you think you and Fanny could test it out for me, for old times' sake?"

Chapter Eighteen

*T*he next morning, I get a text from Dragomir:

Can we stop by at 11?

Replying in the affirmative, I feel a jolt of excited energy far exceeding what's expected from my morning espresso.

In an hour, he's going to be here.

In my apartment.

Not far from my bedroom.

I even out my breath and attempt to keep my cool by making myself presentable. Once my hair is brushed and makeup is applied, I realize I have to clean up my place.

Right now, it looks like the lair of a sex-toy-obsessed hoarder serial killer.

Glancing at the clock every few minutes, I start the epic quest of hiding all the work-in-progress dildos, butt plugs, vibrators, anal beads, and other

Belka paraphernalia. By five to eleven, seeing that I'm not making fast enough progress, I resort to desperate measures. Instead of neatly putting away the remaining items in drawers, I simply kick them under the couch and bed wherever they happen to be.

Everest—a particularly large dildo—ends up jammed under the TV stand.

It's eleven.

Whew. I think I made it.

I do a quick walkthrough and find a nipple clamp prototype being used as a clip for a bag of caramel popcorn.

Crap. What else have I missed?

The doorbell rings.

"Who is it?" I yell as I frantically toss the popcorn in the trash and stash the clamps in the freezer.

"Winnie and Dragomir."

"Coming," I yell and dash for the door, nearly tripping over Boner, who's already in the hallway, wagging his tail insistently.

Catching my breath, I open the door—and go back to hyperventilating.

I mean, come on. Who does this?

Dragomir is wearing a tight shirt that shows off his broad-shouldered, muscular frame in near-anatomical, panty-wetting detail.

The only way this could be worse is if he were wearing a turtleneck.

"Hi," he murmurs.

Before I can act on a wide variety of inappropriate urges that play out in my head, Winnie rushes past me like a bear tornado.

Dragomir says something sternly in Ruskovian but to no avail.

Ignoring him, she gives Boner a thorough sniff and licks him from head to toe, like a lollipop.

Boner seems to be in heaven—that is, until he decides he wants to sniff Winnie's butt but finds that it's much too high for his nose to reach.

Even when he leaps up, he gets only partway to where he wants to be, and then Winnie turns away before he can make another jump.

I voice Boner for Dragomir's pleasure:

"*Ma petite, destin* has us *ensemble* once again—but why did it put your *postérieure piquant* so, so far away?"

With a grin, Dragomir does Winnie's voice:

"It might be for the best, Napoleon Carlovich. I already bear the fruit of your loins."

I grin like a loon. "Call me Stud, *ma petite*. Call. Me. Stud."

Shaking his head, Dragomir pulls out a small box from the pocket of his jeans. "I have the test. Do you want to take care of that first?"

"Sure," I say. "While he's drooling at the sight of Winnie, that swab should yield a ton of saliva."

Dragomir and I work together on this. I hold Boner down, Dragomir offers him a treat to increase the drooling, and as soon as my little friend opens his maw, Dragomir uses the swab, then rewards him with the treat.

All in all, Boner doesn't seem to realize he's gotten a medical procedure.

If only they could all be like this.

Dragomir seals the swab in a plastic bag. "This should do it."

"Great. Why don't we go into the living room?"

He follows me, then stops and whistles, looking around. "Do you have a child?"

"Please don't whistle in the house," I say before I can stop myself.

He looks amused. "Another Russian superstition?"

"Whistling indoors means bad financial luck," I say. "And as you know, I'm seeking funding."

"I'll make sure not to whistle indoors from now on," he says, his lips curving in an agreeable smile. "But you never answered—do you have a kid?"

"No," I say defensively.

I think I know what this is about.

Sure enough, the next question is: "Are you into Disney?"

"Nope. I just like *Frozen*."

He gestures at the large poster of Elsa on my wall, figurines of Anna and the rest of her family on the bookshelf, and stuffed Olaf on the couch. "Clearly."

Great. Next time, besides hiding sex toys, I have to put away all the regular, kid-appropriate toys as well. You never know why someone will judge you.

Dragomir is now looking at the VR headset on the coffee table. "You've been practicing *Beat Saber*?"

I narrow my eyes at him. "Let me guess. You now can do 'Radioactive' on Expert Plus."

His grin is cocky. "Not only that—I bet I can beat your top score."

"You're on. It's a dance off. Or is it a sword fight?"

He shrugs. "Either way, I'll win."

I grab the headset and the controllers and hand everything to him. "Show me what you've got."

As he adjusts the headset for his much bigger head, I check on the dogs to make sure they don't end up under his feet—a tricky VR problem.

I catch Boner giving Winnie his biggest chew-ball, the one he can barely fit in his mouth.

"No." I snatch the ball away. Winnie was no doubt about to swallow the thing whole, which would mean yet another vet trip.

Boner rushes away and comes back with a bone he's been gnawing on for the last couple of days.

"That's better," I say, then check on Dragomir.

He's already got the headset on, and the controllers are in his hands.

Before I can ask if he's ready, "Radioactive" rings out of the headset speakers, and Dragomir begins to move to the rhythm.

Oh, my.

He wields the virtual swords with a regal grace, slicing and dicing the notes in a sleek, athletic mixture of martial arts and dance.

It's a good thing the headset blocks his vision. I'm drooling more than Boner did at the sight of the treat.

A part of me wonders if I could dig out one of my toys from where I've stashed it and use it before the song is through.

"Two hundred thousand points," Dragomir exclaims, breathing hard from excitement.

Wait a second. I don't think I had that many points by the "deep in my bones" line in the song—and that's a problem. I've been too busy salivating over the show he's put on to realize I could actually lose this competition.

Hell, no. I'll just dance and slice my butt off when it's my turn. Failure is not an option.

For now, I might as well enjoy the show—and enjoy it I do. That is, until he stops and announces his final score, which is higher than my record, but fortunately, by just a few points.

"Don't be so smug," I tell him as I readjust the headset to the size of a normal head. "I'm going to be beating your score in a moment."

He doubles down on the smug. "I'm sure you're going to try."

Grimly determined, I put on the headset and grip the two controllers—which in the game world look like two lightsabers, red and blue.

The music starts. The notes fly at me like bullets.

As I slash each one while ignoring bombs and dodging walls, I can't help but wonder what I look like to Dragomir outside VR.

Hopefully fierce like a ninja and graceful like a ballerina.

"I'm waking up to ash and dust," sings Dan Reynolds, and though this is the first line of the song, I'm already beginning to sweat—and I can't wipe my brow like in the song.

When I get to the first chorus and its signature "Radioactive, Radioactive," I'm sweating in earnest, but my score is the highest it's ever been at this point.

I could actually win.

Suddenly, I hear Dragomir shout in Ruskovian. All I can make out are two words: "Winnie" and "Fu!"

Shit.

The bear has breached my game space.

Before I can freeze in place, my right arm finishes slicing a set of notes—and my fist smashes into something hard.

I yelp in pain.

A man grunts.

Bear fur brushes against my leg.

I rip the headset off my head so I can see what disaster has befallen me.

It's worse than I thought.

Dragomir is patting Winnie with one hand, and with the other he's clutching his eye.

An eye that's already beginning to swell up.

Chapter Nineteen

"*L*et me see that hand," Dragomir orders in a voice so commanding I comply on autopilot, which is very unlike me.

Taking my hand, he examines it like a surgeon. "Can you move your fingers?"

I wiggle them, and he nods approvingly. "Do you have an ice pack or frozen peas?"

"One sec." Nearly tripping over Winnie, then Boner, I rush into the kitchen and check the freezer.

The nipple clamps are now nice and cold, but I don't think using them as a cold compress on anything but nipples would work all that well. Since I don't have any ice or peas, I grab a big slab of frozen chicken, slam the freezer door shut before anyone can see the clamps, and turn around—bumping right into Dragomir's chest.

We both stumble back, staring at each other. The

heated energy that's just passed between us feels downright… radioactive.

"Use that on your hand," he says in the same commanding tone, glancing at the chicken in my hand.

"What, no? This is for your face."

"I'm fine. Just do as I say."

Was that a growl? And is it weird that I'm turned on by his bossiness?

"You're acting like I broke my hand," I say in exasperation.

He frowns. "Good point. Let's go get it x-rayed."

"Dude, I just banged it. Your face——"

"It's nothing. Start icing the hand."

I roll my eyes. "How about a compromise? I'll hold the chicken in my 'injured' hand next to your eye."

He sighs. "If that's what it takes."

I sit him down and hold the meat to his eye, all the while wondering just how unhygienic this is.

Can one get salmonella through the eye?

Soon, my fingers feel like they're about to get frostbite, but on the plus side, being so near him gives me a warm feeling in my chest.

After what feels like twenty minutes of nonstop tension, I say through chattering teeth, "I'm freezing and my hand is much better. Can you hold this in place?"

"I'm fine too." He takes the meat and heads over to the freezer.

"Let me do that." I snatch the chicken out of his hand and do my best to hide the freezer and the clamps inside it with my body as I put it away.

He doesn't say anything, so I must be successful.

Blowing out a relieved breath, I turn to face him and assess the damage.

Yep.

Icing or not, he's got a shiner—growing up with two brothers, I'm very familiar with the phenomenon.

"Let's go wash up." I walk over to the sink and use dish soap to make sure no chicken juices are left on my hand.

He washes his face as well, then uses one of his Winnie wet wipes and dries himself with his handkerchief.

Great. Now I can lick his face safely.

Wait, what?

I must be hungry. That has to be it. "You want to order some lunch?"

He nods, watching me with a hooded, amber-toned gaze.

Fuck, he's sexy. Even with a shiner.

Pushing the thought away before I jump him, I grab a few menus off the fridge, and we quickly settle on a pizza.

Order placed, I open and close my hand, feeling for any pain. All good there.

"I'm ready to restart the song," I announce.

"No." The word sounds like a royal decree.

I cross my arms over my chest. "No?"

"I don't want you hurt," he says in a much more diplomatic manner. "I forfeit the competition. You win."

"It doesn't work like that." I know I sound grumpy, but I can't help it.

I need to win. It's a compulsion.

"Please. Don't tax your poor hand anymore. Do it for me?" The beseeching look accompanying the words silences my next objections.

Crap. I hope he doesn't use that look for evil, like, say, seducing me right here and now.

It would work, too.

Alas, no seduction commences. Instead, he looks around the kitchen and frowns. "The dogs have been suspiciously quiet. We should check on them."

"Just to remind you, Winnie can't get any more pregnant," I say, but lead him to the living room anyway.

We get there just in time to witness an amazing display of super-Chihuahua strength.

"What the hell?" Dragomir mutters.

Oh, fuck. All that cleanup effort for nothing.

Boner has somehow managed to extract the Everest dildo from where I'd jammed it behind the TV, and is now dragging the thing toward Winnie—a feat doubly impressive because the silicone shlong in his mouth is almost the size of his whole body.

"It's not what it looks like," I blurt.

Dragomir gives me a look that seems to say, "Your dog is not about to gift a giant dildo to mine?"

I'm about to backpedal more, but then I realize that a) Dragomir looks more amused than judgmental and b) one dildo does not a sex toy company make.

Oh, well.

Let him think I'm into giant fake cocks.

It's not like I'm not.

Panting as though he's just finished a triathlon, Boner triumphantly drops the dildo at Winnie's feet.

Is there some phallic symbolism here or something? Or is this the dog equivalent of a marriage proposal?

Whatever it is, Winnie is happy. Her tail wags so hard it creates a noticeable draft in the room. Without pausing, she grabs the dildo in her maw and sprints into the kitchen.

"Well," I say sagely. "At least it's too big for her to swallow."

Dragomir is not listening. He chases after his dog —which she interprets to be a fun game because she dodges him and rushes back to the living room, dildo still clutched in her teeth.

"You know," I tell him when the two of them dash back into the room. "If you're trying to get Everest back for me, don't. She can keep it. I'll buy myself another one."

There. "Buy" implies I don't have a giant collection of these in a warehouse—and tells him I'm not a pearl-clutcher when it comes to these things. He might as well start getting to know the real me.

Victorian lady I'm not.

He shakes his head, again looking more amused than judgy. "She'll want to play fetch with it in the park."

He's got a point. Not everyone will be as understanding as he is.

To that end, I join the bear hunt, and after fifteen minutes of yelling and chasing, Dragomir finally catches Winnie and I help him extract the dildo from her.

She gives me a betrayed look and lifts her maw, letting out a wolf-like howl.

A slew of treats and a promise of a new toy later, Winnie calms down and walks over to give Boner's muzzle another slobbering lick.

He beams at her. "I have now made an honest bitch of you, *ma petite*."

Another tongue bath from her. "You're my stud forever, Napoleon Carlovich."

The doorbell rings, sending both dogs into a barking frenzy, and I leave Dragomir to calm them down as I go answer it.

It's our pizza.

I bring it in and set it on the kitchen table, then give Boner and Winnie some treats.

"Hungry?" I ask Dragomir as he sits down.

"Starving," he says, grabbing a slice. We chow down on the pizza for a couple of minutes, and then he says, "So, your brother mentioned that you went to MIT. That's impressive."

I shrug. "I was lucky. I set my sights on that school

early on, so I kept my high school GPA a solid 4.0, took all the AP classes, aced the SATs, and did all the right extracurriculars. When I had my interview with them, I made sure to impress, and the rest is history."

He scoffs. "That's not being lucky. That's taking your fate into your own hands. Your parents must be very proud."

I sigh. "You don't know my parents." With a thick accent and my best impersonation of my mother's voice, I say, "Your father and I gave up everything to come to America. Going to a good college is the very least you can do."

Instead of being proud, my parents are disappointed with me—and only in part because of what I've chosen to do for a living.

"I'm sorry." His gaze holds genuine sympathy. "Parents can be tough."

My throat inexplicably closes up, and my next bite of pizza tastes like cardboard. With effort, I rein myself in and say lightly, "Mine are the toughest, that's for sure."

He grimaces. "You haven't met mine."

"Now that's a competition you'll never win," I say. "My parents are borderline evil—that is, to me. They treat my brothers just fine."

"Bullshit," he retorts, a little too harshly for my liking. Taking a deep breath, he continues in a calmer tone. "There's no possible way your parents could be worse than mine when it comes to preferring your siblings—or being disappointed, or anything else."

"Look," I say gently. This is clearly a sensitive topic for him as well. "This is not a competition I *want* to win, but I would."

He stubbornly shakes his head.

"How about a wager then?"

"I'd bet anything," he says promptly.

Anything? Pornographic images dance in front of my eyes, dispelling some of my funk.

"Problem is," he continues, "how would we decide?"

An evil idea occurs to me. "My mother's birthday is coming up. You can come as my plus-one and meet them. Once you admit defeat and run away screaming, I'll win the dubious honor of having the worst parents."

Wait. Did I just ask him to meet my parents?

"Deal," he says before I can backpedal.

Great. Now even if something does happen between us, it will be over after he meets my parental units in all their glory. Then again, maybe that would be for the best.

Nothing *should* happen between us.

"It's been ages since I've been to a Russian birthday celebration," he says.

I blow out a breath. "You're so going to regret this."

He looks unfazed. "What do your parents do?"

I grab another pizza slice. "Back in the motherland, my father was a surgeon and my mother an architect. They now own a restaurant on Brighton

Beach—something they consider a downgrade. They never let my brothers and me forget about the noble sacrifice they made." I bite into the pizza and, still chewing, ask, "How about yours? What do they do?"

Dragomir's lips flatten. "They've never had anything resembling a job—unless intrigue counts."

Huh. That's weird. "They're still in Ruskovia?"

His eyes shift to the color of cold, hard jade. "They are, but they do come to New York on a regular basis."

Okay, maybe he does have bigger issues with his parents than I do.

"How many siblings do you have?" I ask, hoping to lighten the mood.

Nope. Judging by the way his shoulders tighten, I might've just made things worse. "There are ten of us," he says with distaste.

"Wow." I try to picture birthing ten babies and shudder at the gory images in my mind. His poor mom's vag—no wonder she's mean. "Is it a Ruskovian tradition to have such a large family?" I ask cautiously.

He shakes his head. "Just my family's. What about you? I've met Alex, of course. Is there anyone else?"

I smile. "Yep. Vlad."

"Is that short for Vladimir?"

"You guessed it."

"I hope you get along with him as well as with Alex."

"Oh, yeah," I say. "Both of my brothers adore me."

He looks wistful. "That must be nice."

I desperately search for another subject. "Where did you go to school?"

"A university in Ruskovia," he says. "I doubt you've heard of it."

I've barely heard of the country, so yeah. "When did you start your venture capital fund?"

There. That should be a nice, neutral topic.

"A few years after college graduation," he answers.

I quirk an eyebrow, impressed. "Don't you need capital to start something like that?"

His jaw tightens.

Oops. Apparently, I'm not out of the minefield of his past.

"Can you please do me a favor?" he says after a tense moment of silence.

I regard him warily over my pizza slice. "Depends on what it is."

"Don't ask me about my business."

I stuff the pizza into my mouth, channeling the Twix commercial.

Because if I'm not mistaken, that's the exact quote from *The Godfather*, and it plants an idea in my head that I don't like one bit.

Could Dragomir be in the mob?

Chapter Twenty

*a*s I chew, I realize it's not as crazy as it might sound.

He's Eastern European—neatly fitting into the more recent Hollywood stereotype of organized crime —and mysterious as fuck, not wanting to talk about either his business or his family.

Maybe his family is *the* family, in the mafia sense.

That would explain the gold coin he slipped to the veterinarian.

Wait a minute. Could the guy who I thought was a private investigator be an actual investigator—the kind that works for the police or the FBI? Am I going to get approached one day and asked to assist with a sting operation?

Is his venture capital firm a way to launder money?

It's an effort to finally swallow my food.

I wish I'd considered this possibility *before* I invited

him to my mother's birthday. My parents had a run-in with Russian mobsters some years ago, and it wasn't fun. Luckily, Vlad was able to help them out.

Speaking of Vlad, he should be able to shed some light on this. If Dragomir is being investigated by any agency, that's a clue for my snoopy brother.

"Are you upset?" Dragomir asks, and I realize I've been quiet for a while. "If it's that important to you, I—"

"No," I say quickly. "I'm just trying to recall if I took Boner out for a walk in the morning."

At the mention of the word "walk" and his name, my dog begins a happy dance.

Dragomir smiles at Boner, then looks at the bear. "Winnie likes to walk in the afternoon. Want to go together?"

"Sure," I say.

Might not be the worst idea to get a possible criminal out of my apartment. The park is public, so Boner and I should be safe.

"I only have a half hour, though," I say. "I have a meeting with Vlad."

It's not exactly a lie—I'm totally going to drop in and see what my brother thinks about my crazy theory.

Dragomir nods, and we attack the rest of the pizza. Then we prep our charges and go to the park.

As we walk, I ask Dragomir to tell me something interesting about Ruskovia, figuring that's a safe topic under any circumstances.

"Like what?" he asks.

"I don't know. Interesting traditions, maybe?"

He scratches his chin. "We have a holiday where everyone throws ripe grapes at each other—a bit like La Tomatina in Spain, though they use tomatoes for some weird reason."

"Sure," I say with a smirk. "Grapes are logical projectiles, but tomatoes are crazy talk."

"Here's one thing you might find amusing," he says, shortening Winnie's leash before she sticks her nose into the horse poop left by one of the carriages that crisscross Central Park. "We have a bear festival, during which people set out food bears like and even dress like bears."

I grin. "You sure it's not a day dedicated to the misha breed?"

"Positive," he says and tells me about a few more traditions, like everyone's dislike of the color red, thanks to the Soviets, and how Ruskovians toss baby teeth on the roof instead of leaving them under a pillow. My favorite is their stories of Grandpa Krampus—a sort of demon anti-Santa who scares children into being nice.

When we accidentally let a tree come between us, I force Dragomir to circle back. "It's another Russian superstition," I explain. "Two people should not walk on different sides of a tree. Got to pick a side, or we might have a fight."

He touches his black eye. "I feel like the fight has already happened."

Wincing, I apologize for the eye again, and we walk until the doggies do their business.

"Do you have OCD?" he asks as we head back to my apartment.

"No. Why?"

He gestures at the pavement. "You never step on a crack."

"Oh. That's not OCD. Stepping on cracks is bad luck."

"Sure, sure," he says with a grin.

I watch myself walk the rest of the way to my building and realize how automatic my crack avoidance actually is.

Well, whatever. I need my luck to stay good—especially for the rest of this playdate.

When we finally cross the street and stand next to my building entrance, I demonstratively take out my phone and glance at the time. "I'd better go."

He steps closer to me. "This was fun."

My heartbeat speeds up at his proximity. "We should do it again sometime."

Hold up. What am I saying? Didn't I just theorize that he's a mobster? I should figure out a way to uninvite him to my family event, not—

He closes the distance between us.

The cinnamon yumminess of his warm male scent leaps into my flared nostrils and scrambles my brain.

His eyes shifting from light brown to green-flecked gold, he places his hands on my hips.

Fuck.

My hormones take over and I melt into him, eyes never leaving his.

He leans down.

I rise on tiptoe.

Our lips fuse.

uuuuuck.

This. Is. Amazing.

My first ever mouthgasm. My skin pebbles, and as though acquiring a will of their own, my fingers splay over the sizable bulge in his jeans.

Very sizable bulge.

We're talking Everest levels.

Growling low in his throat, Dragomir deepens the kiss, and I feel like I might explode from arousal.

He might be "the one" indeed, because we're nowhere near sex toys and I'm almost ready to come.

My clothes start to chafe, and my fingers go to work on his zipper. Why isn't he naked already? Before I can free Everest from his pants, I feel Dragomir's entire body stiffen. Breathing hard, he lifts his head and steps back, eyes mirroring my frustration.

I gape stupidly at his kiss-swollen lips, then at his almost-undone pants.

Crap.

I forgot we were outside.

I also forgot that I never take a guy's pants off on the first date—not that today was even a clear-cut date.

Flushing, I gulp in some air and back away, out of his Jupiter-like gravitational pull.

Winnie cocks her head at me. "Tsk, tsk, Bella Borisovna. Making puppies in public?"

A slow smirk curves Dragomir's lips as those hazel eyes travel over my body from head to toe. "To be continued?" he asks huskily.

Oh, no. No, no, no. Potential criminal, remember?

"I've got to go," I mutter and pull Boner into the building, my gait unsteady.

I can feel Dragomir's burning gaze on my back.

Boner drags his feet all the way to the elevator. As the doors begin to close, he whimpers and gives Winnie a longing stare.

"I know how you feel, bud," I say hoarsely.

"Oh, *ma chérie*. The Lamians and Chortskys are a match made in *paradis*."

"Not if the Lamians are in the mob," I say and work on steadying my breathing for the rest of the elevator ride.

———

As I drop Boner off, I debate digging up one of my toys, but decide that seeing Vlad is a higher priority than my misfiring libido.

I take a cab downtown and try not to think about what just happened. But my mind is stuck on that amazing kiss anyway, and all sorts of questions swirl through it.

How could I have kissed him mere minutes after thinking he might be a mobster?

Does this mean I'd be okay with becoming a mob wife?

No. No way. Not if it means he'd cheat on me the way Tony did on Carmela in *The Sopranos*. Not that I'd let him. If *I* caught my husband cheating, I'd have him whacked. But crap. I'd then have to run his criminal organization by myself, and that's on top of my sex toy company. No way would I be able to handle both. I'd burn out and resort to drugs. Like coke. I'd be a cokehead in no time, breaking the cardinal rule of not getting high off your own supply.

So, in conclusion, I shouldn't kiss him ever again.

But what if he wants to?

What if, having tasted me, he now wants me so much he's willing to kidnap me? Would I end up on some secluded compound in Ruskovia, where I'd develop the quickest case of Stockholm syndrome in history?

When the cab stops, I rush into Vlad's office like a whirlwind.

He tears his gaze away from his coding, a

concerned expression on his face. "What's the matter?"

I plop down into the chair across from him and explain.

He shakes his head. "I've already checked to see if he's being investigated—and he isn't."

"You have?"

He smiles. "I had to pull some strings, but hey, how many favorite sisters do I have?"

I almost jump up and down from glee. "You don't think he's mafia?"

His smile deepens. "I honestly don't even think there's such a thing as a Ruskovian mob. Not in his home country and especially not in the US."

I begin to feel silly. "Why not?"

"Ruskovia has one of the lowest crime rates in the world. They don't have any jails—or databases of criminals that someone could hack into."

Is Vlad saying he'd be willing to hack into a foreign government's criminal database for me? If so, this might be the last time I ask him to snoop on someone. I wouldn't want to be the reason he gets into trouble.

I fight the urge to chastise. He's a big boy. Instead, I say, "Japan has a low crime rate, but they have the Yakuza."

"Good point. But there also aren't enough Ruskovians in the US to run a criminal organization. Oh, and unlike the Japanese, pretty much all Ruskovians are wealthy. Old money, too—so less motivation for the risks associated with crime."

I exhale in relief. "Okay, in that case, you're right. I guess a Ruskovian mob would be about as likely as one from Monaco."

"Exactly," he says.

"Well, I'm glad. I invited him to Mother's birthday and—"

"Just because he's not in the mob doesn't mean *that* was a good idea," Vlad says with a frown. "He's still an enigma, and that sounds like a date."

I sigh. He's right—and he doesn't even know about the kiss. "Maybe you can dig up something on him if you meet face to face?"

My brother eyes me quizzically. "How?"

I shrug. "Take a picture of him and reverse image search? Hack into his phone? I don't know, it's your area of expertise."

"Bad ideas, all. Unless you don't care if he finds out about my snooping."

"I definitely don't want him to find out."

"In that case, reverse image search is out. If he's anything like me, he has a page set up that will trigger an alert when searched that way. As to the phone, we'd have to steal it to get inside it. I'm not the NSA —I can't just do it remotely."

I get up. "Forget it. We'll stick with the old plan where I try to get you more info. Maybe he'll mention the name of one of his many siblings. Or his parents."

Vlad also stands up. "That's smart."

I give him a hug, remind him that he'd better be at the birthday, and head back home.

———

For the rest of the day, I work on my product designs and grow more and more excited about the upcoming date with Dragomir. The next morning, Alex gives me an update: No word from Marco and team, and no other prospects.

Thanks, bro. A great way to put a damper on my excitement. Despite the fact that Dragomir has recused himself, going on a date with him is playing with fire as far as our funding is concerned.

Busying myself with work may not be the most mature way to deal with my Dragomir doubts, but that's the path I take, and by the end of the day, Belka has a new product: an anal plug with a fluffy squirrel tail sticking out of it, all made out of a dishwasher- and washing-machine-safe material for ease of cleaning.

Which reminds me: I've got to get my mother a birthday gift.

I ponder this for a while.

An overt sex toy would upset her, so that's a no go. But then again, she often complains about neck pain, so why don't I get her something that's allegedly for that?

It doesn't take me long to decide.

Mother will be getting Belka's stiff competition: The Hitachi Magic Wand.

Trademarked back in 1968, this "personal massager" was the vibrator of choice for women at a time when female pleasure—especially masturbation—was more taboo than today. Which means it'll fit perfectly into my parents' household.

And if Mother only uses it on her neck, that's her loss.

Gift chosen, I check my phone.

Score! A text from Dragomir.

He wants to know more details about the birthday.

I text him directions to my parents' restaurant and tell him to meet me there. This way, I can get there early and beg or bribe my family to be on their best behavior—which I realize is inconsistent with the whole "my parents are worse than yours" bet we've made.

I guess I don't want him to run away screaming and never think about me as a romantic possibility, which he is sure to do if he sees my parents uncensored.

Wait, what am I saying? I *should* let him run away screaming. That was the whole—

Should I bring a gift? His text rips me out of my ruminations.

I've got one that can be from the both of us, I reply. *You can bring flowers if you want. Just make sure it's an odd number. For Russians, an even number of flowers is for funerals.*

His reply is a smiley face, which bolsters my earlier excitement.

Next on my list is cheering up Boner. He keeps looking gloomy, likely because he misses Winnie. Luckily, I know just the thing. I put on *Ratatouille*, Boner's favorite animated movie, in the living room.

It works.

As usual, he perks up and begins to pace the room while sneaking glances at the screen that last as long as his doggy attention span allows.

It's a fun mystery as to why he enjoys this particular story. I like to think that he might have dreams of becoming a great French chef, like the rat hero, though a more pragmatic part of me knows the answer might be simpler. He may just think this movie is about a fellow Chihuahua.

Then again, both theories might be wrong. He doesn't like other movies with Chihuahuas, like *Legally Blonde*, nor the ones about French cooking, like *Julie & Julia*.

"*Ma chérie*, don't strain your pretty little brain about it. I'm just a mystery wrapped in an enigma… and bacon, okay?"

———

The morning of my mother's birthday, I get a text from Xenia:

Huge news. Can I come over?

Even though I can guess what the news is, I pretend to be oblivious until she comes over and tells me exactly what I thought she would: Boy Toy has proposed.

"It was so romantic, too," she says when I'm done with all the expected jumping, hugging, and squealing. "Here."

She shows the ring, then a picture of a freezer with a row of four Stolichnaya vodka bottles, where Boy Toy replaced the usual labels with ones that form a phrase: "Will you marry me?"

"Aww, that *is* romantic," I say.

It's also a possible sign someone needs to look into the twelve-step program, but hey, it sure is original.

"I have the perfect gift for the two of you," I say and rush out of the room.

I come back with a tray that Xenia examines dubiously.

"Are these wedding bands of some kind? If so, most look way too big."

"These are cock rings," I say. "Vibrating cock rings."

Xenia looks at the tray, then at me, her expression still confused.

"It's for Boy Toy to wear on a special night," I explain. Then I grab a dildo from the nearby coffee table and show her where a cock ring would go and how to turn it on.

"And it vibrates?" She sounds intrigued.

"Yep. Just pick his size."

Xenia looks wistfully at the extra-extra-large, extra-large, and large. Then her gaze settles on one of the bigger mediums.

"Good for you," I say as she grabs that ring. "Let me know what you guys think."

———

Getting out of the cab next to my parents' restaurant, I pray that I've beaten Dragomir here after all. Murphy's Law has made it so I'm late to yet another family gathering—and I left a half hour earlier than the last time.

Actually, it's likely that I have beaten him. Otherwise, there would be a text from him, and there isn't yet.

My parents' restaurant is called The Hut, which is short for The Hut on Hen's Legs. It's a reference to Baba Yaga, a cannibalistic witch from my childhood nightmares. You know, the perfect association for a restaurant.

Shaking my head, I run up the creaky wooden staircase and slip inside between the decorative hen "legs."

I think my folks are so prudish they're oblivious to the vaginal symbolism they've accidentally created here.

Inside the restaurant, the party is in full swing.

My father's namesake, Boris, is the singer today,

and for some reason, he's belting out a song from his non-Russian repertoire: "Gangnam Style."

I don't speak Korean, but I can still tell Boris has a heavy Russian accent as he butchers the words of the song. On the plus side, thanks to his stocky build and the mirrored sunglasses he's sporting, he actually resembles the original singer—or would if Boris were to shave off that beard. Also, his horse-riding dance moves are spot on. Same goes for the backup dancers on the stage.

As I navigate the dance floor, I'm nearly trampled by elderly Russian people who are horse-riding to K-Pop without fear of heart attacks or broken hips. The party has just begun, but I bet the average blood alcohol level here is already in the DUI territory.

Some of these peeps are distant family, but most are my mother's friends and acquaintances. As one, they give me dirty looks, no doubt because I'm the reason the poor wretches have had to listen to her complaints about me over the years.

My family is gathered at the usual table, all of them, so I'm officially the latecomer again.

"Hi, all," I say in English, figuring that's the language we'll be speaking for most of the night, given Fanny's presence at the table.

My brothers smile at me, as does Fanny—but my parents scowl, as per usual.

Hey, at least they haven't started eating or drinking without me this time—a huge insult in the Russian culture.

"Fashionably late again?" Mother's makeup is so heavy today, a drag queen would be jealous. She's also showing enough cleavage to choke a horse.

Vlad darts her a narrow-eyed look, and Alex rolls his eyes.

I force a smile. "Happy birthday, Mom." I thrust the gift box into her hands. "May you be healthy and prosperous."

There. The high ground.

Let's see how long I can stay there.

Grabbing the box, Mother looks momentarily appeased. Then her features become disapproving once again as she asks, "Where's your date?"

"I told him the shindig starts a little later than it actually does," I say.

"Why?" Father asks. His mustache looks extra bushy today, as does his unibrow.

I take a deep breath. "He's a potential investor, so I want to ask you all not to embarrass me in front of him today."

In other words, I'm asking for a miracle.

"When have we ever embarrassed you?" Mother asks, her eyes flinty.

Is she serious right now?

Figuring a fight isn't going to help my cause, I say, "I'm not saying you have. Just don't do it today of all days."

"We'll be on our best behavior," Vlad says pointedly. At his side, Fanny solemnly nods, and Alex says,

"We'll keep to the topics appropriate for polite company. No religion, politics, or money talk."

"We always avoid those topics too," Mother chimes in. "Besides, if anyone would shame the family, it would be Bella."

I try to think happy thoughts. She gave birth to me. It must've hurt. It's her birthday. I don't want Fanny to run away screaming if we get into one of our infamous rows.

Speaking of Fanny, Vlad leaps to his feet and folds his napkin as if he's planning to leave. Alex looks ready to bolt as well, and Fanny fidgets, extremely uncomfortable.

"Hold on," Mother squeals, seeing where things are headed. "No religion, politics, or money talk, I swear."

Is that an actual compromise from Mother? If so, is a unicorn about to fart a rainbow? If I had to guess why this is happening, I'd say she's trying to stay on Vlad's good side. Now that he's got Fanny, she thinks he's her most direct path to holding a grandchild—an obsession of hers that borders on insanity.

"I'm going to sit," I say and head for a chair farthest away from my parents.

"Don't sit there," Mother says. "It's the corner."

Of course. How could I have forgotten a superstition? Sitting at the corner of the table means you won't marry for seven years.

"Sit next to Fannychka," Vlad suggests.

I gladly comply. I've actually brought a little something for Fanny today, and this will allow me to stealthily gift it to her without getting on Mother's radar.

"Hi," Fanny whispers when I plop next to her. "Nice to see you again."

"Great to see you too," I say, and mean it.

I actually have a platonic crush on Vlad's girlfriend. She's one of the cutest creatures I've ever met—and that includes my dog. With her round, often-blushing face, she all but radiates sweetness and wholesomeness—yet I know she's got a secret wild side and plenty of spunk.

Looking at her and Vlad, I can see why Mother pines for a grandkid from them. With them both being pale, dark-haired, and blue-eyed, it's easy to picture what their potential offspring would look like: an adorable hybrid between a cherub and a vampire.

"I got this for you," I whisper into Fanny's ear conspiratorially.

She looks at me like the proverbial deer in the headlights.

I hand her the bag with my gift. "This is my latest creation."

Appearing even more hesitant, Fanny peeks inside the bag. As soon as she spots the butt plug with a squirrel tail, her eyes widen cartoonishly and her cheeks turn a shade of red I didn't think existed in nature.

"Thanks," she stammers, looking like she wants to sink through the floor.

"No sweat," I reply with a grin. "Vlad wanted a pony as a kid—so you might want to pretend that's a horse tail instead of a squirrel tail."

Vlad must overhear something because he narrows his eyes at me.

Before I can counter with an innocent puppy look, I spot Mother's eyes widening as she looks into the crowd. She then fans herself and bites her lip.

Well, that's weird.

I follow her gaze and immediately understand her reaction.

Dragomir is here, in all his mouthwatering, panty-melting glory.

Chapter Twenty-Two

*W*earing a bespoke suit that accentuates his muscular frame, he's holding a bouquet of flowers so massive someone must've chopped down an entire field of plants for it.

I stand up and wave him over.

Lips curving into a sexy grin, he approaches the table.

To my relief, his black eye is either gone or not visible in the current lighting.

Mother leaps to her feet with such vigor it's a miracle her ample bosom stays inside her dress.

"Everyone, this is Dragomir," I say. "Dragomir, this is—"

"Natasha," Mother says breathlessly.

"I was going to say 'everyone,'" I say with a slight eye roll.

"Hi, everyone and Natasha," he says.

"That's Fanny"—I point at her—"and Vlad." I

gesture at my brother. "You already know Alex, and that"—I nod at Father—"is my dad, Boris."

I check Dragomir's face to see if he's noticed that my parents' names are Boris and Natasha—like from the *Rocky and Bullwinkle* cartoon. Most people instantly realize the connection because my parents actually look like that villainous duo and even have similar accents.

If Dragomir makes the connection, he doesn't show it.

"Happy birthday, Natasha," he says in nearly perfect Russian. "May you have health above all."

Mother looks swoony as she mutters her thanks.

Geesh.

With a regal bow, Dragomir hands her the flowers.

Mother clutches her pearls—literally—then waves over a waiter and hands him the bouquet. Freed, she all but jumps on Dragomir, kissing him on the right cheek, then the left, before hugging him as though she wants to smother him in her bosom.

Father stands up and strides toward Dragomir.

At first, I wonder if he's jealous of the attention his wife is paying to the man and will do or say something to embarrass the family.

Nope. As soon as Mother stops slobbering on my date, Father gives Dragomir the kissing of the cheeks treatment.

Hey, at least he didn't go for the hug. Pretty sure in

another minute, Mother would've been copping a feel.

My brothers, being normal, simply shake Dragomir's hand, and Fanny shyly waves, blushes, and murmurs a hello.

Good job, Fanny. You get to live.

As Dragomir sits on the chair next to mine, the cinnamon notes of his cologne make me want to bite him.

Or lick him.

I'm ravenous, and not for the food.

I want to drag him to the dance floor and rub against him as soon as is socially acceptable—probably after at least a few toasts.

Father grabs the vodka bottle.

Fanny lifts her shot glass, but Vlad gently pushes her hand back down to the table—it's bad luck to fill a glass in the air.

"Now that everyone is here, let's begin." Father flashes a dirty look my way. He likes to drink, and I've made him wait an extra couple of minutes.

Without asking if everyone wants vodka, he pours a round of shots. In his defense, that's the Russian tradition.

"Remember, not too much for yourself," Mother tells him. "You promised."

With a sigh, he pours himself a shot instead of a full glass and says, "As the birthday girl's husband, it falls to me to say the first toast." He thinks very hard, then looks at Fanny apologetically.

"Dear, do you mind if I say this first one in Russian?"

Fanny smiles and shakes her head.

"I'll translate afterward," Vlad says with a slight frown. "We don't want anyone to feel left out."

Father begins his toast.

I lean close enough to Dragomir to nibble on his ear and whisper, "Every shot will have a toast, and there will be a lot of shots."

Dragomir nods.

"If you don't want to look like a wimp, finish every shot you lift in one gulp," I continue. "In general, be careful. If you try to keep up with anyone in my family, you'll be under the table in no time."

What I don't add is: if he gets too drunk, we won't be able to dance.

Dragomir leans toward me, his breath warm on my ear. "This isn't my first Russian get-together. As to anyone going under the table—you'll be there long before me."

"Oh yeah?" I grin. "Challenge accepted."

"I have at least sixty pounds on you," he whispers. "You keep starting fights you can't win."

My grin widens. "Just match me drink for drink, and we'll see what happens."

He shakes his head in exasperation.

I tune back into Father's toast, which is long, even for him.

When the toast is finally over, everyone downs their shots and eats a pickle after—except Fanny. She only sips hers and skips the pickle completely, the former being a big no-no as far as Russian drinking superstitions go, but something we pretend not to notice. A little bad luck is better than losing her to alcohol poisoning.

Everyone serves themselves food, and Vlad translates the toast for Fanny, who's clearly doing her best to keep a poker face.

"Happy perfect day, angel-like being. She who still causes my heart to tremble like a leaf in the wind. She whom I want to caress with my love. The mother of my children. May you have eternal health and happiness…" And so on and so forth, in that vein.

I shake my head at Vlad's translation. Caress with my love? a) TMI and b) That's not exactly what Father said. It's more like "cuddle with my passion," which I guess is also TMI.

"Eat something," I whisper into Dragomir's ear. "Else drinking you under the table won't even be a challenge."

With an eye roll, he takes *sel'edka pod shuboy*—a dish that translates to something like "herring dressed in a fur coat."

"Please send my compliments to your chef," Dragomir says loudly after he tries it. "This is the best version of this dish I've ever tasted."

Both of my parents beam with pride. Though they don't cook the food themselves, they do participate in recipe creation.

I hear Vlad explain the herring dish to Fanny.

"The fish is fermented," he's saying, "and it's served under a layer of shredded cooked beets and eggs, mixed with mayo."

Drowned in mayo, more like.

To her credit, Fanny accepts a small portion and tastes it without wrinkling her nose. The last time I saw her at this place, she was a much more cautious eater. My brother is clearly rubbing off on her—in more ways than one.

Still, she draws the line at *kholodetz*, a jellied meat dish that contains ingredients she finds unthinkable, such as pig snout and ears, chicken feet, and beef tails.

On my own plate is my favorite, *vinegret*—a salad with boiled beets, potatoes, pickles, carrots, onions, sauerkraut, and peas.

As soon as I'm done with my portion, Dragomir offers me more, and I let him put a serving on my plate.

Seeing this, Mother whispers approvingly to Father, "Her date is servicing her. A keeper."

Did she not catch the part where Dragomir speaks Russian?

With a nod at Mother, Father grabs the vodka bottle again. "The time between the first drink and the second ought to be short."

His toast is more concise this time—only long enough for everyone to start yawning—and then we drink.

I sneak a glance at the dance floor. Hopefully, we

can be there soon.

The time between the second and the third shot also appears to be short, and I begin to feel a pleasant buzz. That is, until Mother stands up to make a toast, at which point the buzz is replaced with dread.

"I hope a woman of my years can be forgiven if I think about my family legacy, especially on my birthday," Mother says and narrows her eyes at Alex— probably because he's the only person at the table without a date. Then, glancing approvingly at Fanny and Dragomir, she says, "To the health of my unborn grandchildren."

Even though this is not the first time she's been through this, Fanny blushes.

I half expect Dragomir to choke on his food or at least blink, but he takes it in stride, as though she's toasted to the health of our dogs—which, hey, is not such a bad idea.

Maybe Ruskovians also lack any subtlety when it comes to these things?

We drink the shots.

Vlad refills everyone's glasses and makes a toast next.

Then Alex.

When it's my turn, instead of toasting to the health of our dogs, specifically, I say that we should drink to the health of everyone's pets, "whatever they happen to be."

Annoyingly, Dragomir doesn't seem drunk yet— that or I'm getting too woozy to spot it.

Now would be okay to dance, and I'm about to say so, but then the lights dim.

Crap.

How could I have forgotten about the show when there's one at every celebration? And when I was forced to perform at them as a kid?

Yeah, my ventriloquism wasn't exactly a hobby I picked up on my own, though it's a skill I'm now grateful to have.

These shows take place at every major celebration here, and they're choreographed by my unqualified-for-this mother. As such, they're a hodgepodge of things she likes, including but not limited to ballet, fairy tales, Cirque du Soleil, and the Rockettes.

True to form, showgirls dressed as trees kick up their legs on the stage until our host, Boris—now dressed as Baba Yaga—does his best to dance ballet among them, looking more like a hippo than a witch.

Fanny's eyes grow wider as the show goes on, but Dragomir acts like he sees mustachioed cannibal witches pirouetting around all the time.

From there, it's one of the more common Baba Yaga stories—which itself is very similar to *Hansel and Gretel*. Of course, in Mother's version, it's a ballet, and in my opinion, Hansel is too handsy when he tosses Gretel into the air. I'm just going to tell myself they're step-siblings in this adaptation.

Blissfully, the show ends with Baba Yaga getting burned in a stove represented by orange-clad showgirls.

"Ladies and gentlemen," Boris announces. "The dance floor is yours."

With that, he starts to sing "A Million Scarlet Roses," a Russian slow-dance classic.

This is it.

I want to dance.

In a display of true psychic powers, Dragomir smoothly rises to his feet and extends his hand to me in an unmistakable gesture.

In my peripheral vision, I see my parents nodding approvingly at this, and Mother gives Vlad a pointed glare before gesturing at Fanny.

"May I have this dance?" Dragomir murmurs.

Grabbing his hand, I leap to my feet, and my heart speeds up at the feel of his strong fingers surrounding mine.

He takes a ballroom dance stance.

I put my other hand in his as well.

Wow.

His touch ignites my every nerve ending, his proximity making it hard to breathe.

We begin to sway to the music.

Double wow.

His mercurial eyes are hypnotizing. Claiming.

Is the floor a little shaky today?

I feel a little faint.

Breathless.

Fluttery.

I press against him.

His hard parts press against my soft ones, and my breathing hitches.

If the slow dance is meant to be a seduction, mission accomplished. If it's meant to be foreplay, bring on the main course.

He pulls me closer.

I feel Everest pressing against my belly.

He leans down.

Thanks to my high heels, we're face to face, so it's only a matter of a heartbeat before our mouths engage.

Triple wow.

The room around us seems to disappear.

I'm pure sensation—aware only of his soft lips, his gliding tongue, his large, hard body.

Speaking of the latter, I sneak my hand down and feel Everest over his pants.

How many wows has it been now?

He tears his lips away and whispers huskily, "Not here."

Fuck.

I forgot where I was again. Or didn't care.

On some level, I still don't *really* care—I want him that badly.

Suddenly, the music changes. The slow melody is replaced by the cheerful notes of one of Mother's favorite dances: Lambada.

Based on a Bolivian folk song called "Llorando se fue," this melody has found its way into the repertoires of a bunch of singers over the years, and from the first line Boris belts out, I recognize Jennifer Lopez's "On the Floor."

With a cocky smirk, Dragomir slides his hand to my lower back and pulls me in close—the Lambada position.

Another wow.

Legs arching, we take fast steps from side to side, sometimes turning, sometimes swaying, and all the while moving our hips as much as possible.

Or in other words, dry humping in public.

They didn't call the original inspiration for this song "the forbidden dance" for shits and giggles. It *should* be forbidden—at least on the dance floor of your parents' restaurant.

Especially if said parents already think you're an oversexed nymphomaniac.

"If you go hard, you gotta get on the floor," Boris belts out in his best impersonation of JLo—which isn't very good at all.

However, Dragomir *is* hard. That's the problem. I can feel every inch rubbing against me, and an answering pressure builds in my core.

Wow number three thousand.

I'm about to come. No toys, not even actual touching.

Forget him being "the one." He's more like my personal orgasm trigger—because I'm about to have one right here and now, in the middle of Mother's party.

Dragomir's pupils dilate, his eyes darkening to a rich, deep amber. I think he knows.

"Grab somebody, drink a little more," Boris sings.

I ignore the lyrics and focus on my building orgasm. It's almost there.

I just need a few more dry humps—I mean, sways to the music.

Just a little more.

Almost there.

Almost—

The song stops.

No!

Dragomir pulls away—and I can see why. We've done such a good job with the dancing, people are clapping.

Crap. Crap. Crap.

I catch Fanny's gaze. Blushing, she winks at me.

Fucking fuck.

The next song better give me an excuse to rub against Dragomir some more.

Nope. Not my day.

I recognize what the song is based on the first few notes. Everyone does. Boris is clearly on a Latin kick right now. In his thickest Russian accent yet, he sings, "When I dance they call me Macarena."

As one, Mother's friends and all my distant relatives extend their arms like a horde of zombies.

With a sigh, I do the same, as does Dragomir. Then we flip our palms up along with everyone else.

"They all want me." Boris seems to really enjoy that line, and hey, why *not* keep the hope alive?

Each person puts their right hand on their left shoulder, then repeats the action with their other hand.

My near orgasm is but a distant memory. This is as close as a dance can get to a cold shower.

We put our hands on the backs of our heads.

Shoot me now.

The hands go on our hips, and everyone starts to rotate said hips.

Okay, this is more interesting. With his hips moving that way, Dragomir manages the impossible: actually making the Macarena sexy.

Sadly, he soon joins everyone in a ninety-degree jump to the side, as do I.

Some people do a scuba dive move while others clap. Then the sequence repeats again. And again. And again.

When the song finally stops, I pull him toward me and whisper, "Let's go to your place."

His eyes widen, shifting to golden-green, and his face turns taut. "You mean right now?"

Ugh, he's right. We can't leave right this moment. The second course hasn't even been served. Mother would notice if we skedaddled, and would leap onto the stage, singing, "It's my party and I'll cry if I want to."

Fine.

We'll just keep dancing.

"Ladies and gentlemen," Boris says instead of launching into another song. "Now is the chance for you to grab this microphone and say a toast for our dear Natashen'ka."

Great. They're doing this bit? It's usually super boring.

We return to the table, and Father pours a round of shots.

My great-aunt recites a poem she's composed in Mother's honor.

After the poem is blissfully over, we drink.

The waiters bring out the shish kebab course, so we drink to that.

Someone from Mother's book club wishes her "sturdy offspring," and we drink to that too.

One of Father's usual drinking buddies grabs the mic next. "My friends, it's not good to drink individually, much better to do so as a collective." He raises his vodka glass. "To the power of the collective."

"Sounds like a commie slogan," I mutter as I down my next shot.

"Comrades," the next person says. "Let us have as much grief as there are drops in our glasses."

Cheers. We drink to that.

The next toast is, "Let there be people in your life whom you'd want to toast, not those who make you want to get drunk!"

Another shot.

Then another.

I begin to lose count of both toasts and shots—all I see is that Dragomir is somehow keeping up.

Impressive.

"Can someone tell me a Vovochka joke?" Fanny asks when the toasts are finally over. "I really like them, and Vlad ran out."

I lean toward Dragomir and whisper in his ear, "Vovochka is the Russian equivalent of Little Johnny."

"I know," he says. "I even know some of those jokes."

Does this man never cease to impress?

"I'll go first," Alex says and refills everyone's shot glasses. "'Parents having a fight again?' Grandmother asks Vovochka. 'Yeah,' he replies. 'When Mom came back from vacation, she brought back something called *gonorrhea*. First, she gifted it to Dad, then to Uncle Sergey, then the neighbor from across the street. Now they're all yelling and fighting, but I'm not sure if it's because she didn't bring enough, or because she didn't divide it up fairly.'"

Fanny blushes and laughs, as does everyone else.

We take a shot again.

"I've got one," Dragomir says, and my parents exchange an impressed glance. "Grandmother asks Vovochka why he's crying. 'Mom told Dad he's an ass, and he called her a cow in reply.' Grandmother pats him on the head. 'So what?' He cries harder. 'What animal does that make *me*?'"

Chuckles all around and another shot.

I know I shouldn't, but I can't help myself. "I know one too. But it's dirty."

"Just go for it," Mother says magnanimously.

Everyone's eyes are on me now, so I say, "Math teacher says, 'Vovochka, I will give you 300 rubles. If you give 50 to Vera, 50 to Dasha, and 50 to Elena, what do you get?' Vovochka's eyes gleam excitedly. 'An orgy?'"

More laughter and vodka follow.

"I've got one," Mother says. "'Mom, give me Dad's photo,' Vovochka asks. 'Why?' she replies. 'Because the teacher wants to see the idiot who did my homework.'"

A shot later, Father also tells one: "When six-year-old Vovochka comes back from school, his father asks, 'What did you think of the new teacher?' Vovochka rubs his chin. 'I liked her a lot. Too bad we have such a huge age difference.'"

Yet another round of shots.

The waiters come before anyone can tell any more jokes. They're carrying dessert. Specifically, the cake that's my dog's namesake: Napoleon.

Score. Now it's socially acceptable to leave.

Operation "Dragomir's Place" is back on.

Chapter Twenty-Three

I stand up to make our excuses, but Boris speaks up from the stage. "It's game time, ladies and gents."

Mother claps her hands, waves at Boris, and points at me and Dragomir.

Boris grins. "Looks like we have our first volunteers."

There goes our escape.

Everyone claps as Dragomir and I make our way to the now-cleared dance floor.

Handing me a glow-in-the-dark garter, Boris explains the game to us.

It's the Russian version of what Americans sometimes do at weddings: I'm to put the garter on my leg, and Dragomir's job is to remove it.

Yep.

Vodka is an important prerequisite to this game.

Before either of us can chicken out, the female

dancers surround me, so I have the privacy to put the garter under my dress.

Sticking my leg into the stretchy fabric, I grin wickedly and hike up the garter as far as it will go. No reason to make Dragomir's job *too* easy.

The dancers guide me to sit in a chair.

Boris puts a blindfold on Dragomir. Nice touch. The host then leads Dragomir over to my chair and helps him get on all fours.

Yum. When we finally get to his place, I think I'll want to recreate this whole scenario. Having him taste me blindfolded might be hot.

Dragomir feels around blindly at first but soon discovers my ankle.

Oh my. Heat shoots up my leg from his touch. Then his fingers slide up—and up and up, until he's way up there, under my skirt.

I love this game.

I want to play it for hours.

Everyone around us cheers and hoots, reminding me that this is a public place, so none of my fantasies are about to come true.

Dragomir's fingers brush the inside of my thigh. Then, maybe on purpose, he misses the garter and ends up grasping my thong.

Okay. A little higher and to the left and—

Nope. He realizes his mistake and finally clutches the garter.

"No. Get it with your teeth!"

Did my *mother* just scream that?

"With your teeth," everyone chants. "Teeth, teeth!"

Grinning, Dragomir dives under my skirt.

I gulp in a breath.

His mouth is almost where I dreamed for it to be. I can feel his warm breath through my rapidly melting thong.

Did a soft moan just escape my lips?

To my huge disappointment, Dragomir moves away from my aching clit and grabs the stupid garter with his teeth.

He pulls.

The garter rips on my thigh.

Emerging from under my skirt, Dragomir stands up.

At the sight of the garter in his teeth, the spectators cheer wildly.

He takes off the blindfold and kisses my cheek.

The cheering is so deafening my head is starting to spin.

Letting out a shaky breath, I return to the table on unsteady legs.

"Bye, guys," Alex says, standing up. "I have a big day tomorrow, so I'm going to bolt."

Aha! Dessert has been served, and now Alex is leaving. That means it's completely and totally acceptable to proceed with Operation Dragomir's Place—which is good because I'm as close to bursting from horniness as a woman can get.

"Everyone," I say. "Dragomir and I also have to go."

Vlad kisses my cheeks, and Fanny smiles brightly and waves goodbye.

Mother walks over and gives me a bear hug.

Wait, what?

She hasn't done that in years.

Before I can recover, I get an even bigger surprise. Father not only gives me a hug but also says, "It was so nice to see you."

It must be *The Day After Tomorrow*-level chilly in hell.

Then my parental units' behavior becomes more fathomable.

Mother hugs Dragomir hard enough for him to feel some parts of her that he shouldn't, then slobbers on his cheeks, Winnie style.

As soon as she's done, Father gives my date a similar treatment.

I'm in such a daze as we finally escape that my steps are uneven.

When we pass by Boris, I rummage in my purse for cash, find a hundred bucks, and slip it into his pudgy hand. "Pick Vlad and his date for the next game," I whisper. "Make it the garter again."

Boris nods.

I dart my brother a snickering glance. I'm convinced that my place in his life is to push him to have more fun. And for today, that mission is accomplished. I just hope it's not physically possible to die from blushing. Otherwise, when Fanny goes through what I did on that chair, she just might expire on the spot.

Hey, they might name that type of death after her: the Fanny Pack syndrome. Poor girl. I still can't believe her parents named her Fanny when their last name is Pack.

Maybe mine *aren't* the worst.

"Your parents are sweethearts," Dragomir says as we clear the dance floor.

Is he psychic?

I hiccup. Sweethearts in front of him, maybe. "Mother would sell her soul to the devil for a grandkid as gorgeous as you."

Wait. Did I just say that out loud?

Crap. Like most guys, he's probably going to run at the mention of kids—and I can't have him run. I want to have my way with him.

To my shock, he just smirks. "Excuses, excuses. You're going to lose our bet. My parents are just as obsessed with grandchildren, but yours are still angels compared to them."

Grr. I keep losing competitions. Couldn't drink him under the table. Didn't beat him in *Beat Saber*— unless a black eye counts. And now I couldn't even prove that my parents are worse than his—though I guess in this case, I didn't try all that hard.

As we exit the restaurant, I feel a strange, unpleasant sensation in my stomach. If I didn't know how meticulous Mother is about fresh food ingredients, I'd guess I'd eaten something bad.

Dragomir waves his phone at me. "Fyodor tells me he's stuck in traffic. He thinks he could be here in ten minutes."

"Nah, let's just go now." I point at a cab that's already waiting by the sidewalk.

Dragomir agrees and we dive into it. He rattles out his address, pulls out a wad of cash, and hands the guy half of it. "Get us there quick, and you'll get the other half," he promises.

The cabbie nods solemnly and floors the gas.

As the car jerks forward, I feel a small bout of car sickness coming on, but I don't say anything. Getting to Dragomir's place swiftly is worth the discomfort.

Besides, I know just the thing to keep my mind occupied.

Pouncing on Dragomir, I kiss him. Hard.

His return kiss is scorching.

The cab and the world fall away. All that's left are those sensual lips and the strong, warm, lightly callused hands roaming my body.

After what feels like a minute of bliss, the car lurches to a screeching stop.

We're there already?

Time sure flies when you're on the verge of an orgasm.

Dragomir hands the rest of his cash to the driver and leads me into a swanky skyscraper. On the elevator ride, we kiss again—but it lasts only an eyeblink before we have to get out.

"Welcome to my place," he says as we step into a giant penthouse. Before I can so much as look around, a bear-like creature attacks—and slobbers all over my face. Again.

Yuck. Winnie's doggy breath is potent today. It makes me gag.

I must get cleaned up ASAP. Not only is my stomach rebelling at the smell, but Dragomir won't want to kiss me like this.

Done with me, the bear cockblocker slobbers on her master.

He takes out his wet wipes and offers one to me, but I shake my head. "Can I use a sink?"

With Winnie on our heels, he leads me through a living room where every shelf is covered with trophies.

Hmm. Each golden statue holds something vaguely phallic in its hand. Can you get a trophy in masturbation?

Nah, doubt it. If you could, I'd have Olympic gold by now.

"I'm into fencing," he says, following my gaze.

Fencing. Of course. That makes more sense.

"Hey now," I say, doing my best not to get too much dog drool into my mouth as I speak. "You cheated."

He quirks an eyebrow as we step into the kitchen.

"You had an edge in *Beat Saber* because you're

good with a sword. Or rapier or whatever," I say as I step to the sink to wash off doggie cooties. My foundation and blush are already toast, but I do my best not to wash off my mascara. If I look like a raccoon, Winnie just might try to eat me.

She's already eyeing me with what could easily be hunger.

As I finish washing my face, he holds out a towel for me.

"Since when is being good at something considered cheating?" he asks as I dry myself.

"It just seems unsportsmanlike for a professional to play a novice like that. You're basically a *Beat Saber* hustler."

With a grin, he leans over the sink and also splashes some water on his face.

I use the opportunity to look around the kitchen for any pictures of a wife or girlfriend. Thankfully, there are none. However, there is a photo of him dressed in full fencing regalia.

Oh, boy.

I hadn't realized this before, but those protective outfits are tight. And what's worse, they look suspiciously like turtlenecks.

As soon as I make the connection, my ovaries kick into high gear. I clear my suddenly dry throat. "I need you to keep Winnie busy for the next few hours."

He straightens and dries his face, his eyes darkening as his gaze falls to my lips. "On it," he says huskily.

Reaching into the cupboard, he takes out what looks like a T-rex femur. He hands it to Winnie, crooning something in Ruskovian, and she begins to gnaw on the bone.

He nods at the kitchen exit.

I tiptoe past Winnie into the living room, and he follows.

Alone at last.

Moving with predatory grace, he closes the distance between us and kisses me once again.

The room feels like it's spinning.

Before I know it, I'm ripping off his clothes, and he's peeling off mine.

Finally.

This. Is. Happening.

Without breaking the kiss, he lifts me up. A moment later, my naked back is on the couch, and his eyes are roaming over my exposed skin.

Hey, unfair. He's still got his pants on—but his muscular torso is making up for that sin for now.

As I take in that gleaming, lightly tanned skin sprinkled with masculine dark hair, my mouth waters.

He leans over me. "Are you okay with this?" His voice is rough, his gaze filled with so much heat I shiver.

"Oh, yes. More than okay."

His face suddenly tightens. "We have to be careful. Don't want to follow in our dogs' footsteps."

I moisten my lips. "I'm on the pill."

His expression turns ravenous. "I'm clean."

"Me too," I say, and kiss him before he can waste more time on trivialities.

We dance the Lambada with our tongues.

He bites my lower lip.

I unzip his pants and snake my hand inside.

Everest is silky smooth to the touch, and hard like... well, a mountain.

Dragomir kisses my neck, then gives it a little nibble.

My skin pebbles all over.

His tongue journeys down my collar bone and over to my right nipple.

As I gasp, my hand tightens over Everest, and I begin to stroke up and down.

He groans with pleasure but pulls Everest away as he proceeds to lick his way down to my navel, traveling lower and lower until he's exactly where I want him.

Where I need him.

"Lie back," he commands hoarsely.

I'm all too happy to comply. Here and now, I will find out if he's the one.

When his warm breath touches my clit, I know without a shadow of a doubt that he is.

This is going to be amazing. Better than chocolate and puppies.

He gives my yearning clit the tiniest of licks.

I moan in pleasure.

He flattens his tongue and makes another contact.

Pleasure begins to coil in my core as another moan is wrenched from my lips.

His licks turn into kisses.

My hands fist in his hair. At this rate, I might scalp the poor man.

His kisses morph back into licks.

Letting go of his hair, I come with a cry. The pleasure is so intense that my toes curl spasmodically, and every muscle in my body twitches and shakes.

It's official. My three-year stretch of toy-only orgasms is over.

He looks up at me with pure male satisfaction, his eyes like molten gold.

Heart rate slowing a smidge, I wriggle out from under him. "Now you lie back."

He takes my place.

The room around us spins like a rollercoaster.

Odd. Must be the orgasm afterglow.

Steadying my hands, I rid Dragomir of his stupid pants, then free Everest from the briefs.

Fuuuuuck. Despite Xenia's warning about Ruskovians being well-endowed, and despite having felt it with my hands, I didn't expect Everest to be this huge… or this beautiful.

It calls to me in the way the namesake mountain must call to thrill-seekers the world over. I get why they risk their lives for that climb. Climbing *this* Everest is now on my bucket list—and climb it I will, if it's the last thing I do.

But first, let's see if it can fit into my mouth. It

might be tricky, but I've never shied away from a challenge.

I start with a lollipop lick.

Dragomir groans, and Everest twitches under my tongue, urging me on.

Here we go.

Opening wide, I let in as much as I can.

Wait a second. I don't usually have a strong gag reflex, but something isn't right.

Something activates.

Uh-oh.

It's as though all the prior little issues—the maybe-bad food, the rocky car ride, the dog breath, and the room spinning—decide to come to the surface as one.

Oh my vodka gods. I was in denial about losing yet another contest to Dragomir.

The drinking one.

Dizzily, I extricate myself from Everest and rise up on wobbly legs.

Yep. I'm wasted. And what's worse, the contents of my stomach are rising.

"What's wrong?" Dragomir's face is tight with concern.

"Bathroom," I gasp. "Bathroom! Where is the bathroom?"

He leaps to his feet, but I'm too preoccupied to admire his glorious nakedness.

"Here." He hurries down a hallway and pushes open a door before facing me. "Are you okay?"

I can't answer, as that would require opening my mouth.

Instead, I save all my strength, all my focus on making it to the promised land that is that bathroom.

I do my best to sprint.

Since the vodka has long since decreased the energy consumption of my cerebellum to a snail crawl, my sprint ends with me bumping into the wall. Hard.

No. No. No.

The smack almost makes me cry out and thus open my mouth.

But I don't. Like a hero.

I must finish my epic quest to that bathroom. The stakes couldn't be any higher.

Utilizing every ounce of my willpower, I walk as fast and straight as is possible under the circumstances. If, besides masturbation, they gave out Olympic gold for walking under heavy influence, it would be in my pocket after this.

Skillfully not walking into Dragomir or the door he's still holding, I dive into the bathroom, drop to my knees, and violently pray to the vodka gods at the makeshift porcelain altar.

Strong hands hold back my hair, and soothing words are murmured above me.

I'm so embarrassed that if I could fall through the tiles into another apartment, I would.

This isn't only a prayer, it's a food offering as well —and I sure hope the vodka gods like boiled beets, potatoes, carrots, onions, sauerkraut, peas, and pickles.

Well, everyone knows they like their pickles, but I'm less sure about the rest.

Looking into the altar is a huge mistake.

Another prayer spews from my mouth, Exorcist style.

Then another.

At some point, I run out of spiritual fervor. Shaking, I flush and back away from the altar.

Unable to meet Dragomir's gaze, I wash my face, then grab the bottle of Listerine from the sink and chug it. Next, I take the tube of toothpaste, squirt some into my mouth, swirl it around, and swallow.

"You can never tell any Russians about this." My words come out slurred even to my ears. "They'll revoke my membership."

He gently envelops me in a bathrobe. "Let's get you dressed."

I let him lead me to the living room, where he helps me put on my clothes.

Winnie is here, and like Dragomir, she looks at me worriedly.

"I'm fine," I lie, but my words are even more slurred now.

"Why don't you lie down," he says.

"I want—" I hiccup. "Want to go home. Need a nap."

He frowns. "Wouldn't it be better if you stayed?"

I violently shake my head and feel another prayer coming on. "I'm going to take a cab."

"You are not."

This sounds like a statement of fact, so I don't argue, letting him lead me downstairs and into the already-waiting limo/RV.

"Lie down," he orders as soon as we get inside.

I do, grateful to be off my shaking legs, and he sits next to me and strokes my hair.

"That's nice," I mumble as my lids drift shut.

"Good. Relax."

I do as he says, and a moment later, I'm out.

Chapter Twenty-Four

I wake up in my bed and wish I didn't.

Never. Drinking. Again.

My headache has a migraine, and the taste in my mouth is against the Geneva convention.

How did I get here?

Did last night happen, or was it a cruel nightmare?

Given the smell of vodka in the air, it happened. I must've fallen asleep in the RV. But then what?

Did Dragomir bridal-carry me home?

That actually sounds kind of nice. I hope that's what happened, and not, say, that he and Fyodor carried me together by my arms and legs like a sack of fermented potatoes.

I peek under the covers.

No clothes.

Interesting. He also undressed me?

If so, no big deal. He saw me naked at his place

anyway. It's also possible I undressed myself, but can't remember due to alcohol-induced amnesia.

Hmm. If I undressed myself, maybe I had my way with Dragomir as well?

But no. I'm pretty sure I'd remember that momentous of an occasion. Also, given Everest's girth, I'd feel some soreness, and I don't. Almost the opposite. There's a gnawing emptiness in my girly bits that probably won't go away *until* I get Everest in there—assuming that's possible after my faux pas last night.

With a groan, I sit up and slide my feet into the slippers someone left by the bed.

Boner rushes into the room, his tail wagging too fast for my addled brain to process.

"*Ma chérie*, you smell like the butt of a dog who ate fermented escargot in vodka sauce. *Délicieux*."

I stumble to my feet.

Hmm. My motor control seems to be back. That's a start.

When I reach the living room, the couch catches my attention. The pillows are not where my cleaning lady usually leaves them.

Did Dragomir sleep here?

It's possible. If our roles were reversed, I'd stay to make sure he didn't choke on his own prayer.

"Dragomir?"

No answer, but when I stumble into the kitchen, my theory is confirmed.

A pot of oatmeal is sitting on the stove, a glass of

some strange liquid is sitting on the table, and my coffee pot is loaded and ready to go.

There's also a note on the table:

Off to work. In the cup is a Ruskovian hangover cure. Drink it, and you'll be good as new.

I down the miracle cure. It tastes like Pedialyte with pickle juice, milk, and cherry coke. Not sure how effective this is as a hangover cure, but if someone made me drink this every time, it would be a much better deterrent from drinking than a hangover alone.

By the time I'm done forcing oatmeal into my stomach, I remember what it's like to be human again.

Pouring myself a cup of coffee, I text Dragomir:

Thanks for the breakfast. And bringing me home.

His reply is instant:

My pleasure. Do you have a second for a videocall?

Leaving my coffee on the table, I sprint into the bathroom, apply makeup, and examine my face.

I'm not looking my best, but not my worst either.

Sure, I reply and plop back into the kitchen chair.

A videocall from Dragomir shows up right away.

I accept.

Behind him must be his office—and it's the size of some people's apartments, with several computer monitors occupying a gleaming white desk and a wall of bookcases displaying everything from economics textbooks to fencing trophies.

Piercing hazel eyes scan my face. "The *barabul'ka* must've worked. You're looking better already."

"*Barabul'ka*?" In Russian, that word means "striped red mullet." Which, despite sounding like the haircut of a ginger stripper from the eighties, is a type of fish, also known as a goatfish.

"*Barabul'ka* is the name of the cure," he says.

Was it actually fish broth then, or raw fish blended? On second thought, I don't think I want to know.

"Thanks again." I take a gulp of my coffee. "And sorry about last night."

He stretches back in his throne-like office chair. "Don't mention it."

I quirk an eyebrow. "Can't believe you're not rubbing in your victory. Wish I had that self-control."

His eyes gleam. "Bragging about out-drinking you would be like an opera singer boasting about clearing her throat."

Was that a dig? If so, I'll let it stand. "You have to let me do something for you as a thank-you for taking such good care of me."

I run my tongue over my lips in case my meaning isn't clear.

Mission accomplished. His gaze turns hungry and his body tenses, like he's about to pounce. "What did you have in mind?"

"How about you come over tonight?" I imbue the question with as much lasciviousness as I can. "I'll make you… dinner. I hope you come."

His voice roughens. "I will be there."

"Good," I say, then blow him an air kiss and

hang up.

It's finally happening—and no vodka can stop us this time.

Giddy with excitement, I gulp down the rest of my coffee and rush into the bedroom to set things up for tonight. Clean sheets—check. Romantic music ready to go—check. Sex toys? Will skip for now.

I even set up some LED candles around the bed.

Now I need to go through with my pretext and cook us dinner.

What should I make? No clue, but I do know whom to ask. True, she cooks for dogs now, but she was a human chef before that.

I dial Xenia and bring her up to speed on my recent adventures, then tell her about my culinary dilemma.

"I know just the thing," she says enthusiastically. "Here are the ingredients you should incorporate into all the courses: artichokes, asparagus, avocado, coconut, dates, bananas, eggs, mango, mushrooms, okra, pistachios, sesame seeds, parsley, and celery. For the dessert, just mix walnuts with honey."

Is that four courses if you count dessert? I'm beginning to see why Boy Toy looks so jolly.

"Hon, that's a big list," I say. "Also, what dish can bananas and okra possibly share?"

"Who said they have to be the same dish? These ingredients are known aphrodisiacs from around the globe. For example, the French believe that artichokes warm the genitals."

"So do some STDs."

"Warm, not burn," she says, and I can hear her rolling her eyes through the phone. "Being Russian, you should know how potent walnuts with honey can be. Take one spoonful half an hour after dinner, and have him do the same."

Should I crush some Viagra into that dessert while I'm at it?

"Okay, Dr. Xenia. Now if you hook me up with some recipes to make out of all those things, I'll be golden."

She promises to do so and comes through in an hour.

I order my groceries online, and while I wait for the delivery, I walk Boner and work on some designs. When the groceries arrive, I begin cooking, even though it's too early for dinner.

If I end up with just two courses of edible food by the end of this, I'll consider the effort a success.

I'm in the middle of making a salsa with mango, avocado, and parsley when Dragomir texts me:

Can I videocall you right now?

I agree and rush out of the kitchen to make myself presentable. I barely make it, as he calls me just a minute later.

The moment his face pops up on my screen, I notice his grim expression and my heart sinks.

"I'm so sorry, but I have to bail on our dinner," he says tightly. "My brother has been in an accident."

Chapter Twenty-Five

"*O*h, no! What happened?"

He puts on a wireless headset. "Let me switch to phone mode so I can pack."

Pack?

He proceeds to tell me that one of his brothers is a huge adrenaline junkie who surfs in the most dangerous waters, snowboards the steepest cliffs, and so on. This time, he was base-jumping off the highest skyscraper in Moscow. Something went wrong and he hit his head, at which point he was helicoptered to Ruskovia by their family.

"He's in a coma." Dragomir's voice is filled with so much pain I wish I could reach through the electro-magnetic signals to give him a hug. "I'm flying to Ruskovia tonight."

Tonight? I got so caught up in his story I momentarily forgot about our plans.

I rush into the kitchen and turn off the food before a fire starts.

"What about Winnie?" I ask. "Are you leaving her with Fyodor?"

"No. He's coming with me, and so is she."

"How? I mean, won't the airline have a fit?"

Did he convince them she's a service bear?

"I'm flying on a private jet," he says. "I'll do my best to make her comfortable—though, granted, she really dislikes flying."

"If you want, you can leave her with me," I hear myself saying.

"Thank you, but I couldn't possibly impose on you like that."

He doesn't sound completely certain, so I persist. "Is it even safe to fly in her condition?" I have no idea why I'm trying to persuade him to leave Winnie with me. I mean, a bear in my small apartment? Really?

Maybe I just want him to have a reason to keep in touch… a.k.a. retain a hostage.

"Stress isn't ideal during pregnancy," he admits. "But still, I can't ask you to do this."

"You're not asking. I'm volunteering."

He's silent for a moment. "You don't know what this would mean."

I'm pretty sure I do—and shoveling bear shit is probably part of it.

"If we do this, you have to let me pay for all her food," he says. "She's a big girl, and the expenses of feeding her might—"

"That's fine," I say, fighting the urge to comment on the understatement in the "big girl" comment. I can afford her food, no problem, but if it makes him feel better to provide it, I won't argue.

"I'll also pay a portion of your rent since——"

"Now you're talking crazy. Just bring a bag of food or whatever she needs. If I run out, I'll get more and invoice you when you get back."

"Thank you," he says with feeling. "You don't know how much this means to me."

Great. Now I feel guilty for my nice gesture's ulterior motive.

"When will you bring her here?" I ask.

"In an hour?"

I walk into my closet and look for a bag or a backpack that I haven't decorated with my penis art. "Works for me."

"See you soon," he says and hangs up.

Pocketing my phone, I grab an undecorated JanSport backpack and stuff it with a few choice toys from the teledildonics line Fanny and Vlad tested for me. These toys are meant for use by a man and would allow me and Dragomir to get intimate remotely— assuming I give him the backpack, which I'm not sure I should.

On the one hand, we'd be able to make each other come despite the sudden separation. It obviously won't be as fun as what we would've done tonight, but better than nothing. On the other hand, what if he somehow figures out my company makes these toys?

Then again, how would that happen? As Vlad said, the way Belka is set up makes it impossible to know I own it.

Maybe I'll make the decision when he arrives.

For now, I leave the backpack near the front door and pack some of the stuff I made for dinner in a to-go box for his plane ride.

I spend the next hour reading my email. Apparently, butt plugs in the shape of Woody Harrelson are trending. Does he have a new movie out or something? Well, at least it's not Liam Neeson. I don't know how I would've delivered that bit of news to Xenia.

My doorbell rings.

Boner sprints over there so fast he nearly skids headfirst into the door.

When I open it, the sight of Dragomir in a tight sweater and dark jeans makes my stomach flutter— but then a bear assaults my face with a bucket of saliva, putting a damper on my overactive libido.

"Stop it, Winnie." Dragomir drags her off me. "You're going to be staying with Bella, so you need to behave like a good dog."

He hands me a wet wipe.

"It's okay," I say after I'm drool free. "She *is* a good dog."

Oblivious to us, Winnie licks Boner next.

"*Bonjour, ma petite.* Your tongue is like the perfect

strip of bacon, your drool like a heavenly bone marrow."

"*Zdrastvuyte*, Napoleon Carlovich. You're my favorite kind of dog muffin—stud. You make my puppy-filled ovaries swoon, and my ten nipples hard with yearning."

Hmm. This mental ventriloquism session has escalated quickly. There might be a bit of projection in there too.

"Winnie's things are in here," Dragomir says, wheeling in a huge suitcase.

I blink at the suitcase as he steps outside again and wheels in one more.

Two suitcases? For a dog?

When *I* go on vacation, I only take one—and smaller than either of those.

Misunderstanding my expression, Dragomir opens the suitcases and shows me that one is filled with dog toys, while the other contains a blanket, a bed, and bowls of appropriate sizes, along with some other items meant to keep a bear happy.

I arch my eyebrows. "Is that all of it?"

"Of course not," Dragomir says. He goes out again and drags in a bag of dog food that could easily fit a person my size inside of it—without them having to do any contortions.

Before I can comment on it, he carries the bag into the kitchen, fills up a giant bowl with its contents, and pours water into another equally sized bowl.

As though starved for years, Winnie attacks the chow.

And hey, she might be eating for ten, maybe even fifteen.

"You might want to feed Boner too," Dragomir says. "We don't want them getting jealous of each other."

Agreeing, I fill up Boner's bowls—which look comically small in comparison to Winnie's. As soon as Boner starts munching, Dragomir and I sneak away. We take Winnie's suitcases into the living room and spread her stuff around so that, to quote Dragomir, "she feels at home."

When he's done with the last of the toys, sadness flickers in his eyes—like he's missing Winnie already.

"She'll be okay," I say. "I'll make sure of it."

He steps closer to me, his expression shifting to something far more intense. "I'm officially in your debt."

My gaze cuts toward the bedroom, where everything is set for an epic encounter. "We'll have to figure out how you'll make it up to me."

He removes the distance between us in one step. "I have to run."

"Of course." I stare up at him, my heart pounding in my chest as he lays his hands on my shoulders and dips his head.

I rise on my tiptoes.

The kiss is less hungry than our prior ones.

Instead, it's filled with tenderness—and it seems to make a promise.

A promise of more to come.

He reluctantly pulls away. "I'm sorry. I have to go."

"Of course. Go be with your brother." Did my voice just crack?

Nodding solemnly, he heads for the door.

Remembering the items I've prepped, I run after him. "Take this." I hand him the to-go box. "This was going to be our dinner tonight."

His eyes take on a warm glow. "Thank you. I'll get in touch as soon as I land and take stock of the situation."

Emboldened, I thrust the backpack with sex toys into his hands as well. "Take this too. But don't open it until you have a moment of privacy."

"Okay." He kisses me again—this time gently on the forehead—and steps out.

I close the door with a sigh. On autopilot, my feet carry me over to the living room where I plop on the couch, hold my knees to my chest, and put on *Frozen* for the thousandth time.

At some point, Winnie and Boner waltz into the living room.

Winnie grabs a rubber doughnut toy the size of a truck tire and cozies up next to me, taking up the rest of the couch. Boner joins us on my lap, and by the time the credits roll, I'm feeling better.

Since I'm not sure if Dragomir walked Winnie

before bringing her over, I take both doggies for a walk—and though I usually wouldn't, I bring my phone with me, in case he calls from the plane.

When we enter the park, a familiar king poodle is walking toward us. I remember it because of the lion haircut. This dog was an asshole to Boner the other day.

Yep.

His memory not as sharp as mine, Boner tries to be friendly with the poodle again.

The poodle shows teeth and growls.

Despite being three times bigger, Winnie hides behind me with a whine.

"Pom-Pom, you're not being a nice lady," the poodle's owner says to her charge after I give them both a glare.

Boner's reaction today is nearly identical to the last time. Halting in his tracks, he looks at me with a befuddled look that seems to say, "*Ma chérie*, I thought that I—the stud—was *irrésistible* to bitches."

I pull him back before Pom-Pom can pounce. The snarling creature clearly has rabies.

When the poodle is out of sight, we resume walking, and since I have my phone, I call Xenia and tell her about my day.

"Hmm," she says when I'm done.

"Hmm what?"

"You'll call me a cynical Russian again."

"I'll call you worse if you don't spill it."

"Fine," she huffs. "How do we know there's a hurt

brother in Ruskovia? What if he's going to visit his perfectly healthy wife or girlfriend?"

I squeeze the dog leashes in my hand.

She's talking about a Marco scenario, and I can't believe it didn't occur to me first.

"That doesn't make sense," I say, not sure whom I'm trying to convince. "He had the chance to sleep with me. Isn't that what cheaters want? If we'd done the deed and *then* he had to go, that would be a different story."

"Maybe he's a rare guy with a sense of conscience," she says, sounding less certain now. "When the cheating got close, he felt guilty and jumped on the plane to be with his significant other."

"And left his dog with me? Doesn't fully track."

At least I hope it doesn't. I wish I were as sure as I'm pretending to be.

Xenia sighs. "Maybe I *am* just being cynical. Still, if I were you, I'd keep my eyes and ears peeled when I speak with him."

My stomach feels cold and tight. "Can we talk about something else? What's it like being engaged?"

Xenia is happy to tell me all about her recent conversations with the people in her life and how all the Russians were surprised that a "woman her age" has found someone.

By the time we're done talking, I'm home.

Unleashing the dogs, I walk in and busy myself with VR suit design, then some emails from the marketing department—anything to keep my mind from jumping back to the specter that Xenia has raised.

The problem is, those sneaky thoughts ambush me when I finally get into bed. The sexy setup in this room is a huge Dragomir reminder.

The cold tension in my stomach returns with a vengeance, and as I toss and turn, I realize something.

I wasn't careful.

Somehow, I let my guard down and allowed Dragomir to slither in and wrap himself around my heart. Not that I'm in love with him—it's way too soon for that—but I definitely feel *something*.

Fuck. I'm such an idiot.

Was Xenia right? Could he have picked up on my budding crush, felt guilty about it, and decided to flee before things progressed further? Maybe he's one of those people who think sex means nothing, but if there are feelings involved, that's real cheating.

Any way you slice it, I'm glad he's giving me the space to think it over. It's a bad idea to feel anything beyond lust for him. Recused or not, he's still a potential investor in the project of my dreams, and like he said, business and emotions shouldn't mix. Sex and business aren't a great combo either, but at least that's more excusable.

The man was wearing a turtleneck the first time we met, for fuck's sake.

So is Xenia right? Or is she just being paranoid because she knows I tend to attract assholes? Does it even matter? Even if Dragomir is single, he's clearly hiding something about his past.

That should be a deal breaker in and of itself.

Maybe now that I've realized this, I can sleep.

Nope. Not happening, at least not without some aid.

Getting up, I trudge to the kitchen, nearly tripping over Winnie on the way. She's cuddled around Boner, who seems to be in seventh heaven.

When I finally reach the fridge, I gulp down a glass of milk in the hope that a food coma might help me drift off.

It doesn't work. Instead of sleep, I get heartburn.

Fine. I grab a sex toy at random, get back to bed, and attempt to orgasm myself to exhaustion. Unfortunately, my treacherous mind visualizes naked Dragomir every time I climax—without fail. Stupid mind.

It's not until the toy's low battery indicator starts blinking that I manage to drift off.

Chapter Twenty-Six

As I eat my oatmeal the next morning, I watch my dog doing something peculiar. If I had to guess, I'd say he wants to hump Winnie. He's got that look I know well, the one he wears right before he attacks his sex toy, Remy. However, due to their size difference, he can't even come close to mounting the bear.

He just looks at her butt longingly and whines.

On her end, Winnie either doesn't understand what he wants or pretends not to.

"You've already knocked her up," I remind him.

"*Ma chérie*, what does that have to do with *sexe* time?"

"Touché." I resume eating.

As breakfast goes on, my theory is confirmed. Instead of eating the kibble I've set out for him, Boner stalks Winnie.

Ignoring him, she munches on her food.

With a huge effort, he jumps onto the kitchen chair. That puts him at almost the right height, except the chair is two feet away from the bear's butt, and she doesn't look willing to back into it.

Boner glances down, then at his goal, eyes calculating.

"Don't do it," I say. "You'll break your neck."

Ignoring me, he leaps—but overshoots and lands on Winnie's back.

She doesn't even stop eating.

He looks down, then at me.

"*Ma chérie*, help. *S'il vous plaît.*"

I grab him and set him down on the floor.

If he wants any other kind of help, it's not happening.

He trudges over to his bowl to drown his sorrows in food. Afterward, he humps Remy, but—and I might be imagining it—his usual enthusiasm is lacking.

I glance at my phone.

Nothing from Dragomir.

Wait, why am I even checking?

I dive into work and manage not to think of him too much for the rest of the day. At night, however, I can't fall asleep. It bothers me that there was no call or text from him.

He should've landed by now, I think.

———

When I wake up after another troubled sleep, there's still nothing.

Is this it? Have I been ghosted?

No, that's not logical. I have his dog. But then why is he not calling or texting me?

Finally, a videocall from Dragomir shows up on my phone after lunch, ripping me away from a dildo design.

My finger slides to accept, and I quickly angle the phone to prevent him from seeing what I'm working on.

Familiar hazel eyes peer at me from the screen. Gorgeous eyes, despite how tired and sad they seem.

"Hi," he says, taking me in. "Sorry I didn't get a chance to get in touch earlier."

I look behind him. He seems to be in a living room with a large, expensive-looking rug on a wall behind him—which makes wall rugs another small way Ruskovia is similar to Russia.

"How is your brother?" I ask as my mind frantically tries to figure out what to do with my Xenia-inspired suspicions.

He looks pained. "He's in a coma. The doctors don't know when he'll wake up."

Shit.

He sounds so sincere.

"Where is he?" I ask.

"Here, at the hospital," Dragomir says.

Hospital? The background doesn't look like a hospital.

Wow. If he *is* lying, that's some very bad karma. But how can I tell?

He frowns, peering at me.

Is something of my doubts showing on my face?

"What's your brother's name?" I blurt.

Not very subtle, but hey. If he's making this up, he'll stumble and I'll catch it. Or if he gives me a name, I can pass it along to Vlad to help with his snooping—a win-win.

His frown deepens. "Is something wrong?"

Yeah, that wasn't such a good idea on my part.

"You're at the hospital now?" I ask, deciding to just go for it. "Right now?"

His eyes narrow. "That's what I said a moment ago."

"Then how come it looks like a living room?"

Has someone turned up the thermostat in my apartment? I'm starting to sweat like a pig at a Bikram yoga practice.

He looks at the fuzzy rug behind him, then turns back to face the camera. "It's a private hospital. Why not make the patients comfortable?"

"I guess…"

His kissable lips flatten. "Are you trying to say I'm not in a hospital, even though I'm telling you I am?"

I swallow the sudden lump in my throat. "A rug doesn't seem very hygienic."

If I could rewind time, I'd start this conversation over from scratch and take a different tack.

His gaze hardens. "Are you saying I'm misleading you?"

My stomach twists into knots, and the words spill from my lips of their own accord. "Look, I don't know much about you. When you left so suddenly, I started to wonder if—"

"Enough." He reaches for the phone and turns the camera to pan it around the room.

At first, my living room impression intensifies. I spot a large TV, plush furniture, and an ornate coffee table that belongs in a hospital even less than a rug does. But then a bed comes into view, and my chest tightens painfully at the sight.

It's a hospital bed, albeit the fanciest I've ever seen. Surrounding the bed are stands with what must be intravenous fluids and nutrients, a ventilator machine, a monitor displaying blood pressure and heart rate, and other dread-inducing medical equipment.

My stomach feels cold and hard, like the Siberian tundra.

All this equipment is attached to an unconscious Dragomir.

I gasp in a panicked breath and remind myself it can't be Dragomir. I just saw him a second ago. This dead ringer for him is his brother.

Oh God. His *brother*.

I'm such an asshole. I doubted him at one of the worst moments of his life. If one of my brothers—

No. Can't even finish that thought.

With a jerky motion, the phone pans back to Dragomir's face.

I feel an irrational moment of relief to have proof that it isn't Dragomir in that bed—but my relief is short-lived.

There can be no mistaking the scowl on his face. He's as disappointed in me as I am.

His voice is low and hard. "Satisfied now?"

"I'm so sorry. I shouldn't have—"

"Indeed," he says. "Now if you'll excuse me…"

He hangs up.

I gape at the black screen of my phone for a while.

At some point later, I pinch myself. Hard.

Nope. Not a bad dream. Unfortunately.

So… is this it? Is whatever was happening between us over?

I feel like dog poo—which reminds me of my furry charges.

Ignoring the heaviness in my chest, I make a sandwich, put leashes on the dogs, and go to the park.

———

"You Russkies sure like them bears," John mutters as he takes in Winnie in all her fluffy hugeness.

I shrug and launch into a new story about why he needs to do me the favor of taking the sandwich off my hands.

Looking at me strangely, John takes the food. "Are you okay?" he asks gruffly.

How bad do I look that he's skipped his usual commie insults?

"I'm fine, thank you for asking."

"Well." He takes a bite of the sandwich and swallows it without chewing. "Thanks."

Thanks?

Wow.

Maybe I should play the lottery to get the funds I need for my venture. Between this, the hug from Mother, and that "nice to see you" from Father, I might just hit the jackpot.

"Bye, John," I mumble as I head back home.

On my way back, the lottery thoughts lead me down a chain of ruminations I wanted to avoid.

How badly have I messed things up with Dragomir? Besides never getting his body, have I also doomed my chances of getting the funding for my venture?

I guess time will tell.

A videocall is blasting on my phone when I enter my apartment.

Dogs in tow, I rush in.

As I grab the phone, I will it to be him, calling me back.

Seeing the name on the screen, I plop on the couch in relief.

The universe must've heard me.

It's Dragomir.

Chapter Twenty-Seven

*H*eart hammering, I pick up.

He looks tired but no less scrumptious.

I rein in my excitement. Most likely, he's about to make the arrangements for Winnie or something like that.

"I'm sorry I hung up earlier," he says.

Unleashing the dogs, I blink at him.

"A doctor came into the room," he continues. "I hope you understand."

He didn't hang up on me out of anger? Is the man angling for sainthood?

"I'm the one who's sorry," I blurt. "You're dealing with a tragedy. Obviously, you have no room in your life for my paranoia."

He sighs. "You did have a point. We don't know each other that well, and I realize that's partially my fault. My past here in Ruskovia is... well, I don't enjoy talking about it."

"It's not like we're officially together to justify any paranoia on my part," I say, then wish I hadn't because he stiffens at something in that statement.

Catching himself, he visibly chases away the tension and brings the phone a little closer to his face. "Tell me something... Is there more to your mistrust? Has someone hurt you?"

I swallow through the sudden thickness in my throat. "The last man I dated. He was married, and I didn't know that for the entire year that we were dating."

Dragomir's eyes widen, then narrow dangerously as a vein begins pulsing on his forehead. "He lied to you about it?"

I nod, feeling the hot burn of shame on my cheeks. To this day, I feel like such an idiot. "He was an investment banker at Goldman Sachs, a VP in their mergers & acquisitions department, so he worked crazy hours—or so he said. On my end, I was fresh out of college and busy starting my own career." Or rather, my own sex toy company, but I'm not ready to delve into that topic with Dragomir yet. "We only saw each other once, twice a week at most," I continue, doing my best to keep the bitterness out of my voice, "and almost never on the weekends. He'd always claim he had some urgent client meeting he needed to prepare for, and I'm sure his wife thought that the random weekday evenings and nights he spent with me were just the typical all-nighters at the office."

Dragomir barks something angrily in Ruskovian. It must be a curse word that my ex rightfully deserves, but it happens to sound a lot like something benign in Russian: *crapulence*—the sick feeling you get after drinking or eating too much.

Confirming my suspicion, he mutters "fucker" under his breath in English before looking back into the camera. "I swear on my brother's life that I do not have another woman," he says gravely. "Does that help?"

Another woman? Does that make me *the* woman in his life?

It must. I don't think he'd swear on his brother's life if he were lying. Not ever, but especially not under the circumstances.

"How is he? Did the doctor say anything?" I ask, glad to leave the topic of my ex.

Dragomir's expression darkens. "He explained that the coma was medically induced. The hope is that it will protect his brain from further swelling."

My chest fills with a squeezing ache. "I'm so sorry. I don't even know what to say."

"I can't blame you. I don't know what to say on the subject either." His eyes seem more brown than hazel in this light. "The worst part about this is that I'm so furious with Tigger. What kind of a brother does that make me?"

The brother's name is Tigger? Sounds more like a

nickname, but I file it away anyway before giving Dragomir a reassuring smile. "A human one. If my brothers had even thought about base-jumping from a skyscraper, let alone done it, I'd be livid. And if they'd hurt themselves doing it, I'd probably finish them off myself."

The barest hint of a smile touches his eyes. "I can easily imagine that."

"So can they, I bet—which is why there won't be any Chortskys base-jumping any time soon."

Dragomir nods, then says quietly, "Tigger was always a daredevil, even when we were kids. Whenever any mischief happened in the household, our parents would interrogate him first." His gaze turns distant. "There was this one time when he stole a World War II grenade from a museum and tossed it into a bonfire that he started next to Mother's favorite gazebo. I don't know how he managed to survive, but the gazebo and half the gardens didn't. Our parents hired him a personal nanny after that incident, but he drove her to quit—and five nannies after that."

Wow. And my parents complain about *my* brothers being troublemakers as kids.

"Brothers can be trouble," I say. "When I was six, mine took me with them to Coney Island. I was tall for my age, so they let me ride the Cyclone—a rickety, extremely scary rollercoaster. When we went swimming after, I was so dizzy I nearly drowned and needed mouth-to-mouth from a lifeguard."

He frowns, as if worried about my childhood self,

then shakes his head disapprovingly. "At least they seem protective of you *now*."

"They were always protective of me. It's just that when that incident happened, they were too young to make good decisions—which basically means their protectiveness manifested itself in beating up any bullies who dared pull my pigtails."

"I still say you had it easy with just two brothers to worry about. Imagine nine."

"Wait." I look at him for any sign that he's joking. "All your siblings are male?"

"That they are. It's a source of great pride for Father to have sired so many sons." This last bit is said with distaste.

I whistle. "That's got to be a statistical anomaly. Your poor mother. How did she handle so much testosterone under one roof?"

He rolls his eyes. "Mother never got her hands dirty—that's what the servants were for."

Servants? I recall his mention of his mother's gazebo and the gardens. His family sounds more than merely well off. Just goes to show how true the whole "money doesn't buy happiness" cliché is. He looks distinctly unhappy reminiscing about it all.

"A nanny might've been better than my mom's mothering," I say, unsure if that's going to sound consoling or not.

He scoffs. "Your parents are angels compared to mine."

That competition again? Does he never let up? "They just acted nice around you. They're no angels."

His eyes tighten. "Mine have officially disinherited me. Tigger too. Have yours done that to any of their children?"

I shift uncomfortably in my seat. "No."

"Could they?"

I shrug. "They disapprove of the choices I've made and have let me know it. I'm not sure if they plan to make their displeasure *that* official, though."

A smirk appears on his lips. "So you admit defeat for a change."

"I admit no such thing. Until and unless I meet your allegedly hellish parents, I will not believe they're as bad as you claim."

Then again, do I really want to meet them anymore? Maybe it's better to just give him this one.

The smirk disappears. "They *are* as bad as I claim."

I wish he were here so I could hug him and take at least some of his pain away. "What did you do to piss them off?"

"I wanted to be independent." I've never heard someone channel so much bitterness into five words before. "After college, I handled their investments, but when I made enough capital to strike out on my own, I did just that, and they disapproved."

"That's it?"

Even his sigh sounds bitter. "They like nothing more than getting their way."

So they disapprove of him for basically starting a business. We have that in common—though I'm not going to mention it because I'm not ready for the sex toy company conversation.

"What about Tigger?" I ask. "What's their problem with him? His adventures?"

Dragomir's nostrils flare. "They call it his 'unbecoming behavior.' I suspect that when he comes out of the coma, their first words will be 'we told you so.'"

Hmm. Maybe his parents *are* worse than mine.

He yawns, reminding me of how tired he looked when he called.

"When was the last time you slept?" The question comes out more demanding than I intended.

"Back in New York," he says, suppressing another yawn.

"You should go to bed. You're sleep-deprived and jet-lagged. If Tigger were to wake up, you'd be useless to him in this state."

His faint smile returns. "You're wise beyond your years. Have I told you that?"

"You didn't have to. Now go."

"Thank you," he says and stares at me with a strangely intent expression.

I swallow audibly. Why do I suddenly feel like a fly who got stuck in amber?

"Call me when you wake up?" I manage to say.

"It's a date," he says and hangs up.

I get up from the couch and stumble over to my computer.

Woody butt plugs are still trending.

Alrighty then.

For a while, I busy myself with designing a clit suction device.

If the goal was to forget Dragomir, I'm not sure how much success I can claim. Now that I'm done, I realize the design looks suspiciously like his lips.

Xenia calls me, so I fill her in on everything.

"Sounds like he really doesn't have a side piece," she says when I'm done. "I'm sorry I got you so paranoid."

"You don't need to apologize. I have my own head on my shoulders." And my own baggage predisposing me to distrust men.

We chat some more, then she asks me to keep her posted on Tigger's recovery and hangs up.

I check on my fluffy companions and catch Boner on the kitchen chair again. I think he's waiting for Winnie to come drink so he can try to hump her from the proper height.

"I'd hump Remy if I were you," I tell him.

"*Ma chérie*, how can you compare my baby *maman* to mere *maîtresse*?"

I make myself a turkey sandwich while keeping an eye on him. As expected, Winnie comes to drink but positions her butt so Boner can't even hope to make the jump.

Clever bear.

Looking dejected, Boner jumps off the chair.

Aww. If it weren't for Remy, I'd say my dog is

living in a version of male hell—a sexy female in front of him but always just outside his reach. Then again, theirs is the sexual setup of many marriages, so maybe calling it hell is an exaggeration.

Taking the sandwich to the living room, I turn on Netflix and browse through the offerings. Hmm. Should I watch something with Woody Harrelson—in honor of our bestselling product?

I wonder if he's worn a turtleneck in any of his films.

As soon as my movie is chosen, I start to bite into my sandwich, but my teeth click in empty air.

I gape at my sandwich-less hand.

What the hell? Can you get memory gaps from being too horny?

A whiff of dog breath clues me in, and I look behind me.

Yep.

Eyes completely guileless and muzzle covered in crumbs, Winnie is chewing on what appear to be the remnants of my sandwich.

How did she get it so stealthily? If I could teach her to do that with jewelry, we could be world-renowned thieves.

"Bitchy move, stealing my food," I say sternly. "Besides, haven't you already eaten a tub of dog food today?"

"Tsk, tsk, Bella Borisovna. Appetite shaming a pregnant female?"

I head to the kitchen, stick another piece of turkey

between two slices of toasted bread, and give the doggies some food of their own, so they're also occupied with eating—a surefire way to keep my next sandwich safe.

After the movie and a shower, I put on my PJs and finally get to bed—but not to sleep. First, I want to relieve my pent-up urges with the help of a vibrator from our teledildonics line. The fantasy I have in mind is that Dragomir is operating it remotely, controlling my orgasms from Ruskovia.

I get the brand-new vibrator out of the box and prepare to link it with my phone.

Insanely pink, this toy is made out of a special material that I recently invented. It feels squishy and reminiscent of *kholodetz*—though no pig snout, pig ears, chicken feet, or beef tails were involved in the making of this vibrator.

In fact, no animals are ever harmed in the making of Belka toys. We don't test anything on animals… unless Vlad and Fanny count.

Unlocking my phone, I search for the Belka app Vlad wrote, one with controls for the toy.

Suddenly, a videocall shows up on my screen.

My heart leaps into my throat.

Have I already fallen asleep and am dreaming?

Once again, it's Dragomir.

Chapter Twenty-Eight

*P*ositioning myself so Dragomir can't see the sex toy on my bed, I accept the call.

Behind him is a posh bedroom that must be a penthouse in some hotel. He's sitting in a chair dressed in nothing but a robe, which allows me to salivate at the sight of the firm groove between his pectoral muscles.

His hazel eyes are beyond red and irritated—the eyes of a prisoner undergoing the enhanced interrogation technique that is sleep deprivation. Yet when he sees me, his lips curve in a smile that makes me feel as if I've swallowed sunshine.

"Hi, *squirrelchik*," he says. "You miss me yet?"

My answering grin is goofy. "Did you just call me a squirrel chick?"

He takes on a professorial tone. "The Russian diminutive for Bella is Belochka, which is also the word for a squirrel. Besides the suffix 'chka,' another way to make a diminutive, especially in Ruskovian, is 'chik.' But since you're pretty much an American, I switched it to English and got *squirrelchik*."

I playfully roll my eyes. "Did you just mansplain my pet name to me?"

"Sorry," he says ruefully. "I should've realized you'd understand how I came up with that. You're smarter than I am. And obviously better at Russian."

"And don't you forget it. But more importantly, don't you think the moniker makes me sound a little squirrelly?"

His smile widens. "I can call you *kiska*."

"That's pussy. You know that, right?"

His left eyebrow rises. "It means *little kitty*."

"Female kitty," I say. "Trust me, I'd rather be the squirrel chick—assuming that, in exchange, I can give you a pet name as well."

He cocks his head. "That would depend."

"*Drakonchik*," I say. Parroting his earlier professorial tone, I explain, "Dragomir sounds close enough to 'dragon,' and the diminutive version of that, in Russian, is *drakonchik*."

He frowns. "It also sounds like Dr. A. Konchik. Doesn't *konchik* mean the tip of a penis in Russian?"

"No," I say, doing my best to keep a straight face. "It's a generic word for tip, like that of a pencil, pen, and so forth. But if you prefer, I *can* call you Dr. Tip."

"No, thanks, *drakonchik* is fine."

"Then it's a deal. Now tell me why you're not asleep."

He shrugs, the weariness returning to his face. "I tried. Couldn't."

"That sucks. I hate it when that happens."

A smirk appears on his lips. "It's not *all* bad."

My breathing speeds up. I think I know where this is going.

"When I tired of lying in bed, I ended up looking for something to do, so I opened the backpack you gave me." He turns the camera to show me the sex toys sprawled all over his bed.

Yep. As I thought. But could this actually—

"So, squirrelchik." His smirk turns downright wicked. "Care to explain this?"

Chapter Twenty-Nine

*D*oes he think he can rattle me with the sight of sex toys? Me, the woman who's designed all of them? Or—dare I hope—is my earlier fantasy about to become reality?

I take in a deep breath. "Those are teledildonics toys. 'Tele' is Greek for 'far,' and the dildo part is self-explanatory." I dart a look at the crotch region of his robe. Though it might be my wishful thinking, I think I spot a glimpse of Everest there, tenting the white cloth.

Dragomir's gaze turns a brighter shade of amber, the earlier weariness gone without a trace. "You want to use one of those on me?"

I raise an eyebrow salaciously. "Yes, but you don't get to have all the fun." Turning the camera, I show him the pink vibrator on my bed. "This is a toy that works under the same principle as the ones you have.

With the right app, you can do to me what I plan to do to you."

He brings the phone closer to his face. Based on his expression, I half expect him to bite off a chunk of the screen.

"Okay, then," he growls. "Strip."

Wow. It's *on*. Donkey Kong kind of on.

I take off my tank top, exposing my breasts.

His eyes widen.

Turning my back to him, I stick my butt out and slowly push down my pajama shorts.

His phone nearly falls out of his hand.

I turn around and, as seductively as I can, remove my panties.

I've never done this before, stripping in front of a camera. Who knew it would get me so hot? My nipples are hard, and my clit is throbbing—and the best is yet to come.

"Fuck." Dragomir's grunt sounds pained. "You're perfect."

I teasingly move the camera closer to my face, temporarily hiding my body. "Now it's your turn."

He secures his phone on a nightstand, steps away so I can see his whole body, and drops the robe.

My mind—and more private parts—are officially blown.

Again.

The light in his room highlights every groove in his powerful, gorgeously defined muscles, making me want to lick the screen, touch myself, and maybe fly to Ruskovia.

Yeah, definitely the latter. Teleporting would be even better. The man is ovary dynamite—and Everest is particularly tantalizing. It juts out mountainously at the phone camera, stealing the spotlight with ease.

Does Dragomir have some smart zoom feature on his phone that makes it look even bigger? Or was it that big when it was going into my mouth the other day? How did I not dislocate my jaw?

"Now what?" he asks raggedly.

"Put that on." Finger trembling with anticipation, I point at the extra-large cock ring on his bed. "I'll be controlling the vibration."

As he turns to pick up the toy, I get a view of his tight glutes and muscled thighs—and my arousal spikes another notch.

Someone should build me a statue for the noble sacrifice of letting him be the first to come.

He turns back, cock ring in hand.

I gape as he slides it over Everest.

It's official.

This is the most sexually charged encounter of my life.

The snug ring makes Everest bulge, veins popping up all over.

Would he mind if I started playing with myself?

No. More fun to focus on him first.

Still, resisting the urge is hard. There's something

about jewelry and other small accessories that makes nudity even more pronounced.

Clearing my throat, I launch the Belka app on my phone and quickly walk Dragomir through the process of having my phone be in control of his ring.

Once all is set, I click the prerequisite button on my end, and Everest begins to vibrate—as though affected by an earthquake.

Dragomir's face goes taut, and his mercurial eyes darken with heat.

I up the speed of the vibration a little bit.

Impossibly, Everest looks even more huge and engorged.

Smiling mischievously, I crank the speed to seventy percent.

A dark flush paints his high cheekbones.

Eighty percent.

He groans, his hands balling into fists.

I wait a few moments, then crank up the ring to full power.

Dragomir groans louder, and Everest erupts.

Holy volcanoes. I think I should've nicknamed that thing Vesuvius instead of Everest.

Cum shoots out in a torrent, landing everywhere, including on the phone's camera—which gives his room a washed-out look.

Damn. Maybe we should have used the sleeve? That way, the eruption would've been contained.

I stop the vibration.

Dragomir slides the ring off, then grabs a few

tissues and cleans up the mess. Repositioning the camera, he fixes me with a hungry stare. "Your turn."

Finally.

We quickly link my vibrator to the app on his end, then I slide back on the bed.

"Ready?" he growls.

I touch the vibrator to my clit. "Yes."

Eyes roaming over me, he starts the vibration.

Fuuuuuck. It feels amazing—a hundred times better because he's in control. Masturbation has this in common with tickling—doing it to yourself is substantially different from having someone do it to you.

With a look of purely male satisfaction, he ups the intensity.

A moan escapes my lips.

Though my vision is blurry, I see Everest rise again—which turns me on impossibly more.

"That's it, squirrelchik," he breathes. "Come for me."

I'm about to oblige him—but then his eyes narrow at something behind me, and he shouts in Ruskovian.

My budding orgasm recedes.

What the hell?

Two things happen at the same time.

My nose detects the smell of doggie breath, and Winnie steals the vibrator from my hands with the same ninja skill she'd used on my sandwich.

"Hey!" I shout. "Give that back."

Tail wagging, the bear bolts out of the room.

"Make sure she doesn't swallow that!" I hear Dragomir yell as I leap up in pursuit.

Right. This is the second time she's gotten ahold of a toy covered in my lady juices—and the third toy overall.

I sprint after her.

She vaults over my coffee table with ease, and wags her tail at me, eyes as guileless as usual.

"This is not a game," I warn sternly as I give chase.

She flees, and if her mouth weren't occupied—and more importantly, if dogs could speak—I bet she'd say, "If it's not a game, why is it so fun, Bella Borisovna?"

Since I'm human, and hopefully smarter, I use strategy and eventually corner her in the kitchen.

Boner looks at us, head cocked.

Ugh. I'd better keep the toys hidden going forward. He no doubt wants to play this game now too.

With great effort, I extract the vibrator from Winnie's drooling maw.

She looks longingly at the pink object.

"I'll make you a pink toy that's dog appropriate," I tell her. "But not this."

Boner whines.

"I'll make one for you too."

Winnie still looks sad, so I bribe her with a bacon-flavored cookie, which cheers her up.

Tossing the chewed-up vibrator into the garbage, I

wash my hands, return to the bedroom, lock the door, and reassure Dragomir that she didn't swallow the toy.

"You want to keep going?" he asks.

Does the bear shit in the woods—or steal sex toys?

"Oh, yes."

His answering smile does something indecent to my insides. "Do you have another teledildonics toy?"

I do, but I'm not sure if I should admit it. I don't know how many toys it would take before he starts to suspect I make them myself. Also, now that I'm staring at his nakedness, I want to get myself off ASAP—not hunt down a box, open it, set it up with the app, et cetera.

Pasting on a naughty grin, I slowly slide my hand down my stomach. "How about something more low-tech?"

Everest twitches approvingly. "Yes, squirrelchik." Dragomir's voice lowers an octave. "Make yourself come for me."

"And I want you to do the same for me," I murmur, moving my fingers up and down my aching clit.

He fists Everest.

The orgasm that I was denied earlier returns in a heartbeat—and pleasure explodes through my nerve endings with all the intensity of a nuclear blast.

I moan his name.

He grunts in pleasure.

When my breathing evens out, I catch him

looking at me with a peculiar intensity. Like he's lost in a desert and I'm a lime-cucumber Gatorade.

"I think I need a shower," I say, my voice slightly hoarse.

He blinks, and the look fades, replaced by another indecently sexy smile. "Of course. I could use one as well. Sleep well tonight, squirrelchik."

"You too."

I wait for him to hang up, but he doesn't. He just looks at me, and I catch a hint of that disconcerting intensity in his eyes again—that strange longing that both buoys and unsettles me.

"Go ahead. Hang up," I say.

His lips quirk. "You hang up."

"No, you."

"You first."

Okay, it's official. I *am* back in high school.

Grinning, I wave at the camera and hang up.

Chapter Thirty

*a*s I finish breakfast the next morning, Winnie walks up to me and makes a strange whining sound.

Wait a second.

I've heard that before.

Leaping to my feet, I leash both dogs and zoom outside.

As soon as we're out of the building, I look around to make sure there aren't frail-looking old people around. I don't want them to get heart attacks.

The coast is clear, so I look at Winnie and say, "Kraken."

THPPTPHTPHPHHPH.

I launch into a sprint, both dogs in tow, hoping to outrun the smell, but the fart coming out of Winnie's butt keeps on going and going.

When we stop at a red light, Boner shoots Winnie what must be an impressed look. I bet he'd sell his soul to be able to pass even ten percent of that much gas.

At least the wind blowing in my face takes the majority of the fumes away. Even so, it feels like we're walking through a horrific graveyard where sick eggs and cabbage come to die.

"Thanks for the warning," I tell Winnie when we've traveled far enough away from the stench. "If you'd done that in the apartment, I'd have to move— and I'd lose my security deposit for sure."

Winnie doesn't hear me. Her attention is on something to the side.

I follow her gaze and freeze.

It's a black cat about to cross our path, and there's no one nearby to break the curse, so I'll have to turn back like an idiot.

As usual, Boner pretends the cat doesn't exist— which is fair. This cat to him is what a lion would be to me. Then again, if a lion turned up in Central Park, I'm not sure I'd act like he didn't exist.

Spotting Winnie, the cat arches its back and hisses.

Whimpering, Winnie rushes to hide behind me.

The cat stops hissing, turns back, and runs for its life—no doubt thinking, *That bear bitch is acting crazy. Safer to stay away.*

Whew. Bad juju averted, we walk on—that is, until I see Pom-Pom, our enemy poodle, running at me all by herself.

Crap. The owner must've dropped the leash, and the beast is now roaming free.

Stupid black cat must've brought this on, after all.

Winnie is behind me before I can even blink.

Oblivious to his past interactions with the evil poodle, Boner wags his tail.

Pom-Pom snarls and speeds up in our direction.

My heart drums frantically as I pull Boner back. I don't know what to do. Even if I pick him up, we could be in trouble. Despite their goofy appearance, king poodles are big dogs, able to hurt not just Boner but me as well.

Boner must finally realize the danger. He tucks his tail between his legs and whines, loudly.

Encouraged, Pom-Pom lunges toward us.

I scoop up Boner and prepare to fight for our lives.

The curly-haired beast is almost within biting distance.

Suddenly, a blood-chilling growl vibrates the air.

It's what a hellhound would sound like if you really, really pissed it off.

At first, I think the horrific sound is coming out of Pom-Pom.

But no.

Pom-Pom halts in her tracks, eyes widening.

I do a double take.

Winnie is no longer hiding behind me. She's put herself between us and the attacking dog, and as hard as it is to believe, the growling is coming out of her maw.

Actually, given that whole "rid Ruskovia of

wolves" bit, maybe it's *not* so hard to believe. Winnie's whole demeanor has changed from cute and cuddly to crap-your-pants feral. In this, she's a lot like a bear too —they look cute, but can be deadly scary if you get on their bad side.

And that's what *this* is.

Winnie has just gone mama bear on this poodle's shaved ass, protecting me and Boner.

"Step any closer, and I let go of her leash," I tell Pom-Pom triumphantly.

The poodle isn't suicidally stupid. Turning on her heel, she tucks her tail between her legs and sprints away—right into the arms of her panting owner.

Exhaling in relief, I set Boner down on the ground.

Back to looking like a sweetheart, Winnie licks Boner's face and resumes walking like nothing has happened.

———

Back home, I'm disappointed not to find any messages from Dragomir on my phone. There is, however, a missed call from my mother—which is worrying. She almost never calls me, preferring to send family event invites as Facebook messages.

Has something happened?

I remember the black cat, and my breath speeds up. Swiftly, I call her back.

"Hi, honey," she says, picking up. "How are you?"

Honey? How are you?

Who is this, and what has she done with my real mother?

"I'm fine, Mom," I say cautiously. "Is something wrong?"

"Of course not. I just realized I haven't spoken to you in a while."

Understatement much?

"I'm good," I say. "How are you?"

"Great, great. How's Dragomir? How are things between you two?"

Ah. Things click into place. This call is an invest-ment in the "hold a cute grandchild" project.

"Dragomir isn't so good," I say and tell her about Tigger's accident.

"That's horrible," she says with genuine feeling. "Tell him and his parents that I wish Tigger a speedy recovery."

"Sure." And I will—if I ever meet his parents.

"You know," she says, "I have a great remedy that they should try."

Oh, boy. Mother's remedies can be out there, even for Russians. And for some reason, they're very urine-oriented. I once had to pee on her leg when she got a rash, and there was that time when Alex got the stomach flu and she managed to convince him to *drink* urine—but at least it was *his* urine that time.

"I'm sure the doctors know what they're doing," I say.

If I tell Dragomir to pee on his brother, I don't

think he'd get it. He might even think I'm into golden showers, which I'm not.

"What's the harm in trying my poultice?" Mother asks.

"Depends on the poultice…"

If it's raw lamb meat, like her acne remedy, he could get E. coli poisoning or worse.

"Have a nineteen-year-old virgin girl chew up a pound of cabbage, two onions, five cloves of garlic, and a stalk of parsley. Warm the poultice to body temperature and cover as much of Tigger's skin as possible for a few hours."

Virgin? How would that help, medicinally? Do hymens help girls produce some magic enzymes in their saliva? Also, why does this remedy sound like a recipe for a human dumpling—sans flour?

Hey, at least the virgin doesn't need to pee on anyone. That's a first.

"I'll pass this on to Dragomir," I lie. "Thanks."

"You're welcome. Now go and call him, so they can get a head start. It can be hard to find virgins these days."

Was that a dig at me for losing my virginity at eighteen, or a complaint about the morals of millennials?

"Sure," I say. "Thanks, Mom. Bye."

I hang up but don't call Dragomir. He might be sleeping off his jet lag. Instead, I check my email.

Interesting. Alex tells me we have a meeting with Marco and his people next week—I was wondering if he'd left for Ruskovia with Dragomir.

I make a note of the meeting on my calendar and throw myself into suit design, only stopping to feed the dogs and myself.

When my brain begins to hurt from the work, I get up and prepare the bedroom in case Dragomir calls me again.

Instead of a vibrator, I unbox a clit suction gizmo and lay it on the bed. Next, I put on my sexiest bra and panties, and slip into a cute dress.

Just as I'm about to go watch some Netflix to kill the time, my phone rings.

Can it be?

I grab the phone.

Yes!

A videocall from Dragomir.

Chapter Thirty-One

*H*e's in that penthouse-like bedroom again, looking much better rested—and proportionally more delicious.

"Hi, squirrelchik."

"Hi, drakonchik," I reply with a grin. "How did you sleep?"

He returns my smile. "Very well. Thanks for tucking me in."

"It was my pleasure. Literally. How is your brother?"

The smile disappears. "Same. The doctors are of no help. He might come out of the coma today, tomorrow, or in a few weeks—they really don't know."

"That sucks." I sit on my bed. "Let me know if I can do anything to help." Besides sparing him Mother's remedy.

He also sits on his bed. "You're doing it already. Speaking with you gets my mind off things."

I feel so fluttery it's a marvel I don't float to the ceiling. "In that case, call me any time, day or night, whenever you want to talk."

"I might just take you up on that. Especially since I'm still on New York time."

"Isn't the time difference huge?" I ask.

He nods. "Ten hours."

"You should probably start getting used to local time. It's not good for your circadian rhythm to sleep during the day and walk around at night, like a vampire."

He sighs. "I guess I can be superstitious myself. I can't help but feel that if I shift to the Ruskovian time zone, it'll be like accepting that Tigger isn't going to recover any time soon—and thus bring it about."

Not for the first time, I wish I could reach out and hug him through the internet. Once my VR suit is complete, hugging at a distance will definitely be one of the applications. As is, I have to try some other means of cheering him up.

"Tell me something about Tigger," I say softly. "Some pleasant memory."

Dragomir's mouth curves slightly. "Well, for a start, he was almost always the striker on our football team. He scored more goals than I could count."

Goals? Aren't they called touchdowns?

I raise an eyebrow. "You sure you mean football?"

"Ah. Sorry. I meant soccer, of course. My father's

dream was to have enough sons for a soccer team. He got his wish: with the exception of the goalie who was a cousin, my brothers and I made up the team. For a while anyway."

He proceeds to tell me about their athletic adventures, and it seems to lift his spirits—especially when he talks about the time they managed to defeat a semi-professional team from Russia.

As I listen, I again get the sense that his family is enormously wealthy. The soccer field in the stories was "theirs," their coach sounds professional, and that team for the critical game was flown in from Russia.

"What about you?" he asks. "Did you and your brothers play sports?"

I shake my head. "The closest we got was playing hockey on the Xbox. In general, we played a lot of competitive video games, anything from fighting to racing. I think that's how Alex got his passion for game design."

He smiles. "Is that how you learned to be so competitive?"

I grin. "Doubt it. I beat them effortlessly in pretty much every game." I wiggle my nimble fingers. "I have above-average hand-eye coordination and outstanding reaction time."

His smile widens. "Don't forget your above-average, super-amazing humility. I doubt anyone can compete with that."

"Well, yeah. And here you thought I was just the

sexiest woman you've ever met. I'm not—I'm also the most humble."

Heat glimmers in his eyes. "I probably shouldn't encourage you, but you really *are* the sexiest."

I bat my eyelashes at him. "Right back at you— and I'm not sure you realize it, but you've just opened a Pandora's box."

He cocks his head. "You want to know about the women I've dated?"

"I've told you about my ex. It's only fair."

He must agree because he says, "Not much to tell on my end. There weren't that many women in my life, and none of those relationships were serious— with the exception of my last one." His face darkens. "She worked at my parents' fund, and when I lost my inheritance, I lost her too." He clears his throat. "It's for the best, really. She was clearly interested in the wrong things."

Yeah—and her loss is my huge gain.

He brings his phone closer to his face. "Now you have to tell me something personal. It's only fair."

"*Frozen*," I blurt after racking my brain for something to share besides the fact that I own a sex toy company. "It's my favorite movie."

He takes this a lot more seriously than I would've if our roles were reversed.

"I can easily believe that," he says. "It's a story about rebellion and self-actualization, isn't it?"

I pretend to be shocked. "You've never seen *Frozen*?"

He looks genuinely chastened. "I've heard the song. Does that count?"

"No, it doesn't," I say with mock grumpiness. "You now have a homework assignment. You have to watch it."

He nods—either still taking me at face value or acting at Oscar levels. "Consider it on my to-do list."

"You'll thank me later," I say. "What about you? What's your favorite movie?"

He rubs his chin. "It's hard to pick a favorite, but one I rewatch the most is *The Princess Bride*."

"Inconceivable!" I say with a grin. "Actually, it's very easy to conceive. It's got all that fencing, not to mention Robin Wright as Buttercup. She's one of my favorite actresses."

He raises his eyebrows. "She is?"

"Have you seen her as General Antiope in *Wonder Woman*? Or Claire Underwood in *House of Cards*?"

"I have and she's great. But she's not the reason I like that movie—and neither is fencing. I like the messages in it."

I frown. "It's got messages?"

"Yeah, sure. Such as 'life's not fair.'"

I nod. There is that.

"More importantly"—he gives me a meaningful look—"it teaches that good things happen to those who wait."

I blink at him.

Is he talking about his lack of serious relationships? Am I the good thing that's happened to him after he's patiently waited? If so, I think he's just compared the act of meeting me to Inigo Montoya getting bloody revenge on his father's killer—yet I still feel warm and fuzzy.

Since I don't feel comfortable asking him to clarify, I instead inquire about what kind of music he likes.

Turns out, we have a similar taste in music. We even bond over our love of Russian rock bands that Americans have never heard of—like Nautilus Pompilius. We also both dislike Russian pop except for a few select bands, like t.A.T.u.

When we finish talking about music, we move on to books, and here, too, our tastes have a lot of similarities—the exceptions being the engineering books that I read for work versus fencing and investing books on his end.

As we keep talking, I get the feeling that he wants to know every little detail about my life. It makes me feel increasingly guilty that I'm not telling him about my company. Then again, he still gets cagey when the conversation veers in the direction of his past in Ruskovia, so I guess that makes us somewhat even, especially if he *is* hiding something there—something that I no longer think is another woman.

After we talk for what feels like hours, I steer the conversation to sexy times. Flipping my hair over my shoulder, I ask, "Are you ambidextrous?"

"Sadly, no," he says. "Why?"

I waggle my eyebrows lasciviously. "I want to be accurate when I imagine you touching me."

He sits up. "I will first touch you with my left hand. Then—when you tell me it was the most mind-blowing experience of your life—I'll finally admit I'm *not* left-handed."

I grin at his favorite movie reference and turn the camera to show him the clit suction device I've prepared on my bed. "Would you like a repeat of our teledildonics adventure?"

He turns his own camera to show me the toys on *his* bed, ready to go. "As you wish."

"Oh, I wish." I walk to the bedroom door and lock it this time. "And I get to go first."

Chapter Thirty-Two

*W*e strip as though our clothes were on fire.

His fingers dance on his phone screen as he sets up the clit suction to be under his app's control.

I sprawl on the bed and ready the device.

"You're amazing," he says, his voice awed.

My eyes roam over every groove of his muscles before settling on Everest. "You're not so bad yourself."

His eyes gleam. "Ready?"

I bring the gizmo to my clit. "Yes."

He reaches for the controls on his phone. "Close your eyes and picture me sucking on you."

Great idea. I do as he says, but before I can let my imagination go wild, the suction begins.

Fuck. Fuck.

The image of his soft lips sucking on my clit is all

too easy to bring to mind thanks to how well-designed the toy is.

The intensity of the suction increases. I picture him puckering those lips and inhaling deeply, as though he wants to give my clit a hickey.

An intense orgasm starts to unfurl in my core—and that's before the vibration begins.

Wow.

The vibration is harder to picture him doing—unless I convince myself he's a cat shifter and that is his purr.

The orgasm doesn't care how realistic my fantasy is, though. It explodes through my nerve endings, making my toes spasm and wrenching a moan from my lips.

"Good girl," he murmurs hoarsely.

Attempting to catch my breath, I open my eyes—and do a double take at the sight of my lady parts. The suction was so strong it drew more than the usual amount of blood to my clit, engorging it to almost the size of a tiny penis.

I've never played with this toy in a well-lit room before, so this is good to know. It might also be a good thing that Dragomir isn't here to see me up close. I imagine some guys might get eeked out if their woman were to sprout a penis.

Then again, I doubt Dragomir would be one of those guys. If nothing else, compared to Everest, some actual penises might look like clits.

I lick my lips. "Your turn."

He examines the toys on his end. "Do you have a preference?"

"The sleeve." I point at the gizmo that looks like a pocket made out of a squid.

He takes the thing, lubes it up, and stares at me with visible eagerness as we sync it with my app.

"This time you're going to close your eyes," I say. "Put yourself inside that, and picture being in my pussy."

Something no one knows is that I designed that particular toy based on my own vagina. It's the exact dimensions in terms of depth, width, and elasticity. I also did my best to get the texture just right. It took countless hours of fingering myself and toy prototypes —but I'm always willing to make sacrifices on behalf of womankind.

Of course, I can't tell Dragomir any of this without revealing my secret.

Speaking of secrets, I hope Vlad never finds out this particular factoid. While helping Fanny test my teledildonics line, he stuck his penis into a sleeve just like this one.

Yeah, I'm not going to think about that.

Eyes closed, Dragomir slides Everest into the sleeve. I watch closely—if the toy tears, I might have a big problem down the line.

Nope.

It's a snug fit.

My vaginal walls squeeze in jealousy.

"How does it feel?" I ask huskily.

Dragomir's face contracts in ecstasy. "Squirrelchik…" His voice is a soft growl. "Your pussy feels amazing."

It better.

I initiate the patented back-and-forth motion of the sleeve.

He stiffens.

Reveling in my power, I up the intensity.

He groans.

Why, oh why didn't I make the sleeve see-through? I want to see every detail. Oh, well. I add a little vibration to the up-and-down motions.

He exhales, loudly.

It's my turn to stiffen.

Did I just hear a knock? Is it the dogs?

Nah. Boner doesn't know that particular trick—and I doubt Winnie does either.

Probably my imagination.

Forgetting all about it, I raise the intensity all the way.

The buzzing is super loud now, but I think I hear a female voice speaking Ruskovian.

What the hell? Does he have a radio on?

I should really say something, but I can't take my eyes off Everest—which engorges impossibly more.

Remarkably, the sleeve accommodates it.

Whew. If I had any subconscious concerns about Everest fitting inside me, they're gone now—replaced with a yearning for him to return and try this very thing with the sleeve's inspiration.

Dragomir's neck cords, his fists tighten, and with a grunt, he comes into the sleeve.

When he opens his eyes, they look wild.

"That was fucking fantastic," he rasps, his breath ragged.

Suddenly, there's a screech of a door opening.

Eyes widening, Dragomir looks away from the camera.

There's a loud feminine gasp.

Turning around, Dragomir yells something in Ruskovian.

There's a squeal that sounds like the Russian word for "sorry," followed by the sound of a door slamming shut.

I peer into the camera. "Do I need to be jealous?"

He turns back, his face edged with a hint of color. "No, sorry. That was just the maid. No doubt wanted to clean the room."

"Crap. That must've been the knock I heard. I thought it was just my imagination."

He grimaces. "She's supposed to wait until guests hang a 'please clean' sign on the door."

"She probably thought you were out," I say. "You really should start locking those doors—the hotel might now have a harassment suit on their hands."

"This isn't a hotel," he says. "I'm staying with my parents."

Huh. More evidence of his family's wealth. Their guestroom looks like a penthouse, and they have a maid who's supposed to adhere to signs put out by guests.

As I ponder all that, Dragomir removes himself from the sleeve and locks the door.

"Where were we?" he asks, returning to the bed.

I grin mischievously. "We were about to switch the video to our laptops, so we can use our phones to make each other come at the same time."

He likes that idea, and we do what I suggested.

A couple of times.

Finally, we're both completely worn out. Panting, I lie there, my bones so jellified I can barely hold the phone straight.

"How was it for you?" he asks over a yawn.

"Reminds me of the sixty-nine position." I mirror his yawn. "It's difficult to work app controls when you're screaming in ecstasy."

His gaze sweeps over my body with rekindled hunger. "I'm sure it will get easier with practice."

"Definitely," I say, and even though some part of me wants more, my clit is begging for mercy. Reluctantly, I suggest, "How about tomorrow?"

He gladly agrees, and we return to the "you hang up" dance from the other day, until I eventually relent and do so.

In the dream-filled sleep that follows, I find myself in his arms, having dozens of orgasms nonstop.

Chapter Thirty-Three

*O*ver the next few days, videocalls with Dragomir become a routine. Outside of video, if I want to talk, I call or text him—and he always gets back to me within five minutes or less. It's actually eerie how good he is with responding, better than anyone else I know. I like to think it's because I'm a priority in his life. Of course, it's possible he's just one of those people who see their phone as an extension of themselves, but the fact that he doesn't take it to walk Winnie makes me doubt that.

Either way, each time we speak, we learn more about each other, and every night, we use my teledildonics toys to make each other come.

If I had any doubts that the world needs the VR suit I'm working on, they're gone now. If the suit already existed, this time apart would be that much more bearable—and what's true for us would also be true for soldiers overseas, fishermen on long-term expeditions, patients under quarantine, and so on.

Still, given the current levels of technology, our relationship is as blissful as a long-distance one can be, except for the fly in the ointment: the fact that his brother still hasn't come out of his coma.

"The doctors say the swelling in his brain is going down," Dragomir tells me one evening, "but they're still not certain when he's going to regain consciousness."

And though he doesn't say it, I can hear the unspoken "if" in his words.

———

The following week is our meeting with Dragomir's company.

"We had some technical questions for you today," Marco says to kick it off.

He's looking at Alex as though I don't exist, so I pointedly say, "I'll be sure to answer any questions you may have to the best of my ability."

"It has to do with VR sickness," Marco says, still looking at Alex. "How is your system going to prevent it?"

Alex looks at me.

I tip my head in thanks to him. "First things first. Let's define the problem."

Everyone's attention finally swings toward me.

Marco clears his throat. "VR sickness is an illness that people get when using virtual reality. Right?"

I inwardly sigh. By recusing himself, Dragomir has left a person in charge who clearly knows nothing about VR.

"That's not really the common definition of that phenomenon," Alex says before I get a chance to reply—and it's just as well.

Out of the two of us, he's more diplomatic.

Marco glances at the tech guy in glasses—Eugenius, if I recall correctly.

"VR sickness isn't a medical condition," Eugenius says. "If you stop using VR, the symptoms go away."

Marco frowns, making me wonder if he's bringing this up to have an excuse not to give us the funding.

"If I may," I say, my voice laced with honey. "I took a course on VR back in school, so I can easily define the problem. As well as explain how we will overcome it."

Marco looks like I've peed in his soup.

"Going back to the definition," I continue. "VR sickness is a set of symptoms some people experience when using VR, symptoms that are similar to that of motion sickness. In fact, the two conditions have a lot in common because in both cases, the underlying cause is the person's brain receiving conflicting messages about motion and the body's position in space."

Everyone nods, and Marco grudgingly waves for me to go on.

"First and foremost, current VR hardware and software as a whole have already made huge progress combating this problem. The number of spatial degrees when tracking the user's body has gone up, latency has been reduced, and graphics performance is better across the board." I look around to make sure I haven't lost anyone. It seems like I haven't yet, but might unless I get less technical. "Having said all that, I should point out that our product will actually have a huge advantage when it comes to VR sickness, because we will have the body suit. When wearing the suit, the person's brain is more likely to be tricked into thinking that VR is happening for real—therefore removing the key underlying cause of the symptoms."

From here, I launch into a laundry list of software tricks we plan to use to minimize this problem further, and then I give the floor to Alex to reassure everyone that he can make said tricks a software reality.

What I don't mention is that we have an extra reason why VR sickness is not a major concern for us. Moving around inside VR is the biggest trigger for the malaise, and our users will be having sex—a more stationary endeavor compared to activities such as sword fighting, dirt bike racing, and other game staples.

"Thank you," Marco says, but he doesn't look like he means it. "How about eye strain? Isn't it another issue with VR?"

He's totally fishing for problems. "Our product

will cause less eye strain than our competition's, and here's why."

Tired of Marco's shit, I give them a boring-ass lecture on vergence-accommodation conflict—the key reason for eye strain—and then I go into industry-wide solutions before mentioning a few things that will be unique to us.

The funny thing is, because of the planned sex content, eye strain is another non-issue for us—but I can't play *that* card.

Clearly regretting his question, Marco nonetheless tries to throw me a few more curveballs, but I just bat them all away until he reluctantly concludes the meeting.

———

"You're good," Alex tells me in Russian as we get tea in the coffee shop where Dragomir and I had our first date.

"Did you get the feeling he was trying to sabotage us?" I ask.

He nods. "But you stopped him. That's what counts."

"Stopped him this time. I'm worried about what he might pull next."

Alex pats my shoulder. "In you, Marco has bitten off more than he can chew. I'm sure of it."

We grab a table, and the conversation pivots to more personal matters—specifically, my brother's love life. Apparently, ever since meeting Dragomir, Mother has been on Alex's case for being her only child who's still single. That leads Alex to probe for the latest on me and Dragomir, so I fill him in on our long-distance relationship.

"Are you done snooping on him then?" Alex asks after hearing all about how wonderful things are between us.

I blow on my tea as I ponder this. For some reason, I haven't thought about this recently. "I don't believe he has another woman," I say finally. "But I do think he's hiding something. I just haven't had a chance to dig deeper into his past."

"Smart girl," Alex says. "Trust but verify."

———

When I get home, a package is waiting for me.

It's a gift from Dragomir—a snowman outfit for a dog Boner's size.

And not just *any* snowman.

It's Olaf, from *Frozen*.

Chuckling, I put the outfit on my poor dog.

"*Ma chérie*, you know those *histoires morbides* of dogs eating their departed owners? Something tells me said owners made those dogs wear outfits like this—and that the humans didn't die of causes *naturelles*, if you catch my drift."

Winnie looks Boner over with a confused expression.

"Napoleon Carlovich, you know I think the world of your studness, but I'm sorry to say, you're not stud enough to pull off that outfit."

I strip the outfit off Boner before he can rip it into shreds.

Next time I'm Elsa for Halloween, I'm bribing him with bacon to wear this for a few dozen pictures.

Chapter Thirty-Four

For the next week and a half, Dragomir and I continue our evening video sessions. Then one day, he calls me in the afternoon.

I pick up immediately. "Is everything okay?"

"Tigger is out of the coma." Dragomir's voice brims with excitement.

Heart fluttering, I sit down. "Tell me everything."

He proceeds to explain how it happened. Apparently, Tigger opened his eyes a few hours ago and recognized Dragomir, the person who happened to be at his side at the time.

"He's very lucid, all things considered," Dragomir continues. "He'll need some physical therapy and the like, but the doctors are now extremely optimistic."

Is it selfish that I want to ask him when he'll be returning to the US?

Yes, very—which is why I don't. Instead, I tell him the truth: how happy I am for him and his family.

From the stories he's told me about Tigger as a kid, I feel like I already know the daredevil.

"Thank you," Dragomir says. "I'll go be with him now. Just wanted to share this news with you."

He hangs up, and I get back to work, where my joy translates into a particularly creative solution for the VR suit's nipple-squeezing problem.

———

On our videocall that evening, Dragomir gives me another update on his brother. Apparently, Tigger plans to tackle his physical therapy with the same zest he approaches his dangerous stunts, which bodes well for his recovery.

The updates I get in the following days are each more heartwarming than the next. Tigger's rehabilitation progresses like a dream, and in no time at all, he and Dragomir are taking walks in their family's gardens.

A few days after the walks start, Dragomir videocalls me outside the usual time again.

I eagerly pick up. "Hi!"

His hazel eyes are bright. "Guess what?"

"What?" I ask, but I think I know.

"Tigger has been eager to return to New York, and as of today, the doctor has approved it."

A weight that has been sitting on my shoulders all these weeks seems to lift.

I'm going to see Dragomir again. Touch him for

real instead of in my fantasies. Do all the dirty things to him that I've planned.

"How long is the flight?" I ask, not even trying to hide my excitement.

"I'll be there in two days," he says, then frowns. "Having almost lost Tigger, our parents have decided to accompany us to New York, and they need some time to get ready."

Two days.

Forty-eight hours.

Two-thousand eight-hundred and eighty minutes.

Have I been this psyched ever in my life?

"My first destination upon arrival is your place," he says.

My heart leaps, but I make my face playfully stern. "Your first destination is my bedroom."

His eyes gleam pure gold. "As you wish."

"And no left-handed business. Bring your A-game. I want your dominant hand and cock from the start."

His face goes taut, his voice dropping to a low growl. "Oh, squirrelchik, you don't have to worry about that. I've wanted you since the moment I laid eyes on you, and my desire has only grown stronger over the past two months."

I stare at him. Can a surge of lust rob someone of speech? All I can do in reply is fan myself, like a Victorian lady.

"I'd better run," he says hoarsely. "See you soon."

He hangs up, and I just sit there, reeling. I, too, have wanted him since that first meeting. The time between then and now has been like one torturously long foreplay session.

The idea that we will finally consummate whatever's going on between us makes me shiver with excitement.

Chapter Thirty-Five

*A*s I wait for Dragomir's return, I don't masturbate—even though I really, really want to. I don't want any soreness down there until Everest is in the picture. Instead, I channel the pent-up sexual energy into work, creating a slew of giant dildos in a not-so-subtle tip of the hat to the object of my desire.

I also prep for the big event itself. I shave hair from any place on my body where I find it displeasing, and nicely groom the rest. I turn the bedroom into a tantric shrine with mood-setting candles and music, and—though this might be going a tad overboard—I do yoga poses meant to make my body extra limber.

When a call from Dragomir finally appears on my phone screen, I'm like a hormonal bomb ready to blow—pun intended.

I slide my finger to accept. "Hi!"

"Hey. I'm at the JFK airport, and I have news."

That news better be that he's on his way to my place. "What's up?"

"You know how you wanted to meet my parents?"

I frown. "I wanted to prove mine are worse than yours, sure. Why?"

Even as I ask, I have a sinking feeling about this.

"Well, I told my brother about you, and he wants to meet you—and when our parents heard that, they asked to be included."

"Uh-huh," I say warily. "And when is this meeting supposed to take place?"

"Tigger doesn't like airplane food," he says apologetically. "Neither do our parents."

I curse myself for holding off on masturbating. "It's today, isn't it?"

"Are you free in a couple of hours?"

"Well, yeah." I've blocked out my work calendar for the rest of today, and if I'd bothered to put in a reason, it would've said 'to fuck Dragomir's brains out.'

"It's probably for the best," he says unconvincingly. "It's only fair that you meet them before we take things between us any further." He clears his throat. "You might just change your mind about me afterward."

"Why would I? Even if your parents are the reincarnations of Stalin and Hitler, what does that have to do with you?"

He exhales audibly. "In that case, could you bring Winnie with you? My brother and parents have brought Winnie's siblings with them. I'm sure she'll appreciate being reunited with her family for an evening."

I look at the nearby bear, who's oblivious to our conversation. "Their dogs are her relatives?"

"Well, yeah," he says. "The dogs of everyone in my family are from the same bloodline. Haven't I mentioned that before?"

"No. You just said Winnie was of the purest misha bloodline."

"Ah, right. My bad. If it's too much trouble, I could—"

"I'll bring her," I say, though a part of me is wondering if he wants me to bring the dog so he can break up with me without leaving me a hostage.

But no. Who asks you to meet their parents *before* a break-up? If anything, he might want Winnie back because he still thinks his family will scare me away.

"I'll text you the time and the place," he says. "Thank you for being so understanding."

Understanding, my foot. I'm so horny I'm about to rub myself against the kitchen table.

"I'll see you," I say and hang up before we get into the "you hang up first" loop.

Then I run into my walk-in closet and frantically search for an outfit that might impress evil incarnate, also known as his parents.

Chapter Thirty-Six

*W*hen Winnie and I exit the cab, Dragomir is standing by the entrance of The Doro—the most expensive restaurant in the city. His thick, dark hair is windswept, his stubble is a little longer than usual, and his tall, muscular frame is clad in a casual yet elegant outfit of dark jeans and an ivory turtleneck.

A turtleneck.

Hormones help me. I might just attack him on the table in front of his family.

Before I can blink, Winnie pulls on the leash with all the power of a hungry bear—and I nearly trip as she drags me over to her master, whose face she licks like an ice cream cone.

I watch jealously. It must be nice to be a dog and have that behavior be socially acceptable. I, too, want to lick his face—and the rest of him—but unlike Winnie, I have to wait.

"Come here," Dragomir says to me once he's freed himself and cleaned his face.

Grinning, I go in for a hug. It quickly turns into a kiss that takes my breath away and ratchets up my horniness to moose levels.

"They're already inside," he murmurs, reluctantly extricating himself from my clutches. "You ready?"

I nod.

He puts his hand on the small of my back as he leads me into the posh restaurant.

Is it wrong that I want to lick that hand?

Once inside, I look around and whistle under my breath. With all the paintings and statues on display, the high-ceilinged marble hallway we walk through reminds me of the Metropolitan Museum of Art.

As if to heighten the MET association, a pair of burly doormen greet us in the most outrageous uniforms I've ever seen: capes and bicorns of the Carabinieri, but with the garish colors and pantaloons of the Vatican Guard.

Interesting. This restaurant's reviews didn't mention these uniforms, but I have to admit, they add to the ambiance. Goofy outfits aside, these dudes look like they can double as bouncers should someone try to run away from this place's notoriously astronomical bills.

As one, the doormen/bouncers nod politely at us and open the large doors that lead into the dining hall.

My breath catches.

In the entire restaurant, only two tables are set. At one table are three people—most likely Tigger and the parents. At the other table, one slightly lower to the ground, are two ginormous dogs eating out of big bowls.

"A canine table?" I whisper as Winnie's tail turns into a helicopter rotor at the sight.

Dragomir shrugs. "My family tends to pamper their dogs."

If his treatment of Winnie is an example of this, "pamper" might be an understatement.

Fascinated, I examine everyone.

The dogs at the table make Winnie seem like a normal bear in comparison. One has a distinctly snooty posture despite sporting a funny haircut that makes it look like a throw pillow made out of a grizzly, while the other resembles a panda, thanks to its black and white spots. And, for some unfathomable reason, it's wearing goggles.

The humans are just as interesting. Dragomir's mother is a pale, round-cheeked beauty who reminds me of the women portrayed by the Renaissance painters—an impression possibly influenced by the ambience of the restaurant. Both of the men at the table look eerily like Dragomir, though the father has a mustache and wears a grouchy, sourpuss expression, while Tigger's eyes gleam with all the mischief Dragomir has attributed to him.

Hand still residing on the small of my back, Dragomir leads me to the human table.

They all stand to greet us.

"Everyone, allow me to introduce Bella," Dragomir says. "Bella, this is my mother, Bronislawa; my father, Stanislaus; and my brother, Anatolio."

I desperately repeat all the names in my head to make sure I remember them. Like other Ruskovian words, the names are vaguely but not quite Russian. Vampires from Russian fiction might have such names.

The brother's grin is contagious. "Nice to meet you, Bella. Please call me Tigger. Everyone else does." Like Dragomir, he speaks American English without an accent.

The mother darts Tigger a disapproving glare. "So informal," she says with a mixture of British and Slavic accents. "This country is a bad influence on manners. Next thing you know, we will all be holding our knives in the left hand!"

Oh, no. Knives in the left hand? The universe would surely implode.

Bronislawa examines me from head to foot, frowns, then extends her hand limpidly, as though she expects me to kiss it—Godfather (or is it Pope?) style.

I awkwardly fist bump her instead.

She looks at me like I've licked her face.

Tigger turns his chuckle into a cough, and Dragomir's eyes crinkle in the corners.

Bronislawa pulls her fisted hand away.

The father—Stanislaus—says nothing throughout, just stands there, scowling.

Dragomir says something to him in Ruskovian. The father looks at me, almost imperceptibly inclines his head, says something in Ruskovian with cold politeness, and sits back down.

The only words I make out are "Bella" and "pozor," the latter meaning "disgrace" or "dishonor" in Russian. Hopefully, it means something else in Ruskovian. In Prague, signs that say "pozor" actually mean "warning"—not that such a word choice works better in a phrase like "Nice to meet you, Bella."

Judging by Dragomir's glare, his Daddy-O might've indeed said something mean to me.

Oh well, it doesn't count if I don't know what that something is. Thus far, my parents are still worse. No one here has complained about nonexistent grand-children, nor shamed me for my passion in life.

"Our father doesn't speak English," Tigger whispers to me conspiratorially, and I get the feeling he means "doesn't deign to speak English."

"Why don't you take Winnifred to her kin and then join us," Bronislawa says imperiously.

I follow Dragomir as he leads Winnie to the doggie table. She gets more excited the closer we get, and when we're a few feet away, the panda dog with goggles turns Winnie's way, barks, and wags its tail.

"That's Caradog," Dragomir says as they exchange face licks and butt sniffs. "He's Winnie's brother and Tigger's best friend."

"I could've guessed," I say. "But what's with the goggles? Does he go skydiving too?"

Dragomir shrugs. "Might be to improve eyesight or to protect sensitive eyes. We'll have to ask my brother."

Done with Caradog, Winnie turns to the snooty, throw-pillow-looking bear.

The creature pretends Winnie isn't there.

"That's Gruffydd, my parents' dog," Dragomir says with an eye roll. "He's Caradog and Winnie's father."

Fortunately, Winnie has a thick hide and recovers from Gruffydd's snub quickly—and hopefully without any daddy issues. She simply gives Caradog's butt a parting sniff and takes her place at the table, where something yummy-smelling is already waiting in a bowl.

My mouth salivates, and this time, not only from the sight of Dragomir. If what passes for dog food at this place smells so amazing, the human food is bound to be divine.

We return to the human table and take a seat next to Tigger.

"I hope you don't mind, I ordered the big cheese plate," Tigger says, rubbing his hands together.

As though waiting for that announcement, a person wearing the same funky outfit as the bouncers shows up from the kitchen, a huge wooden board in his hands.

It turns out to be the cheese plate in question—and it's the biggest such plate I've ever seen, with cheeses of every color, smell, and consistency, from soft to rock hard.

Stupid turtleneck. The thought of something "rock hard" break my concentration and speed up my breathing.

No. Got to fight it. Don't want his parents thinking I'm some nympho.

Mumbling something that might be grace in Ruskovian, Stanislaus reaches for a moldy-looking, blue-colored morsel that smells like an army of unwashed feet. As he grabs it, I see his face in profile, and something about it seems vaguely familiar, though I can't figure out why.

Bronislawa goes next, daintily plating herself some of the five different soft cheeses.

I wait for Tigger and Dragomir to go next, but Dragomir pushes the plate toward me.

"Bronislawa," I say, doing my best to sound like the angel that I'm not. "Is there a cheese you'd recommend?"

There. Olive branch.

"My name is pronounced Bronislawa," she says, which to me sounds just like what I said.

"Bro-nis-la-wa," I carefully enunciate.

"No. It's Bro-nis-la-wa." Again, she says it exactly as I did.

You know what? She can shove that olive branch. "Thanks for correcting me. Is there a cheese you think I should try?"

She points at a yellow, sickly looking slice at the

edge of the plate. "How about plain American?" What she seems to leave unsaid is, "Like you."

I'm about to correct her about my Americanness when I feel Dragomir squeeze my knee under the table.

Is he nuts? Between his turtleneck and that squeeze, I lose my ability to think for a moment.

When the hormonal surge recedes, I recall that Ruskovians don't like Russians, which is what I was about to out myself as.

Fake-smiling at Bronislawa, I grab the American cheese and give it a taste.

Wow. It's so good I moan in pleasure. While it's recognizable as American cheese of the type someone might melt onto a burger, it's the tastiest example of its kind and therefore amazingly good.

It's like the Platonic form of American cheese—what every other slice of this substance aims for but never achieves.

Bronislawa whispers something to Stanislaus in Ruskovian, and I recognize one word: *shlyuha.*

In Russian, that means *slut.*

Was that a reference to my moan? What are the odds that word happens to mean *saint* in Ruskovian?

Given Dragomir and Tigger's frowns, not very high.

I do something pretty childish. I feign a sneeze that contains two words: *sama shlyuha.*

In Russian, it means *you're the slut.*

Bronislawa's eyes widen—the Ruskovian and

Russian must be close enough for her to understand what my sneeze sounded like. Dragomir and Tigger appear to be suppressing smiles, while the father is as stone-faced as ever. Before anyone can say anything, Tigger animatedly grabs a sample of each cheese, and Dragomir goes straight for a purple substance that I assume is also some form of fermented mammalian baby feed.

"Ready for the next course?" Tigger asks, quickly demolishing his portion. "Culinary adventures are the only type I'm allowed to have right now."

As soon as everyone nods, he claps his hands and another funnily dressed dude runs out of the kitchen, carrying a giant tray. On it are five steaks with mashed potatoes and assorted vegetables—a pretty basic offering for a place this fancy.

I wait for everyone to start eating before I carve myself a piece of the meat and stick it into my mouth.

By the Michelin star.

A foodgasm explodes through my taste buds.

I have no idea what animal I just tasted, but it's deliciously soft, perfectly juicy, and heavenly earthy.

I revel in pleasure until I spot Bronislawa staring at me with disapproval again.

What?

Did I moan again?

No. It's worse than that.

I'm holding my knife in my left hand.

It's official.

I'm a filthy barbarian.

Chapter Thirty-Seven

I switch my utensils from one hand to the other, and in the hopes of covering my faux pas, I ask, "What kind of meat is this?"

"Fawn," Tigger says.

"Venison," Bronislawa says at the same time.

I wait for someone to show that they're kidding, but they do not.

Great. I've just enjoyed eating Bambi.

Avoiding the meat from that point on, I try the mash and the veggies—which, unsurprisingly, also turn out to be the best I've ever had.

"Do you not like the meat, dear?" Bronislawa asks me.

"No, Bambi is delicious," I say. "I'm just not very hungry."

She cocks her head. "Are you sure that's it?"

"What else can it be?"

She shrugs. "Just wondering if you're watching what you eat."

I nearly choke on a Brussels sprout. "Excuse me?"

Is she saying I'm fat?

She wrinkles her nose. "You seem like a model or an actress. Don't they always watch what they eat?"

Given the distasteful way she says the words *model* and *actress*, she might as well have said *bimbo* and *whore*.

On the plus side, she didn't call me fat.

"Bella is an entrepreneur," Dragomir says pointedly, his tone noticeably cooler. "An MIT graduate, in fact. In case you're unaware, that's the most elite technical university in the world, with a seven-percent acceptance rate."

I almost want to thank Bronislawa for being a bitch. I never thought having a guy defend me like this would be such a huge turn-on. Dragomir has just earned himself all kinds of sexual favors.

Wait, who am I kidding? Between how horny I already was and his turtleneck, I'll be turning whatever tricks he wants in the bedroom, no defending required.

"Tigger," I say, deciding to change the topic before I spontaneously combust, "do you know of any fun New York adventures—ideally those that don't involve risking life and limb?"

"Flying air balloon," Tigger says without hesitation. "You can jump off with a parachute attached to the basket. That way, you don't even need to know how to use one."

He proceeds with more ideas along those lines, and I pretend to be interested, though I'd never in a million years do any of it. I like my skull not fractured, thank you very much.

To pass the time, I stealthily run my hand up Dragomir's thigh under the cover of his napkin, then higher and higher until I feel Everest yearning to Hulk out of his pants.

Dragomir's jaw flexes, but he keeps eating his Bambi steak and does his best not to show anything to his family.

Impressive.

Eventually, I take pity on us both and pull my hand away.

A loud bark comes from the doggie table. We all turn and see another bouncer-dude run out of the kitchen, carrying another tray.

That's a new definition of pampered.

On a whim, I throw my voice close to where Winnie's maw is, making it gruff and heavily accented:

"Pace yourself, Caradog Gruffyddovich. Eating kitten stew too quickly can cause heartburn."

Tigger and Dragomir laugh, but the parents look at me like I've sprouted a nipple on my forehead.

I eat in silence from then on, and when everyone's Bambi but mine is devoured, my phone vibrates.

It's a text from Dragomir:

Do you admit it now?

I make sure no one can see me reply and type out:

Admit what?

When Dragomir sneaks a peek at his phone, he rolls his eyes.

Do I win the worst parents contest?

I think about it for half a second, then reply with a resounding *no.*

At almost the same time, Bronislawa leans toward her still-scowling husband and rattles out something in Ruskovian, occasionally darting glances my way.

I make out a couple of words and phrases that have meanings in Russian besides the aforementioned *pozor,* including "rebellion," "just a phase," and "can do better."

Dragomir must overhear because his expression turns livid and he leaps to his feet.

"I've given up dessert," he says coldly. "We'd better go."

Tigger gives his parents a disappointed once-over, then stands up too. "The doctors told me not to overindulge, so I have to run as well."

Bronislawa gives both sons a disapproving glare. "If you must."

"A pleasure, as always," Dragomir says, his voice dripping with sarcasm.

We get Winnie and her panda-like brother and head out.

As we get to the fancy doors that lead out of the dining hall, Winnie makes the now-familiar whining sound.

Dragomir doesn't seem to have heard it.

I sneak a glance over my shoulder. Both Bronislawa and Stanislaus are giving me the stink eye.

Fine. That was their last chance to avoid my revenge, and they blew it.

Pretending to drop my purse, I kneel to pick it up, take in a deep breath, and whisper at Winnie, "Unleash the Kraken."

THPPTPHTPHPHHPH.

Dragomir's eyes widen as he gapes at Winnie's fart-generating butt.

With a doggy grin, Caradog rips an even louder flatus—and I didn't think it could get any louder than Winnie's.

Dragomir's determined expression reminds me of firefighters heading out to combat a blaze. He firmly grabs me and Tigger by the elbows and drags us out, along with the still-farting dogs.

Even though I'm holding my breath as we rush out of the hall, the foulness somehow manages to penetrate my senses, and it's so bad I start to regret what I've done.

To my shock, instead of running for their lives, the bouncers/doormen pull out gas masks from somewhere—maybe their pantaloons—put them on, and rush inside.

In the distance, I hear Bronislawa and Stanislaus making gagging sounds and Gruffydd howling—or also farting. It's hard to tell which.

By the time we get outside, the dogs have thankfully run out of gas.

Holding a handkerchief against his nose, Dragomir hails his limo-RV. It must've been circling the block all this time.

With a screech of tires, the vehicle halts and we leap in.

"Fyodor, punch it," Tigger shouts.

As the RV launches forward, everyone finally resumes normal breathing—except the dogs. They've been enjoying the aroma the whole time.

Once we catch our breaths, Tigger begins to chuckle. "Can you imagine the look on Mother's face?"

Dragomir's eyes crinkle, and all three of us burst out laughing.

"Where are we headed?" I eventually ask.

"A bar?" Tigger suggests.

"No," Dragomir says sternly. "You're still healing, so we're going to drop you off at your hotel."

He doesn't say it, but I'm sure the next stop is one of our places. At least it better be.

Tigger throws out a bunch of alternatives to heading home, but Dragomir shoots them all down.

Turns out, Tigger's hotel is just a couple of blocks away from my apartment. "I recommended it to him," Dragomir explains after we drop Tigger off. "I stayed there recently because my place was getting fumigated. It was actually when we first met."

Ah. That explains why I only ran into him that one time at the park.

The RV comes to a full stop next to my building.

My heart begins to hammer wildly in my chest. "Will you come up... for some tea?"

The look Dragomir gives me seems to say, "Does a bear have weaponized flatulence?"

I bite my lip. "Let's go then."

Ruffling Winnie's fur, he tells her, "Fyodor will take you home. I'll see you tomorrow."

Tomorrow? He's planning to spend the night with me? My heartbeat is at panic attack levels as we exit and sprint to my apartment.

Boner gives us a disappointed look as we enter. "*Ma chérie*, where is *ma petite?*"

"One second," I tell Dragomir and shepherd Boner to the kitchen, where I give him a bowl of his favorite food to distract him from his missing crush.

Once Boner is happily munching, I dash back, grab Dragomir by the hand, drag him into my bedroom, and lock the door.

Ignoring the room's romantic décor, Dragomir looks at me with a hunger that matches my own.

For a few moments, we engage in a stare-off, gunslinger style. Then both of us pounce.

Our lips meet in a deep, ravishing kiss, and caterpillars turn into horny butterflies in my belly. The room spins around us as if we were in a NASA training machine.

We rip off each other's clothes without breaking the kiss, and I'm vaguely aware that I might've torn his turtleneck.

Whatever. I'll get him dozens of replacements.

With a growl that sounds like "you're so fucked, squirrelchik," Dragomir picks me up in a bridal carry, then lays me out on the bed and pauses to run his heated gaze over my naked body.

Dizzy with anticipation, I visually devour him as well—every coiled muscle, every mouthwatering angle, and last but definitely not least, the mountainous glory of Everest.

When his gaze finally returns to my face, his eyes are the darkest I've ever seen them. Muscles flexing with panther-like grace, he joins me on the bed.

Finally.

Here. We. Go.

Chapter Thirty-Eight

*H*e kisses my neck. Or rather, sucks on it.

I scrape my nails over his back.

He moves the kiss over to my left nipple and nibbles on it until I moan in pleasure.

I can feel his satisfied smile on my nipple. Then his tongue traverses down my breast, past my belly-button, and down to my eagerly awaiting clit.

After all the tension, the pleasure this causes is indescribable. Compared to his tongue, my clit suction device sucks ass.

My eyes roll back.

If tongues could take IQ tests, I'm sure Dragomir's would fall in the two-hundred range, along with other geniuses—it's that deviously clever.

Is he teasing me?

Fuck that.

I fist his hair to keep him steady and buck against his tongue.

Score!

The orgasm crashes into my every nerve cell, and I cry out his name.

When he looks up, there's a smug expression on his face.

He *was* teasing me. Evil.

Growling low in my throat, I pull him into a deep kiss, tasting myself on his lips as I begin to stroke Everest with my hands.

Stroke it softly, that is. Two can play the teasing game.

He stiffens—in every sense of the word.

Echoing his earlier movements, I slide my tongue down to his neck, move lower to his right nipple, oh-so-teasingly circle the areola, then give his nipple a light nibble.

Both Everest and the nipple harden, and I continue my journey farther down, over his wash-board abs and down the landing strip until I reach his balls.

With an evil grin, I give them a catlike lick.

The balls tighten with excitement.

There we go. I give Everest a slow lollypop lick and get rewarded by a twitch that would've sent a rockslide downhill had this been a real mountain.

His hands grip my hair, and his breath turns ragged. "I want you so fucking bad."

I scan Everest, my own breath unsteady from excitement. The last time I took this whole thing into my mouth didn't go so well. But I want to do it again anyway. Surely, it was the alcohol in my system that got me in trouble, not my gag reflex.

Still, in part to tease, in part as a precaution, I take him in carefully, slowly, the silky-smooth skin hard and hot on my tongue.

Did it just get even bigger and harder? Is there blood left for the rest of Dragomir's body to function?

He groans, and I proceed giddily. Having played with Everest remotely for weeks, I've learned exactly what makes it tick, and I use that carnal knowledge now, driving Dragomir to grunt my name in pleasure.

The problem with teasing when you're as horny as I am is you're torturing yourself as much as your victim.

When the pulsing ache in my core grows unbearable, I look up into his amber eyes. "I want you inside me."

He moves like a whirlwind. Before I can take another breath, he has me on my knees.

That's some serious manhandling skill.

He licks my opening from behind, his tongue extending a couple of inches into my crack.

Wow.

So dirty. So hot.

"You ready, squirrelchik?"

I can only whimper.

He ever-so-gently presses Everest into me.

Holy mountain climb.

As ready as I am, there's a moment when the

stretching is uncomfortable. Thankfully, it passes quickly, replaced with bliss.

He grabs my ass cheeks possessively, pulling them apart.

Okay, this is getting hotter by the second.

Panting, I look over my shoulder.

His eyes burn with need and his naked body is utterly glorious—reminiscent of a Greek god's statue.

The first thrusts are slow and gentle.

I back into him, eager for harder rhythm and sharper sensations.

His callused hands squeeze my ass cheeks, and his thrusts grow hungrier, more urgent.

I ball my fists in the sheets.

He speeds up more.

My moans of pleasure turn into screams as the tension in my core builds to a crescendo.

Crying out his name, I come. At the same time, he thrusts even deeper, and I feel his release in a warm burst inside me as he groans out his pleasure.

Releasing my ass, he hugs me from behind.

I collapse onto the bed. He reluctantly lets go of me, and I use what little strength I have left to roll over and look up at him.

He sprawls next to me, holding himself up on his elbow. Though he's still breathing unevenly, there's a tender expression on his gorgeously chis-eled face.

"That was unbelievable," I murmur, suddenly feeling uncharacteristically shy.

He sweeps a stray lock of hair off my forehead. "*You're* unbelievable."

Flushing, I poke a bead of sweat that's gliding down his flexed deltoid muscle. "You're staying the night, right?"

What I really want to ask is, "Will you stay forever? Do you think this thing between us—whatever it is—can work?"

His gaze softens. "If you'll have me, I'll stay tonight... and tomorrow night, and the night after that."

Wow. Are we on the same wavelength? I want to probe further, but I'm afraid to. In the afterglow of sex, men say all kinds of things they don't mean.

With effort, I gather my scattered wits. "I think I need a shower." The words come out more seductive than I meant.

His eyes grow hooded. "I'll take you."

Matching actions to words, he gets up, picks me up in a fireman's carry, and strides decisively for the shower.

As I luxuriate in the warmth of the water streaming down on us, Dragomir begins to lather me with soap.

A girl can get used to this.

When I'm nice and sudsy, he rinses me off, then washes my hair—throwing in a moan-inducing head massage that would make the best hair salons proud.

It's official. I want to keep this man as my spa slave.

And sex slave, of course.

With an evil grin, I start to return the favor.

Damn. Lathering his hard muscles with soap gets me hot and bothered all over again, and judging by Everest's reaction to my ministrations, Dragomir might also be amiable to another go.

"Can you put lotion on my back?" I ask as I towel off. "I get so dry without it."

He looks me over appreciatively. "Now?"

"In the bedroom." I imbue my words with carnal promise, then grab the bottle of lotion with one hand and Everest with the other.

His eyes widen as I gently lead him out that way.

"Always wanted to lead a guy by his dick this literally," I say in a sultry voice. "Didn't have access to an appropriately sized victim until now."

Everest jerks in my hand.

"Glad to be of use," Dragomir growls.

When we reach the bedroom, I let Everest go and leap onto the bed, ass up. "I'm ready."

He clears his throat. "For lotion?"

Turning, I pretend to clutch my nonexistent pearls. "What else?"

He grabs the lotion roughly, and I turn away, my heart rate speeding up.

Instead of attacking me, which is what I half expected, I hear him squeeze the lotion bottle.

Oh my.

Instead of merely moisturizing me, he embarks on an honest-to-goodness erotic massage, starting with my shoulders, moving down my back and legs, and finishing with an orgasmic foot rub.

"Is there going to be a happy ending?" I gasp when he runs out of body parts to give a spa treatment to.

He turns me over.

"First, I need to lotion the front."

Teasing again? I guess I started it.

His attempt at teasing is brutally successful. By the time he finishes massaging the lotion into my breasts, I'm ready to beg for his cock on my knees.

Moving with his signature athletic grace, he puts the lotion away and covers my body with his.

As Everest juts into my belly, I suck in a breath to start that begging, but before I can say a word, he dips his head so his lips brush my ear.

"*Now* you can get that happy ending," he whispers.

Hells yeah.

I grab Everest and all but shove it inside myself, ignoring the initial, near-painful stretch.

Oh, yeah. That feels good.

Dragomir takes over from there, his thrusts slow and sensual.

More teasing?

He looks into my eyes and intertwines his fingers with mine.

Okay. So not teasing.

I like this.

If the last session is best described as a hard fucking, this seems like something else entirely.

The word "lovemaking" comes to mind, but I banish it for now, not ready to evaluate feelings and put labels on things in the middle of such bliss.

He gradually speeds up, and I forget all about tricky terminology as an orgasm twice as strong as the last one bursts through me, forcing me to scream. Again.

I want him to finish too, so I put my Kegel-ball-trained muscles to good use and squeeze Everest for all I'm worth.

Nostrils flaring, Dragomir comes again, then hugs me tight, like he never wants to let me go. I bury my face against his neck, inhaling his warm male scent.

Fuck, this man is everything.

"Another shower?" I whisper after what feels like an hour of heavy-duty oxytocin production.

"I'm not sure we should bother." He cups my left breast, and I feel Everest growing once more—a feat I didn't think was physically possible. "How about you bring over all your toys so we can play?" he continues.

Instantly as horny as an Amish teen who's discovered Pornhub on his Rumspringa, I rush to obey and bring *all* the toys I own.

As I dump them on the bed, I realize the pile is huge.

Suspiciously huge.

Oops.

To my relief, Dragomir doesn't so much as raise

an eyebrow—as though he's used to women owning enough toys to stock an adult store.

Should I tell him I made these?

I really, really want to.

Before I can utter a word, Dragomir grabs a vibrator that catches his fancy, presses the "on" button, and touches me with it.

Never mind. I can always come clean when not on the verge of another orgasm.

Or another.

Or another.

After about ten, I stop keeping count. All I know is that the sun is rising when we finally pass out, tangled together in a sweaty heap.

Chapter Thirty-Nine

"Squirrelchik, I have to work," a voice says from a far distance.

I reluctantly pry open my heavy eyelids.

Judging by the sun in the room, it's way past my usual wake-up time.

Dragomir is standing by the bed, dressed in a suit.

Hmm. Did Fyodor deliver that for him this morning, or did he wake up a while ago and go shopping in tatters of yesterday's clothes?

"I'm sorry," he says. "I really have to go."

Oh right. That. Even though my brain is not fully functioning, I push down the covers to expose as much of myself as I can. "Are you sure you must go?"

A muscle in his jaw flexes. "I wish I didn't. Thanks to the trip, I'm way behind on some projects. I've already skipped all the nonessential meetings today, but the next batch are mission-critical investments."

Shit. I've completely forgotten that I've slept with a potential investor.

Well, I guess the djinni with two backs is out of the bottle now.

"Fine, go," I say with a mock frown and cover myself up. "You *will* make this up to me when you get back."

"Oh, I will." His eyes are filled with scorching heat. "In the meantime, I've left you some breakfast in the kitchen. You should eat and rest some more. You'll need your strength when I come back to atone for my sins."

With that, he exits the room, leaving me flushed and panting.

After I cool off, I debate falling back asleep, but my stomach rumbles so I go check on that breakfast.

Wow. Dragomir has covered all the bases. On the table are Eggs Benedict, waffles, five types of jam, a carafe of freshly squeezed orange juice, a teapot, and a large coffee.

He really meant that whole "get your strength" business.

Before eating, I fill Boner's bowl and call him over.

The little guy trudges into the room and looks around as if hoping to see something. Not finding whatever it is, he hangs his head and listlessly starts on his chow.

Aww. He must be missing Winnie. I'll ask Dragomir to bring her over soon to cheer him up.

After I stuff my face with enough food to sustain

me for the next two nights of nonstop orgasms, I take Boner for a walk.

He's definitely not his usual self. Longingly sniffing every patch of grass Winnie has peed on, he ignores all the other dogs we come across and is ready to go back in a quarter of the usual time.

At home, Boner manages to look miserable as he drinks his water—and that takes acting skills, especially for a perky-eared Chihuahua.

"*Ma chérie*, I can't go on without *ma petite* for much longer. If she doesn't come back, I will throw myself off the fridge."

I take out my phone and text Dragomir:

Let's have our dogs hang out at your earliest convenience.

As I wait for a reply, I move the kitchen chair away from the fridge—just in case.

As usual, Dragomir doesn't take long to get back to me.

I can get Fyodor to walk them together this evening.

I convey the good news to Boner and tell Dragomir that the joint walk should be great.

Dog's needs met, I let myself yawn. Loudly.

Not sleeping all night is catching up with me.

Well, the beauty of owning your own business—at least a remotely run one like mine—is that you can take a chill day whenever you want.

Today, I want.

I locate a sleeping mask, but before I can turn off my phone, it rings.

It's a call from Vlad.

Since we haven't spoken in forever, I pick up.

"Hey, you," I say with a smile.

"Hey, sis. How're things going?"

"Great. Dragomir is back."

"Ah, finally. When did that happen?"

I fill him in on the recent events. When I get to last night's dinner, he asks me to repeat the names of the brother, the parents, and even the dogs a couple of times—as though he's taking notes.

Clearly, he still plans to snoop on Dragomir as per our earlier plans. I don't clarify this, though. In fact, I pretend to have forgotten all about it. It might be silly, but it helps me deal with the gnawing sense of guilt. I've gotten to know Dragomir, have earned his trust, and therefore should respect his privacy. There's also this: I've come to care about him so much that I'm afraid to learn something sketchy.

No, that's crazy talk. At least the guilt is easy to rationalize away. If Vlad snoops without my prompting him to do so, how is that my fault? I mean, I can stop him, but he likes snooping so much he might do it even if I ask him not to.

There. Making deals with my conscience has never been this easy. I might well be on my way to becoming a sociopath.

"You there?" Vlad asks, pulling me out of my reverie.

"Sorry. What have you been up to?"

"Working too much," he says. "But that's about to change. Fanny and I are going camping."

I move the phone away from my ear and stare at it uncomprehendingly. "Camping? As in tents, ticks, bugs up your ass—all that?"

"I'm not asking you to come with," he says as I bring the phone back to my ear. I can almost hear him roll his eyes on the other end. "It's Fannychka's idea. She's taken a day off and wants an overnight adventure that would let us unplug completely from the day-to-day grind."

I scratch my head. "I think she just wants to be alone in the woods with you, her big strong protector."

"And what's wrong with that?"

"Sorry, enjoy it," I say and save my tirade about how he could accomplish something similar by getting them both earplugs, shutting down his Wi-Fi router, and sticking his phone in the microwave. "How are things going between the two of you? Camping seems like a big step… at least to me."

"Amazing," he says—and given how reluctant my brother normally is to share his feelings, those words blow my mind. That is, until he continues, saying, "I think she's the one. You know?"

For some reason, mercurial hazel eyes flit through my mind. "Yeah. I think I know exactly what you mean."

He clears his throat. I guess he's just realized he's gone over his emotion-sharing quota for the century. "I still have some packing to do for tonight's trip, so I'd better get to it."

"Enjoy. And stay away from bears."

He hangs up with a chuckle.

I smile at the phone. When I asked Vlad to help me with the app for the teledildonic sex toys, the last thing I expected was for him to find his other half in the process.

Feeling warm and contented, I yawn yet again.

Right. Too much sex and too little sleep.

I put on the sleeping mask and pass out as soon as my head touches the pillow.

―――――

The stupid doorbell rings, waking me from a wet dream that featured Dragomir in a spandex turtleneck, armed with futuristic sex toys that I hope I can recreate when I next sit down to work.

The ringing continues as I put on a robe and walk over to the door, stepping over Boner—who's the most excited I've seen him in years. "Who is it?"

"Fyodor," says a voice that sounds just like Dragomir's butler. "My apologies, I have Lady Winnifred with me, and she's eager to take care of her biological needs."

Lady Winnifred? Has he never witnessed a session of the Kraken?

As if to confirm, Winnie barks, and Boner goes even more berserk with glee. Bear pheromones must be making him cuckoo.

"One sec," I say and rush away to make myself more presentable before returning with Boner's leash.

When the door opens, there's frantic barking, butt sniffing, and snout licking.

"*Ma petite*! *Destin* has bathed you and brought you to me."

I give the leash to Fyodor. "Thank you."

He nods in his butlery way and departs.

I check my phone.

Yep. Dragomir had given me a heads up about this home invasion. I guess he didn't think I was lazy enough to sleep half the day away.

There's also a text from Fyodor:

I'm coming over.

I'll need to teach him to wait before just showing up the next time. I could've been out. Then again, I wouldn't want Boner to miss out on Winnie time on my account, so maybe I'll give Dragomir a copy of my keys... strictly for Fyodor, of course.

A voicemail from Vlad catches my eye next. He called me an hour ago.

Hey, sis. I finally found out something about Dragomir. Call me back soon. You'll want to hear this.

Shit.

My hands visibly tremble as I frantically dial Vlad.

I get his voicemail.

I text him to call me *now* and wait a nail-biting minute.

Then another.

Then a half hour.

The doorbell rings. It's Fyodor. He hands me Boner's leash and departs before I can talk to him about the protocol for next time—or ask pointed questions about Dragomir.

Freed from the leash, Boner beelines for his sex toy, Remy, and begins humping away.

Does this mean Winnie didn't give him any? I thought she might—distance makes even dog hearts grow fonder. Then again, for all I know, maybe she did, but he got oversexed and needs to burn the remainder of it off.

Done with Remy, Boner lies down, closes his eyes contentedly, and softly snores.

Still no sign of Vlad.

What the hell?

Then I remember. The stupid camping excursion. He's probably there already—with no phone reception.

Damn it. What is it that he's learned?

I begin pacing as my earlier concerns about Dragomir resurface.

To this day, he acts cagey about certain topics. Is Vlad's discovery related to that? If so, what is it?

Dragomir swore on his brother's life that he didn't have another woman, à la Marco, but what if that was a lie?

He also never gave me an explanation for that private detective guy with the camera. What was that about? And why did Dragomir use gold coins with the veterinarian? Is he from the criminal underworld, after all?

Lots of questions, no answers.

I glare at my phone. Vlad said the camping thing was overnight. Does that mean they will also hike in the forest tomorrow?

Just how long do I have to wait before I learn whatever he's uncovered?

I stop pacing and call Xenia.

"You should just ask him," my friend says when she's fully up to speed.

"Ask Dragomir. Just like that?"

"Yeah. That way you get answers today."

"Maybe…"

"No maybe. Do it."

"Fine," I say with a sigh.

"Good. Now that that's settled, tell me about the sex."

I do, and I can almost visualize her reaching for the vibrator that I got her, but then swearing she'd never.

"How is Boy Toy treating you?" I ask when I realize I've been talking about myself nonstop. "Do you have your own stories to share?"

"You know I don't kiss and tell," Xenia says, much to my annoyance.

"No, I don't," I lie.

"Some things are private," she says defensively.

"I've just told you everything. Ever hear of quid pro quo?"

"You don't mind talking about that stuff. I do."

"You suck."

"I do." She giggles girlishly. "With Boy Toy. Happy now?"

Actually, the image I now have in my mind might ruin Christmas forever, so maybe it's for the best she's decided not to overshare.

My phone chirps, making my heart leap.

"I just got a text from Dragomir," I breathlessly tell her.

"Go check what it says. If he does have another woman, I'll help you kick his ass."

"Deal," I say and hang up.

The text from Dragomir doesn't shed light on anything. It merely says:

Working late. Please have dinner without me.

Grr.

I do as he says, then watch *Frozen* to calm myself down.

The doorbell rings.

Pointed questions swirl through my head as I sprint over to open it.

As soon as I lay my eyes on Dragomir, however, the questions die on my lips.

Fuck. Me.

He's wearing a tight black turtleneck.

He must've changed before coming over.

Unless… is this another wet dream?

Stepping in, he pulls me to him and crushes his

mouth against mine, devouring me with his lips and tongue as his hands squeeze and knead my ass.

Okay. It's real.

Questions? What questions?

Kissing as if our lives depend on it, we stumble over to my bedroom, leaving our clothes behind like the porn version of Hansel and Gretel—minus the incest.

As soon as we tumble onto the bed, a repeat of last night's sextivities begins—except, unbelievably, it's more intense this time.

By four a.m., I've had enough orgasms to feature in the Guinness Book of World Records, and feel like a squeezed orange that's been run over by a truck.

Okay. Now that the sex is over, I'll ask what I wanted to ask.

I yawn so hard I almost dislocate my jaw.

Maybe we talk after I rest my head in the crook of his shoulder?

Yeah. That's the plan.

I cozy up against him and close my eyes.

————

I wake up because of the stupid sun on my face.

Dragomir is nowhere to be found, but there's a note on my vanity:

Didn't want to wake you again, but had to run. Might be another late night. Enjoy breakfast and gather strength.

Dragomir.

Enjoy breakfast, my foot.

I never confronted him, and now I have to wait until evening?

Actually, by this evening, Vlad had better turn up.

Reining in my frustration with effort, I eat the scrumptious spread Dragomir has laid out with the apparent goal of fattening me up. Then I take Boner out for a walk and try to nap again.

Nope.

The questions prevent me from sleeping, so I channel the anxious energy into my work.

When I get hungry, I make a sandwich, but before I can bite into it, my phone rings.

Could it be?

Yes!

Finally.

It's Vlad calling.

I'm about to learn Dragomir's secret.

Chapter Forty

"*W*ho does that?" I ask Vlad as soon as I hear his voice. "How could you leave me a voicemail like that and disappear from the face of the Earth?"

"Sorry," he says, but doesn't sound like he really means it. "It wasn't the sort of information I wanted to discuss over the phone."

I narrow my eyes. "Oh, no, you don't. You're not making me shlep to your office. In fact, make me wait another second, and I'll make you regret it. Remember my tenth birthday?"

"Chill out. Let's at least jump on a videocall. At least those apps pretend to care about privacy enough to use encryption."

Gritting my teeth, I hang up and switch to video.

"Spill it," I say as soon as I see Vlad's face. "Now."

"Okay, so here's the deal. As I was waiting for

Fanny to get ready, I did some digging with the aid of the names you gave me."

I narrow my eyes at him. "And?"

"And hit paydirt."

"And?" My voice spikes in volume.

"And I learned who he really is. *What* he is."

"*What* he is? If you say 'a werewolf,' or make some other joke, I'm going to choke you."

He gets closer to the camera. "The truth might actually sound like a joke, but I assure you, it's not. I'm still adjusting to this, to be honest."

I feel a hollow sensation in the pit of my stomach. "What is he?"

"*Knyaz*," Vlad says solemnly.

I blink. "Say what?"

"*Velikiy knyaz.*"

I blink faster. "Still don't get it."

Vlad frowns. "It means the same thing in Ruskovian as in Russian. The Grand Prince."

At this point, I'm blinking in Morse Code. "A prince? Like Hans?"

Vlad quirks an eyebrow. "Is that the villain from *Frozen*?"

"Seriously?"

He and Alex make fun of my favorite movie, but there's a time and a place for these things. "How can Dragomir be a prince?"

Vlad shrugs. "You know how Ruskovia has a ruling monarchy?"

I nod. That's one of the few things I knew about that place before I met one of its citizens.

"Dragomir's last name wasn't always Lamian. That's what he changed it to when he moved to America. He was born a Cezaroff." He looks at me for signs of recognition. Not finding any, he adds, "As in, the Cezaroff dynasty. As in, a royal prince."

My brain strains to process this.

A prince.

A royal.

"Is he married?" I ask numbly.

"No," Vlad says. "I think his noble status is the only thing he's hidden from you. Everything else he's told you is true—including the fact that he was disinherited. That's public knowledge."

"Yeah, sure," I say bitterly. "He just understated what was on the line a bit—the ability to rule a freaking country."

"He wasn't really going to rule anyway," Vlad says. "Too many older brothers."

Older brothers. Of course. Things begin to click into place—such as why Stanislaus's profile looked so familiar when we had dinner the other day.

I've seen it once before, on that gold coin Dragomir gave the veterinarian.

And there's more. The initials on his hankie: D. C. It must stand for Dragomir Cezaroff.

Other little things make more sense now too. His perfect English, the stories about his family employing servants and owning gardens, gazebos, soccer fields…

"You okay?" Vlad's tone is gentle.

Oh, right. I'm still on the call.

I shake my head. "I better go and wrap my head around this."

He leans in toward the camera. "Do you want me to come over?"

"No. Thank you. This is something I need to deal with alone."

As much as I could use a brotherly hug, I need to go online and check all this out for myself, because a part of me still hasn't accepted it.

"I'm sorry," Vlad says, and this time, he does sound like he means it.

I give him a weak smile. "Unlike Mother, I never shoot the messenger. Besides, it's not like you found out he's married."

I wish I could be as serene as I'm trying to seem.

"Just let me know if there's anything you need," Vlad says. "I could hack into his—"

"Thank you, but no. Can we talk in a bit?"

"Of course."

"Okay, then, bye."

Rushing to my computer, I search the name *Cezaroff*.

A deluge of results pops up.

The majority are articles in Ruskovian that my browser easily translates. One is about Dragomir Cezaroff winning a fencing contest as a teenager. Countless others are about his troubles with his parents.

More interestingly, there's some stuff in English. Apparently, being royals has put the Cezaroff family on the radar of gossip magazines in the US and abroad. While not as popular as their British equivalents, these princes are still interesting enough to obsess about.

I scan the English stuff and find nothing about Dragomir—perhaps because of his disinherited status?

They do love his other siblings, though. Tigger—under his full name of Anatolio Cezaroff—is a particular staple. There are write-ups about his crazy adventures, coverage of his recent accident (with clickbait titles like "Will he die?"), and speculations about the women he's been seen with.

In fact, the most recent article puts him in The Doro on the very night of our dinner there. The writer claimed that his next stunt would be a feat of overeating.

Wait a second.

I recognize the picture of the person who wrote this article.

It's the camera guy, the one I thought was a private detective. Now I see what he was after. He was hoping Dragomir would either do something newsworthy or lead him to a story about his more newsworthy relatives.

More things fall into place.

That strange design made out of diamonds on Dragomir's Patek Philippe watch is the Cezaroff family crest, and the Ruskovian writing on it is the family motto: "In tradition, strength."

The funnily dressed people I mistook for bouncers/doormen at the restaurant were actually the royal guard—which might explain why they had gas masks ready to go.

Even the dogs are famous. The misha breed was originally created for the royal family centuries ago. To this day, every Cezaroff gets the purest-blood misha puppy in existence. In fact, the royal family is famous for always having one around—a bit like the Starks with their direwolfs on *Game of Thrones*. Dragomir didn't lie when he said he didn't name Winnie. Only the king—or tzar—has the naming privileges, and Dragomir's snobby father would obviously use a fancy name.

The more I learn, the stupider I feel for not figuring it all out on my own. I also get progressively angrier.

Leaping to my feet, I pace the apartment.

We've known each other for two months, yet he's hidden something of this magnitude from me. I told him how much it hurt me when the last man I dated lied by omission, yet he proceeded to do the same.

How could he?

This entire time, I didn't even know his real name.

And to think I almost fell for the guy. Or did fall—which might be why this hurts so much.

I stop pacing and ball my hands into fists.

This is what I get for being stupid enough to trust. I should've known better.

Dragomir was attracted to me—that's a red flag right there. I always attract asshats, yet I thought this time might be different. Einstein was right when he said that "the definition of insanity is doing the same thing over and over and expecting different results."

Well, my insanity ends now.

Or soon.

I still have to face him.

I spin around.

Yeah, that's a great idea. I'm going to march to his work and give him a piece of my mind. Why the fuck not? He deserves my wrath.

Feeling a modicum better, I rush into my closet and put on the sexiest outfit I own—a killer black dress. I top it with a short biker jacket and slip on a pair of high-heeled boots.

Let him see what he's about to lose.

Next, I smear on makeup, war-paint style.

As I stride for the door, Boner steps into my path and whines pitifully.

Great. The poor dude misses Winnie already.

I feel a surge of guilt that really shouldn't be mine to bear. Given what I'm about to do, Boner is going to lose access to Winnie—but it's not my fault.

Hopefully, Boner will move on.

Hopefully, both of us can.

Still, driven by the guilt, I grab Boner's leash.

Seeing this, he perks up a little, as I knew he

would. A leash outside the usual walk time means adventure, and he loves those.

———

With Boner on my lap in the cab, I fume all the way to Dragomir's office. As I enter the lobby of the building, Boner has to run to keep up with my furious strides.

Stepping into the elevator, I glare at the buttons.

It's just occurred to me that I don't know where Dragomir actually is. The only area I've been to here is the conference room where Alex and I pitched Project Morpheus.

Deciding to start my search there, I take the elevator to that floor and sprint over to the room.

No Dragomir. However, Marco is there, with the whole team from our meetings.

Fine.

If I have to beat Dragomir's location out of Marco, so be it.

Taking in a deep breath, I barge in.

Chapter Forty-One

*M*arco's greeting is a sneer. "Bella. What a coincidence. We were just talking about you."

Confused, I halt within strangling distance of him. "I'm not here for you."

His mouth flattens. "You would be if you knew the topic of our discussion."

I pinch the bridge of my nose. "What are you going on about? I don't have time for—"

"I was just telling everyone your secret," Marco says, rudely cutting me off.

My secret?

Is this about me sleeping with his boss? If so, that's not going to be a—

"You own a company named Belka," Marco announces, and I freeze in place. "A company that makes filth." He steps so close to me I can smell stale coffee on his breath. "So you see, we can't in good

316

conscience invest in a project that has *you* as its member."

As I reel from this, there's a low growl at my feet. Like me, Boner dislikes Marco's tone.

"Where is Dragomir?" I demand.

"Why?" Marco asks. "He recused himself. Our decision is final. You don't need to bother him with more lies."

"Lies?" I bare my teeth. "You'd know, wouldn't you?"

Everyone in the room seems to be on the edge of their seats. It's not every day you can witness a show like this in a corporate setting.

Marco looks indignant. "What is that supposed to mean?"

I pin him with a dagger-like stare. "Does your Ruskovian woman know about the American one? How about vice versa?"

Marco whitens, and the people around us begin to whisper among themselves, some of them frowning.

"She's lying," Marco says, not very convincingly.

"I'd be happy to email the proof to everyone in the room." I pull out my phone and wave it in the air.

I'm bluffing, of course. I have no idea if Vlad has proof, or if I even care to ruin Marco's life to that degree.

Marco tries to snatch at my phone, but I yank it back and give everyone a speaking look.

Judging by the expressions all around us, no one believes Marco anymore.

The growling from below is replaced with a strange sound.

Marco glances down and begins to curse in Ruskovian.

I follow his gaze, and my eyes widen.

It's Boner. He's hiked up his leg as high as he can and is relieving himself on Marco's foot.

Good boy. That's what assholes deserve.

Marco's expression turns livid, and I see his leg pull back—presumably to kick my dog.

My hand jerks forward instinctively, and next thing I know, I have Marco's soft, shriveled balls in my grasp.

Yuck.

"Kick him and you'll sing falsetto," I snarl.

Marco looks ready to kick *me* now, so I prepare to squeeze for all I'm worth.

"Leave them alone," Eugenius says. He's pointing his phone at Marco, no doubt recording a video.

Reddening, Marco mutters obscenities under his breath but pointedly stills his leg.

I pull Boner away, mouth "thanks" at Eugenius, and let go of the grossness in my hand, making a mental note to Purell my palm until it's raw.

"You better leave," Eugenius says to me.

Yep. Marco has sixty pounds on me and might decide to risk violence despite the presence of his colleagues.

I walk out, keeping my back straight, and ponder what to do as I get into the elevator.

318

The post-adrenaline crash is hitting me hard, and I don't feel ready to face Dragomir anymore. Nor do I really need to. If Marco knows about the sex toys, Dragomir must too. Add to that my unseemly behavior just now, and I'm certain it's over.

Sprinting out of the cursed building, I hail a cab.

Midway to my house, my phone rings.

It's Dragomir.

For a second, I'm tempted to pick up, but what would be the point?

It's over. A confrontation would just prolong the pain.

I let the call go to voicemail.

Unable to help myself, I listen to it a few seconds later. His message is short: *We should talk.*

My reply text is equally terse and to the point: *No, thanks, Your Royal Highness.*

He calls again, and I let it go to voicemail.

He texts next: *Call me.*

I don't. Instead, I ignore another call, then turn off my phone.

For the rest of the way home, I pet Boner to calm myself down, and when I step into my apartment, I beeline straight for the living room.

With the way I'm feeling right now, I have to take out the big guns: *Frozen.*

Sadly, I'm still feeling shitty when the credits roll. Worse even—and I didn't expect that. I thought it would be like when I broke up with my married ex. It hurt, sure, but I also felt liberated once I pulled off that Band-Aid.

Not this time. This time, it feels like the Band-Aid I've tried to pull off is sandpaper that some evil genius has crazy-glued to my heart.

Why am I feeling this way?

Is it because Dragomir has wormed his way deeper into my heart than my ex ever had? Or—and this is unsettling—is it because his lie is less malevolent and therefore doesn't warrant my reaction?

My stomach feels icy as I ponder that further.

Could it be I'm not feeling liberated because a part of me knows that I'm not so blameless myself? After all, Dragomir isn't the only one who's omitted information. I haven't told him about my sex toy business, and an argument could be made that my lie is more selfish—in the beginning, I hid the truth so I could get his fund to invest in my venture.

Leaping to my feet, I begin pacing my apartment, memories of our long-distance phone conversations kaleidoscoping through my mind—along with all the different ways he's brought me to orgasm.

When I nearly trample Boner, I sit down and take out my phone.

Time to be honest with myself.

I still want Dragomir, lies or not.

The question is: does he still want me? When he called before, was it so he could break up with me, or did he want to apologize about concealing his true identity?

If it's the latter, I think I might need to forgive him.

In fact, I might've forgiven him if I'd succeeded in storming into his office—assuming Dragomir had said the right things.

My pulse racing, I turn my phone back on.

It's the moment of truth.

I call Dragomir back.

The call goes to voicemail.

My heart feels like it's shrinking.

Is he retaliating for my not picking up?

I wait five minutes, staring at the phone the entire time.

He doesn't get back to me.

My heart shrivels further. He's always gotten back to me within five minutes before.

Maybe he's in a meeting? Or walking Winnie sans phone, as per his custom?

Just in case, I call again and leave a voicemail: *Call me.*

Five minutes later, I also text the same message.

Maybe he has the world's richest man in his office? Or is negotiating some billion-dollar deal?

A nail-biting hour passes without any reply.

The meeting and dog-walk excuses seem more pathetic with every passing minute.

Two hours later, I have to admit it.

I fucked things up, and there may be no going back.

Chapter Forty-Two

I want to cry, but I fight the urge. Boner is sensitive to my mood, and the poor thing is already suffering from bear withdrawal.

Grabbing my laptop, I dive into work instead.

Nope. I'm so distracted with uselessly checking my phone every two seconds that I can't design the most basic of butt plugs.

I take Boner for a walk instead of pointlessly pacing the apartment, but since I bring my phone with me, it's an hour of wallowing in self-pity and incessant phone checking.

When Boner is done with all his bathroom needs, I take us home, but instead of entering my building, I stop, filled with sudden determination.

The walk has cleared my head enough to make a decision.

If Dragomir won't answer my calls, I'm going to confront him face to face. If he wants to end things, he'll have to do it in person. Not that I will accept rejection meekly—I plan to fight for us if I have to.

Hailing a cab, I direct it to Dragomir's offices again.

When we get there, I grab Boner under my arm and rush to the same meeting room in case luck is with me and Dragomir is there.

He isn't.

The people from earlier are, though. Thankfully, Marco isn't among them.

Setting Boner on the floor, I prepare to enter, but Eugenius spots me and steps out into the hallway.

"You've already heard?" He sounds impressed.

My eyebrows squish together. "Heard what?"

"The funding," he says, looking slightly confused. "It's just been approved."

I rub my eyebrows. "But Marco—"

"Was fired," Eugenius says with distaste. "He was the driving force for that initial rejection. The rest of us actually felt safer investing in your venture when we found out it wasn't just your brother who could run a successful business."

I should be ecstatic about this, but I'm not. Not if this money has cost me the man I care about.

"Where is Dragomir?" I barely resist the urge to shake the information out of Eugenius.

"He left right after he let Marco go," Eugenius says.

"So where is he?" I demand.

Frowning, Eugenius adjusts his glasses. "Is everything okay?"

Does he want me to shake him? "I just need to talk to him. Please. It's important."

The guy shifts from foot to foot. "The boss doesn't explain his comings and goings to us. It seemed to be a private matter, something urgent."

Urgent private matter.

Do I dare hope? Could he have gone to my place to have the same conversation I came here for?

"Thank you, Eugenius. I'm looking forward to working with you guys."

Ignoring the blush on his face, I rush back, and when I jump into the cab, I check my phone.

Nothing.

Ugh. Why did I think Dragomir would go to my place without calling? Of course he wouldn't do that.

For all I know, the funding was his parting gift.

Still, though I've done my best to ready myself for the disappointment, my chest tightens painfully when I get to my place and don't see Dragomir at or near the building. The pain grows to Everest levels when I get to my door.

He's not here.

I wasn't the urgent personal matter, after all.

How conceited of me to think that I was. Not only are his parents in town, but his brother is still in recovery.

Oh, shit.

What if something's happened to him?

That sort of emergency could explain the radio silence.

Grabbing a very confused Boner, I run out of my building again—this time heading to Tigger's hotel, which fortunately happens to be nearby.

"I'm here to see Anatolio Cezaroff," I pant at the hotel clerk.

He peers at me down the length of his nose. "Mr. Cezaroff wasn't expecting visitors."

I exhale in relief. "So he's okay? He was recently injured, and his brother Dragomir is missing, so I thought that maybe something—"

"Let me see if I can get him on the phone," the clerk says snootily. "What is your name?"

"Tell him I'm Bella—Dragomir's Bella."

At least I hope that last bit is or will be true.

The guy dials a number with his pinky and waits a few seconds. "Hello. There's a lady here who says she's Dragomir's Bella."

He waits a couple of seconds, then quickly describes what I look like.

"He said he's coming down," he informs me after hanging up. "He also said that if you're not Bella but some crazy stalker, he'll press charges."

A stalker? Is that a joke, or something Tigger actually has to deal with? More importantly, if Tigger isn't the emergency, where is Dragomir and why is he ignoring my calls?

Could he have moved on to another woman so quickly?

No. He's not like that.

Prince or not, I know him. I know what his core is like.

An unthinkable option occurs to me, and a jolt of adrenaline spikes my heartbeat.

What if Dragomir is in some kind of trouble?

What if he's been hit by a car? Or his RV has gotten into an accident?

My mind has clearly been primed by worrying about Tigger, but now that it's gone to that dark place, I can't get rid of the paralyzing fear.

Wait. No. I'm being stupid. Tigger wouldn't be chilling in his hotel if Dragomir were hurt.

Unless… he doesn't know.

I all but bite my nails until Tigger steps out of the elevator.

Spotting me, he grins—not something he'd do if Dragomir was in trouble.

"Do you know where he is?" I blurt, all but tackling him by the elevator doors.

His grin widens. "You mean Dragomir?"

"Obviously."

"He didn't tell you?"

I bite my lip. "I might've told him not to call me earlier, so…"

"Oh." Tigger's grin disappears. "What happened?"

"Never mind that. Where is he?"

Tigger frowns. "With Dr. Delomalov, of course."

At first, the word *doctor* sends my anxiety through

the stratosphere, but then the full name registers. That's the—

"You really have no clue?" Tigger darts a glance at Boner. "I thought of all people, you'd expect this." He grins again. "'Commoner impregnates royal'— that's what all the Ruskovian papers will say once they find out."

"Dr. Delomalov is the veterinarian, right?" I say breathlessly.

"That he is."

"Winnie's gone into labor?"

"Bingo."

My breath whooshes out in relief.

This explains everything.

Dr. Delomalov's office has no cell reception, so if Dragomir has been there for the past few hours, he doesn't even know that I'm ready to talk.

"I need to get to that office," I tell Tigger urgently. I turn to the clerk. "Can you get me a taxi?"

"How about *I* give you a lift?" Tigger suggests. "I rented a Lamborghini and still haven't gotten a chance to test it out."

"Sure. Whatever gets me there fastest."

"I'll tell the valet to get the car out for you," the clerk says.

We step outside, and a few minutes later, a black Lamborghini pulls up—the latest model with all the bells and whistles.

The valet opens the car door for me, and I scramble inside.

Hmm. The seatbelts look like those in a race car. I'm not a huge fan of going fast—is it too late to mention that?

Warily strapping in, I open the window for Boner and check my phone.

Still nothing.

Tigger gets behind the wheel, looking unsettlingly excited.

"You've driven this thing before, right?" I ask.

"Does it matter? Brace yourself."

"Wait. I don't like the sound of—"

Turning the wheel sharply to the right, Tigger floors the gas.

With a smell of burning rubber, the Lamborghini tears forward at Mach 1 speed—or whatever pace the supersonic jets fly at. Gravity flattens me into my seat, and Boner whines as I squeeze him against my chest. The wind through the open window is like a hurricane, so I release my death grip on Boner long enough to press the button to close it.

"Dude," I say when the wind tunnel effect is gone. "When I said 'whatever gets me there fastest,' I meant *alive*."

In the time it takes me to say those words, we clear four blocks.

"Don't worry," Tigger says, zooming through a yellow light. "Live a little."

Living is the goal.

Boner looks on the verge of throwing up. "*Ma*

chérie, I've changed my mind about suicide. Can you get this insane *humain* to slow down?"

"Is there a complication with Winnie's delivery?" I ask Tigger in the hope that he'll slow down if forced to talk.

Nope. He doesn't slow so much as a mile per hour. "I don't think so. Dragomir just wanted to be safe."

Wanting to be safe is clearly a concept Tigger doesn't get.

I don't ask anything else—we have a higher chance of survival if he focuses on the driving.

The rest of the ride is like a scene from *The Fast and the Furious* and will be the source of my future nightmares. The only good thing I can say about it is that it's over quickly.

Very quickly.

"Go," Tigger says when we come to a tire-burning stop. "I'll park and come up."

Knees wobbly, I make my way to the vet's office, shell-shocked Boner under my arm.

When I step inside, Dragomir is sitting there.

He looks so worried you'd think it was his wife giving birth, not his dog. But at the sight of me, he leaps to his feet.

"Hi," I say uncertainly.

His hazel eyes gleam. "Hi."

I inhale a big breath. I'll need all the air to say what I want to say.

It's now or never.

Chapter Forty-Three

*B*efore I can get a single word out, the door opens and Dr. Delomalov rushes out.

"Joyous occasions, truly," he says with a wide grin. "The bitch done. Birthed fifty-teen pups. Want to envision them?"

"Of course," Dragomir says eagerly.

"Me too," I say.

What I really want is to talk to Dragomir, but I'm not sure he'll be able to focus on my words until he makes sure Winnie is okay.

And, of course, I *am* mega curious about the puppies. I'm not dead inside.

We follow the doctor down the hallway and into a room where Winnie is lying on a big dog bed. She looks tired but happy—and she's surrounded by her new family.

The puppies have their eyes closed and look vaguely like koala bears, both in terms of looks and coloring—and each is at least five times the size of their father.

If the dogs' genders had been reversed, this pregnancy would've been impossible.

I set Boner on the floor, clutching his leash.

My heart is filled with enough joy to power a Tesla for a trip to Disney World. Some of the pups are already nursing, and Winnie is licking one youngster who isn't. Spotting Dragomir, she wags her tail, and when her gaze falls on Boner, the wagging turns into outright windmilling.

Yipping excitedly, Boner pulls on the leash.

"Can I let him near them?" I ask.

"Yes, but carefully," Dragomir says.

Well, yeah. We wouldn't want Winnie to go into mama bear mode. That shit is scary.

Preparing to pull Boner back if necessary, I let him approach the newborns.

Winnie eyes him intently.

Boner sniffs one of the pups, licks it almost reverently, then steps back and gives me the most confused look.

"*Ma chérie*, how are they bigger than *moi*? Please say I'm such a stud I broke the laws of *physique*."

We all ooh and ahh over the pups for a while. Then Tigger joins us and begs Dragomir to give him one.

"They're going to live with me until Winnie is ready to part with them," Dragomir says sternly. "I'm not going to take babies away from their mother—not even for you."

Tigger rolls his eyes. "I didn't mean now."

Dragomir rubs his chin. "You'll have to bring Caradog so I can be sure he's going to be nice to the pup. I also want to check that his shots are up to date."

Tigger exhales in exasperation. "Obviously."

"In that case, maybe," Dragomir says. "Depends on your behavior."

Tigger switches to Ruskovian for his reply, and the two brothers start to bicker—but it sounds more like good-natured ribbing than a fight.

I tug on Dragomir's sleeve.

He gives me an apologetic look. "Sorry about that."

"No worries. Can we talk?"

Dragomir nods, and Tigger arches an eyebrow.

"In private?" I look at Tigger pointedly.

"Dr. Delomalov," Dragomir says. "Is there a place Bella and I can get some privacy?"

"Come," the veterinarian says and opens the door.

I thrust Boner's leash into Tigger's hands and follow the doctor, swaying my hips for Dragomir as a way to butter him up before our chat.

When we reach a big wooden door, the doctor opens it and we step into a cramped office.

As soon as the doctor leaves, Dragomir locks the door.

I find the action insanely hot—and reassuring.

A man doesn't lock himself in with a woman he plans to scorn.

Hopefully.

Gathering my courage, I launch into my spiel. "I'm sorry. It was shitty of me not to take your calls." And I mean it. Thinking that he'd done the same to me really sucked.

Jaw tight, Dragomir closes the distance between us. "No. I'm the one who's sorry." His voice is low and earnest. "I wanted to tell you about my heritage so many times, but I kept putting it off."

"Why?" The question isn't bitter. I'm genuinely curious.

He grabs my hand and squeezes it tight. "Because it's always ruined things in my life. I didn't want to lose you over it. Ironic, right? I almost did lose you— because I hid it from you."

My breathing picks up at his warm touch, but I ignore it—I have to speak coherently for the next part. "I take it you know about my sex toy company?"

He smiles. "I've known since the day after you gave me your name."

I gape at him. "You have?"

"Since we're coming clean, I might as well tell you. I have access to the Ruskovian equivalent of the CIA. I wanted to learn more about you—so I did. I hope you can forgive me for that invasion of privacy."

"Well, as far as the invasion of privacy goes, I've done the same to you," I admit sheepishly. "How about we call it even, then? On the snooping and the omitting of information."

He brings my hand to his lips and kisses the back of my knuckles. "I wholeheartedly agree."

I do my best to focus on something other than the tingles radiating down to my core. "Wait. So if you've known about my business all along, how did Marco find out about it just now?"

"My parents, I'm sure. They undoubtedly used the same service to look into you after our dinner."

I sigh. "Doesn't sound like they liked me."

"Take it as a compliment."

Relieved, I smile. "So they don't decide whom you date?"

"Hells no."

"Good. And just to double check—the person you're with doesn't have to be royal, like you?"

He shakes his head. "That's what my parents would want, but not me. In fact, if they liked you, I'd be worried."

My smile becomes a grin. "I bet I could make them like me if I got to know them better."

He grins back. "And I bet yours will still like me more than mine will ever like you."

I bristle. "That's not fair. Mine already love you more than they do me. They're not fans of my business—something I never got the chance to tell you."

His smile vanishes. "Ignore what anyone thinks. Your toys are amazing. You have serious talent and should be proud of it." Framing my face with his palms, he says solemnly, "I want you to always be yourself, and don't ever apologize for it."

Wait a sec. That sounds like a takeaway from *Frozen*. Does that mean he's watched it?

Before I realize what the fuck I'm saying, the words fly out of their own accord.

"I love you."

His face goes taut, his hazel gaze turning a golden shade of amber. "I love you too. Squirrelchik…" His deep voice is husky. "You're a person worth melting for."

Oh. My. God.

It's official. He's watched *Frozen*.

My overfull heart feels like it's pulling an Olaf.

Rising on tiptoes, I throw my arms around his neck and drag him down for a kiss. One that I hope is the best of his life. The kind that will make him think of the ending of *his* favorite movie—specifically, the moment where Grandpa says, "Since the invention of the kiss, there have been five kisses rated the most passionate, the most pure. This one left them all behind. The end."

Except our kiss isn't pure. It isn't PG, like *The Princess Bride*.

Maybe not even PG-13.

Then Everest rises and Dragomir takes over, clearing the doctor's cluttered desk with one swipe of his muscular arm—and the rating of our movie quickly escalates to triple X.

Epilogue

DRAGOMIR

*L*ooking like a fierce Valkyrie, Bella swings her red lightsaber at my head.

I parry her attack with my blue lightsaber, and sparks fly at the intersection of our blades. Before she recovers, I riposte, my blade scoring a hit into her shoulder.

She growls and exposes her breasts.

Fuck. Those breasts. Perky, perfectly pliant, with those oh-so-suckable nipples, they—

No. Must not look there.

She's using her feminine wiles as a form of psychological warfare. Effective psychological warfare at that—I've lost count of how many unwelcome erections I've gotten during our matches.

Well, two can play mind games.

"Ninety-nine hits now, squirrelchik," I say tauntingly. "One more, and you have to yield."

Nostrils flaring, Bella swipes at my midsection.

I parry effortlessly. "You're letting your anger drive you again." I know full well this will actually fuel the anger more, which is the point. "Make your mind calm, like water in a well."

Rolling her gorgeous blue eyes, she performs a decent feint.

If I didn't have as much fencing experience—or if more of her were exposed—she might've gotten me. As is, I parry again but don't yet deliver the finishing blow.

Like a cat, I like to play with my beautiful prey. I find this leads to all the benefits of makeup sex without actually fighting.

Well, unless you count what we're currently doing as that.

She performs another extremely effective attack, especially for a beginner.

Fuck. I might be getting cocky. That swipe could've gotten me—which would mean I'd have to exclusively wear turtlenecks for a month, including tight and scratchy ones.

Then again, if *I* win, she'll have to walk the puppies—or the Chort Pack as we've been calling them, in part as a tip of the hat to Bella's family name, but more so because the word *chort* means *demon* in both Russian and Ruskovian. Walking the Chort Pack is a fate anyone would want to avoid, as it's quite similar to herding the proverbial cats… if the cats were on catnip laced with amphetamines.

Bella makes the rest of her clothes disappear.

Fucking fuck.

All the blood rushes away from my brain.

I want to lick every curve, trace my tongue over that delectable stomach all the way down to—

She attacks so furiously her lightsaber whooshes an inch from my ear.

Fine. If she's going to play dirty, so be it.

Casting the same magic spell as she did, I make my own clothes evaporate.

Her eyes widen. My squirrelchik denies it, but she finds the sight of me naked distracting as well.

Still, she attacks competently—but I'm ready.

Executing a flawless *passata sotto*, I drop beneath her lightsaber. My free hand is now on the ground to provide me with support and balance, and my eyes get an exquisite view of her pretty pink pussy.

Must stay focused for another moment.

Before Bella realizes what's about to hit her, I straighten my sword arm and make the final stab.

She curses like a Russian sailor.

With my squirrelchik, competitive is a vast understatement.

I jump to my feet. "What did you say?"

"I yield," she grumbles. "Happy now?"

"Thank you. Now if—"

Before I can finish my thought, she makes our lightsabers disappear and replaces the room with an open sky.

Ah. I know what she wants.

Grabbing her, I take flight like Superman with his Lois Lane, except I'm soon buried deep inside her.

Clouds float around us as she moans in pleasure.

When we both come, we hover in the sky, holding each other.

"Ready to get out?" she murmurs, stroking my face.

I kiss her fingers one by one, then take off my VR goggles.

Across the bedroom of my private plane, she also takes off her headgear and climbs out of her VR suit.

I take off my suit as well. What we've just tested is the early prototype that came out of Project Morpheus, and if everyone enjoys it as much as I do, it will be a huge success.

"Remember, don't look out the windows," I tell her. "It'll ruin the surprise."

She nods, her full lips in a slight pout.

"Oh, come on. We're landing in a few minutes. You can see Ruskovia from up high when we fly back to the States."

"I guess…"

Despite the orgasm I've just given her, she's still a little sore about losing, but it'll make her eventual win that much sweeter. With the current rules—a hundred hits for me versus one for her—and the progress she's making, that win is inevitable.

I'd better shop for some turtlenecks.

I dress first, then wait until she does so as well. My

eyes mourn her luscious nakedness disappearing from sight, but my brain is glad.

She's so beautiful I can't think around her as is.

Once she slips on the engagement ring I've given her, I unlock the bedroom door, and as usual, the Chort Pack rush into the room like a horde of Tasmanian devils.

Boner and Winnie follow them, beaming with parental pride.

Now bigger than an average bulldog, the adorable pups begin destroying anything and everything they can get their paws on, but I just stare contentedly, a goofy grin on my face.

"Fu," Bella says when Mephistopheles—the pup we plan to house with Tigger—tries to chew on Bella's stilettos.

Mephistopheles stops.

The demon spawn revere Bella—or at least she's the only person who can get them to behave, if only for a couple of seconds.

"Beginning descent," the pilot announces on the intercom.

Bella and I strap ourselves in on the luxurious bed, and the furry family surrounds us with all their love and warmth.

When we land, I wait for Bella to put on the heavy clothing that will shield her from the Ruskovian cold, then hand her a blindfold.

She reluctantly covers her eyes. "The surprise better be worth it."

"I hope it is," I say, then clasp her shoulders and carefully guide her off the plane.

"You can see it now," I say, positioning her just so.

She rips off her blindfold and gapes at the structure in front of us.

I half expect her to quote her favorite movie and say, "I never knew winter could be so beautiful," but she seems to be struck mute.

I must say, even *I'm* impressed, and I was the one who commissioned this to be built in the first place.

A replica of the ice palace from *Frozen* stands one hundred feet tall, glimmering majestically in the light.

"Wow," she breathes, then spins around to face me. "Is that…?"

"Yes, it's for you."

"Do you think we could——"

"Hold the wedding here? Yes."

And as she throws her arms around me, beaming with joy, I imagine our life together in the years to come: Bella in my arms, challenging me in and out of bed… our children riding on Winnie's back… the countless other surprises I will create for her.

It's a glorious future—and to think, it all began when a Chihuahua molested my dog.

Sneak Peeks

Thank you for reading *Hard Ware*! If you enjoyed Bella and Dragomir's story, please consider leaving a review.

Can't get enough of the Chortsky family? Read Vlad's story in *Hard Code*, and Alex's story in *Hard Byte*!

Misha Bell is a collaboration between husband-and-wife writing team, Dima Zales and Anna Zaires. When they're not making you bust a gut as Misha, Dima writes sci-fi and fantasy, and Anna writes dark and contemporary romance. Check out *Wall Street Titan* by Anna Zaires for more steamy billionaire hotness!

Turn the page to read previews of *Hard Code* and *Wall Street Titan*!

Excerpt from Hard Code by Misha Bell

My new assignment at work: test out toys. Yup, that kind.

Well, technically, it's to test the app that controls the toys remotely.

One problem? The showgirl who's supposed to test the hardware (as in, the actual toys) joins a nunnery.

Another problem? This project is important to my Russian boss, the broody, mouthwateringly sexy Vlad, a.k.a. The Impaler.

There's only one solution: test both the software and the hardware myself... with his help.

NOTE: This is a standalone, raunchy, slow-burn romantic comedy featuring a quirky, nerdy heroine, her hot, mysterious

Russian boss, and two guinea pigs who may or may not be into each other. If any of the above is not your cup of tea, run far, far away. Otherwise, buckle in for a snort-water-up-the-nose-funny, feel-good ride.

———

"Me?" Eyes widening, he steps back.

I'm committed now, so I barrel ahead. "It makes sense. I presume you trust yourself not to toss me into the Harbor. The privacy of the project isn't compromised. And, well"—I blush horribly—"you have the right parts for it."

Unbidden, my eyes drop to said parts, then I quickly look up.

The elevator doors open.

"Let's continue this in the car," he says, his expression turning unreadable.

Crap, crap, crap. Is he hating the idea? Hating me for even suggesting it? Ugh, how awkward is it going to be if he says no?

Am I about to get fired for coming on to my boss's boss?

We get into the limo again, sitting opposite each other this time.

He makes the partition go up. "Just to clarify: I test the male batch, acting as both giver and receiver, right? I actually already tested one of the pieces on myself after I wrote the app, so I could in theory do the same with the rest of them."

Yes! He's actually considering it. I want to jump up and down, even as the blush that had slightly receded on the walk from the elevator returns in all its glory. "That wouldn't be good end-to-end testing, and you know it. You wrote the code; that makes you biased."

His nostrils flare. "Then how?"

Even my feet are blushing at this point. "You just act as the receiver. I act as the giver, and record the testing data. It's the proper way these things are done."

His eyebrows lift. "That's stretching the definition of the word 'proper' way outside its comfort zone."

"Look." I try to mime his accent as best I can. "If you want to quit, I understand."

A slow, sensuous smile curves his lips. "I don't shy away from a challenge."

Can my panties really melt, or is that just a saying?

———

Order your copy of *Hard Code* at mishabell.com!

Excerpt from Wall Street Titan

A billionaire who wants a perfect wife...

At thirty-five, Marcus Carelli has it all: wealth, power, and the kind of looks that leave women breathless. A self-made billionaire, he heads one of the largest hedge funds on Wall Street and can take down major corporations with a single word. The only thing he's missing? A wife who'd be as big of an achievement as the billions in his bank account.

A cat lady who needs a date...

Twenty-six-year-old bookstore clerk Emma Walsh has it on good authority that she's a cat lady. She doesn't necessarily agree with that assessment, but it's hard to argue with the facts. Raggedy clothes covered with cat hair? Check. Last professional haircut? Over a year ago. Oh, and three cats in a tiny Brooklyn studio? Yep, she's got those.

And yes, fine, she hasn't had a date since… well, she can't recall. But that part is fixable. Isn't that what the dating sites are for?

A case of mistaken identity…

One high-end matchmaker, one dating app, one mix-up that changes everything… Opposites may attract, but can this last?

———

I'm all but bouncing with excitement as I approach Sweet Rush Café, where I'm supposed to meet Mark for dinner. This is the craziest thing I've done in a while. Between my evening shift at the bookstore and his class schedule, we haven't had a chance to do more than exchange a few text messages, so all I have to go on are those couple of blurry pictures. Still, I have a good feeling about this.

I feel like Mark and I might really connect.

I'm a few minutes early, so I stop by the door and take a moment to brush cat hair off my woolen coat. The coat is beige, which is better than black, but white hair is visible on anything that's not pure white. I figure Mark won't mind too much—he knows how much Persians shed—but I still want to look presentable for our first date. It took me about an hour, but I got my curls to semi-behave, and I'm even wearing a little makeup—something that happens with the frequency of a tsunami in a lake.

Taking a deep breath, I enter the café and look around to see if Mark might already be there.

The place is small and cozy, with booth-style seats arranged in a semicircle around a coffee bar. The smell of roasted coffee beans and baked goods is mouthwatering, making my stomach rumble with hunger. I was planning to stick to coffee only, but I decide to get a croissant too; my budget should stretch to that.

Only a few of the booths are occupied, likely because it's a Tuesday. I scan them, looking for anyone who could be Mark, and notice a man sitting by himself at the farthest table. He's facing away from me, so all I can see is the back of his head, but his hair is short and dark brown.

It could be him.

Gathering my courage, I approach the booth. "Excuse me," I say. "Are you Mark?"

The man turns to face me, and my pulse shoots into the stratosphere.

The person in front of me is nothing like the pictures on the app. His hair is brown, and his eyes are blue, but that's the only similarity. There's nothing rounded and shy about the man's hard features. From the steely jaw to the hawk-like nose, his face is boldly masculine, stamped with a self-assurance that borders on arrogance. A hint of five o'clock shadow darkens his lean cheeks, making his high cheekbones stand out even more, and his eyebrows are thick dark slashes above his piercingly pale eyes. Even sitting behind the table, he looks tall and powerfully built. His shoulders are a mile wide in his sharply tailored suit, and his hands are twice the size of my own.

There's no way this is Mark from the app, unless he's put in some serious gym time since those pictures were taken. Is it possible? Could a person change so much? He didn't indicate his height in the profile, but I'd assumed the omission meant he was vertically challenged, like me.

The man I'm looking at is not challenged in any way, and he's certainly not wearing glasses.

"I'm… I'm Emma," I stutter as the man continues staring at me, his face hard and inscrutable. I'm almost certain I have the wrong guy, but I still force myself to ask, "Are you Mark, by any chance?"

"I prefer to be called Marcus," he shocks me by answering. His voice is a deep masculine rumble that tugs at something primitively female inside me. My heart beats even faster, and my palms begin to sweat as he rises to his feet and says bluntly, "You're not what I expected."

"Me?" *What the hell?* A surge of anger crowds out all other emotions as I gape at the rude giant in front of me. The asshole is so tall I have to crane my neck to look up at him. "What about you? You look nothing like your pictures!"

"I guess we've both been misled," he says, his jaw tight. Before I can respond, he gestures toward the booth. "You might as well sit down and have a meal with me, Emmeline. I didn't come all the way here for nothing."

"It's *Emma*," I correct, fuming. "And no, thank you. I'll just be on my way."

His nostrils flare, and he steps to the right to block my path. "Sit down, *Emma*." He makes my name sound like an insult. "I'll have a talk with Victoria, but for now, I don't see why we can't share a meal like two civilized adults."

The tips of my ears burn with fury, but I slide into the booth rather than make a scene. My grandmother instilled politeness in me from an early age, and even as an adult living on my own, I find it hard to go against her teachings.

She wouldn't approve of me kneeing this jerk in the balls and telling him to fuck off.

"Thank you," he says, sliding into the seat across from me. His eyes glint icy blue as he picks up the menu. "That wasn't so hard, was it?"

"I don't know, *Marcus*," I say, putting special emphasis on the formal name. "I've only been around you for two minutes, and I'm already feeling homicidal." I deliver the insult with a ladylike, Grandma-approved smile, and dumping my purse in the corner of my booth seat, I pick up the menu without bothering to take off my coat.

The sooner we eat, the sooner I can get out of here.

A deep chuckle startles me into looking up. To my shock, the jerk is grinning, his teeth flashing white in his lightly bronzed face. No freckles for him, I note with jealousy; his skin is perfectly even-toned, without so much as an extra mole on his cheek. He's not classically handsome—his features are too bold to be described that way—but he's shockingly good-looking, in a potent, purely masculine way.

To my dismay, a curl of heat licks at my core, making my inner muscles clench.

No. No way. This asshole is *not* turning me on. I can barely stand to sit across the table from him.

Gritting my teeth, I look down at my menu, noting with relief that the prices in this place are actually reasonable. I always insist on paying for my own food on dates, and now that I've met Mark—excuse me, *Marcus*—I wouldn't put it past him to drag me to some ritzy place where a glass of tap water costs more than a shot of Patrón. How could I have been so wrong about the guy? Clearly, he'd lied about working in a bookstore and being a student. To what end, I don't know, but everything about the man in front of me screams wealth and power. His pinstriped suit hugs his broad-shouldered frame like it was tailor-made for him, his blue shirt is crisply starched, and I'm pretty sure his subtly checkered tie is some designer brand that makes Chanel seem like a Walmart label.

As all of these details register, a new suspicion occurs to me. Could someone be playing a joke on me? Kendall, perhaps? Or Janie? They both know my taste in guys. Maybe one of them decided to lure me on a date this way—though why they'd set me up with *him*, and he'd agree to it, is a huge mystery.

Frowning, I look up from the menu and study the man in front of me. He's stopped grinning and is perusing the menu, his forehead creased in a frown that makes him look older than the twenty-seven years listed on his profile.

That part must've also been a lie.

My anger intensifies. "So, *Marcus*, why did you write to me?" Dropping the menu on the table, I glare at him. "Do you even own cats?"

He looks up, his frown deepening. "Cats? No, of course not."

The derision in his tone makes me want to forget all about Grandma's disapproval and slap him straight across his lean, hard face. "Is this some kind of a prank for you? Who put you up to this?"

"Excuse me?" His thick eyebrows rise in an arrogant arch.

"Oh, stop playing innocent. You lied in your message to me, and you have the gall to say *I'm* not what you expected?" I can practically feel the steam coming out of my ears. "*You* messaged *me*, and I was entirely truthful on my profile. How old are you? Thirty-two? Thirty-three?"

"I'm thirty-five," he says slowly, his frown returning. "Emma, what are you talking—"

"That's it." Grabbing my purse by one strap, I slide out of the booth and jump to my feet. Grandma's teachings or not, I'm not going to have a meal with a jerk who's admitted to deceiving me. I have no idea what would make a guy like that want to toy with me, but I'm not going to be the butt of some joke.

"Enjoy your meal," I snarl, spinning around, and stride to the exit before he can block my way again.

I'm in such a rush to leave I almost knock over a tall, slender brunette approaching the café and the short, pudgy guy following her.

———

Order your copy of *Wall Street Titan* at annazaires.com!

About the Author

I love writing humor (often the inappropriate kind), happy endings (both kinds), and characters quirky enough to be called oddballs (because… balls). If you love your romance heavy on the comedy and feel-good vibes, visit mishabell.com and sign up for my newsletter.

Made in the USA
Monee, IL
24 July 2021